PRAISE FOR JE

"Jen Michalski is a member of an exclusive club: that very small group of writers who could put out a novel, a novella, a story collection, a cereal box, a greeting card—and I'd read it all. She writes masterful, elegant, controlled works of fiction, yet she's unafraid to write movingly, to write passionate people with problems—the kind of characters who are, let's be honest, the reason we read with such hunger."
> – Amber Sparks, *The Unfinished World*
> and *May We Shed These Human Bodies*

"*The Summer She Was Under Water* introduces us to the vivid Pinskis, a family unwilling to be honest about its past and ill-equipped to alter its future. Jen Michalski movingly captures the way mother and fathers, sons and daughters, sisters and brothers jab at and dance around each other, alternately trying to soothe and to wound."
> – Pamela Erens, *The Virgins* and *Eleven Hours*

"Jen Michalski is a writerly heavyweight and with *The Summer She Was Under Water*, we're seeing her at the very top of her game."
> – Nate Brown, editor, *American Short Fiction*

"There are no easy answers here but instead a family's dysfunction laid bare in all its messiness and heartbreak—and also its moments of occasional, near-accidental grace."
> – Katharine Noel, *Halfway House*

"Jen Michalski has an extraordinary gift for revealing all the crooked tributaries that come together to form the ocean of the self. *The Summer She Was Under Water* brims with heat and longing and secrets, and yet again Michalski has delivered a story that dazzles and devastates."
> – Laura van den Berg, *Find Me*

Queen's Ferry Press
8622 Naomi Street
Plano, TX 75024
www.queensferrypress.com

Published 2016 by Queen's Ferry Press

Cover art by Scout Cuomo, "She Went Swimming" (Acrylic on Birch)
Cover layout by Brian Mihok
Interior layout by Adam Robinson

First edition May 2016
ISBN-13: 9781938466687

Printed in the United States of America.

THE SUMMER SHE WAS UNDER WATER

Jen Michalski

2017

For Carol—

Warmest wishes,

Contents

FRIDAY

1.

"I think the car is on fire," Eve says. Smoke tendrils curl out from under the hood of Samantha Pinski's Volkswagen Jetta.

"It's just overheating," Sam answers. They are at the precipice of the soft, winding dirt road that leads up to her family's cabin on the hill. She flips on the heater and hot air from the engine pours into the interior like batter into a pan. "We'll make it."

Tree branches whip the sides of the car on the narrow path as the sun shines and recedes repeatedly through the leaves. Sam thinks how much it would suck if her car breaks down right here, right in the middle of the road, blocking it for everyone else coming up to their cabins on the hill by the lake on Fourth of July weekend or at least for her brother Steve, who's coming up later, and the look on her father's face as he tries to fix it because he thinks he can fix everything although he will probably make it worse. And it will all be her fault because in her rush to pick up Eve she forgot to check the antifreeze at the gas station. Eve rolls down her window and blots her forehead with a McDonald's napkin as Sam holds her breath, trying not to inhale the fumes escaping from the hood. But then they are on level ground, and the familiar red-and-white wooden cabin appears through the windshield before it disappears behind a cloud of smoke.

"Jesus Christ," Sam hears her father say somewhere down the rutted, grassy hill, where the ground slopes to meet the creek below. She gets out with an old towel and touches the hood with it, searching for the latch. "Didja put antifreeze in it like I told you?"

She feels her father beside her, sweaty, emphysemic, grabbing the towel from her and wrenching up the hood in one motion. Smoke thins, and Karl Pinski materializes like a genie. He is hard and heavy across the front, like someone has stuffed a lead pillow under his shirt. The only thing that is soft is the lumpy flesh of his face, and his thick dark hair, combed back with Brylcreem, like a mobster's. He chews at the filter of his cigarette as it burns close to his lips and leans over to pull off the antifreeze cap.

"I'll look at it after lunch when it's cooled down," he decides, dragging on his cigarette, as the car hisses. "Driving a car like that—what the shit's wrong with you?"

Almost twenty years have passed since Sam has been at the family cabin and the creek it overlooks. Eve has come, too, for the holiday weekend, but when she leaves Sam figures she will stay a few more days, maybe a week. Maybe the whole summer. She's not teaching the mini-semester. She's now single. Her plans feel pretty open, in a crossroads kind of way.

Sam looks down the hill at the old pontoon boat, which still floats like a soggy bread slice on the narrow waterway that joins the lake, along with the motorboat, always broken. Various inflatable tubes that somehow her parents had managed to fill with their shallow lung capacity litter the dock. Sam's mother and Eve meet in the middle of the hill, Eve twirling her sunglasses casually between her fingers, her combat boots and fatigue jacket out of place next to Sam's mother's sandals and matching shirt and Capri pants, Eve nodding at the older woman's monologue. Despite their differing views on fashion, Sam imagines Eve would be a good daughter for her mother, and vice versa. She watches as her mother touches Eve's arm lightly, drawing her in, sharing a throaty laugh.

"Sam, do you need any help?" Eve looks over her shoulder. Sam pretends not to hear her. Already she has been excluded, reduced to bystander in her own family. She reaches deep into the trunk, fiddling with a duffel bag, until she feels Eve standing next to her.

"You okay?" She feels Eve's hand on her back.

"Yes." She smiles, slamming the lid. "I see you've met Mom."

"Yeah, she's met Mom." Sam's mother has lumbered up the fifteen feet of pine cones and gravel and grass. The hard, blue-collar features of her face are hidden behind her big sunglasses, her straw hat. She is holding huge bottles of suntan lotion and bug spray. "You better put some of these on, Eve. You look like you haven't seen outside for the last twenty years."

They join Sam's father down on the dock, where an old, weather-beaten picnic table has been dragged. He sits anchored at one end, his own legs slathered with suntan lotion that rests in clumps on his leg hairs, his feet small in a pair of rubber sport sandals that Sam's mother likely picked up at Kmart before the trip, along with a faux-Bahamas shirt and khaki drawstring pants. He inhales, looking at Eve, nodding his head.

"Eve, this is Karl, Sam's father," Sam's mother says, like he is retarded, and everyone is quiet in acknowledgment.

"I think I got the boat figured out," he says, addressing no one in particular.

"Oh yeah?" Sam's mother sits across from him, tapping out a cigarette. "What was wrong with it?"

Sam's parents are probably the last people on earth who smoke. However, they aren't normal smokers. Sam's father awakes in the middle of the night to have a cigarette; her mother has smoked while on the patch. There is nothing more visceral, more affected, more rewarding to her parents, she thinks, than sharing their lives with a good cigarette. It was a miracle every summer that they didn't burn down the cabin with their smoldering cigarettes that lived like fireflies in every available ashtray.

"Duddin' matter what was wrong with it." He shrugs. "You wouldn't know what it was, anyhow."

"Do you need any more help with it?" Sam remains standing while Eve joins the smokers, pulling her own pack of Marlboros from her purse.

"What, you know something about boats now, too?"

"Jesus, Karl," her mother butts in. "Can't people offer you a hand, even if they don't know nothing?"

"Why would that be helping?" He scrunches his face up at Sam's mother, who shakes her head.

"Dad." Sam touches Eve's shoulder. "Eve is my friend from Baltimore."

"So do you teach at Hopkins, too, Eve?" Sam's mother asks.

"No. I don't teach at Hopkins. I just work in a coffee shop."

"Oh." Sam's mother looks confused. "Do you know Michael?"

"Nope. Not personally."

"Sam was supposed to get married to him, you know," Sam's father says. He is sanding some rust off a piece from, presumably, the boat. "I guess I shouldn't be complaining. It's not like we coulda given her a big fancy wedding or nothing."

"You could have had it here." Eve looks at Sam and smiles. "It certainly is beautiful."

"That's an idea. Right on the dock," Sam's mother agrees.

"What a logistical nightmare that would be," Sam snorts. "Can you imagine trying to get everyone up that road? Where would they park? Where would they stay?"

"In little rafts and donuts—they could sleep on the lake under the moonlight," Eve explains. "Boy, for a writer, you sure have little imagination."

"It's a moot point." Sam turns toward the house. "Since I broke up with him. I'm getting a beer."

"Can you bring the cooler down, Sam?" her mother instructs. "Put that pitcher of ice tea in it for me and your father, and whatever you girls want."

Sam drags their bags through the screened porch and into the cabin. The cabin, two hours north of the Pinski home in Baltimore, has been in the family for generations, built pipe by pipe, before the road was laid, lumber and shingles and nails floated downstream on rafts in the Conowingo Creek during the days her grandfather and father and uncles had off from the steel mill. The cabin is a place Sam knows almost as well as herself; it has evolved, addition by addition, in the same way her limbs have grown awkwardly outward. A case for beauty could be made, for each, Sam considers, but only if one considered very hard.

Sam winds through the living room and two bedrooms, built one after another along the way, like a makeshift parade dragon—before reaching the last room in the back. Inside it a sliding door opens onto a deck that snakes along the front of the cabin, facing the vein of water. The room has been used for entertaining over the years—there is a padded bar from the seventies in the corner, along with her brother Steve's elaborate stereo system that he lorded over her as a teenager in the late eighties. Various sofas from the Pinski home have found retirement here after their springs broke or their cushions started to reek or their patterns became hopelessly out of style. One of the sofas has a stowaway bed in it, and it is here where Sam has slept for most of her adulthood. The crocheted owl still hangs on the wall, as well as a Bananarama poster that she had put up in her teens. On the bar remain a few ancient, dusty, mid-priced bourbons and vodkas, along with a bottle of Peppermint Schnapps, its contents solidified. She can smell citronella but can't find its source.

Sam stops in the adjoining room to leave Eve's bags, the room she and her older brother Steve shared growing up. There are two beds, one of them in the loft, but no window. The fights over who got to sleep in the loft, even though it was the hottest and most suffocating place in the house, were legendary and started even before the Pinskis drove up to the cabin. Both Steve and Sam would corner their mother privately in the kitchen or in an aisle at the grocery store, pleading their case for the right to stay in the loft. Eventually their mother made up a calendar for the whole summer, breaking down the days that Sam or Steve would have it, but that did not stop them from bartering and trading—a McDonald's coupon for a free sundae from a classmate's birthday party, a handful of Bazooka Joe gum carefully stockpiled for such an occasion, and sometimes just the more traditional forms of negotiation—hair pulling and stomach punching.

Sam remembers the nights in the loft, dangling a thin rope, to which was tied an army figure or a recovered toy from the southern creek bed, down to the lower bed where Steve waited sprawled on top of the sheets. Sometimes he would be a bear, and his fist would devour the army figure or algae-spotted Barbie head while he growled, or he would be a tornado, grabbing the end of the rope and swinging the figure wildly into space. Sam would concentrate on the spinning object until it made her dizzy and she'd have to pull the rope up, lie in bed still for a few moments. Sometimes Steve would be quiet, listening to their parents fighting, their father breaking an oar on the kitchen counter, heaving the toaster oven against the wall. Steve's fists would ball, whiten, while the rope swung limply between them. Sam would climb down into his bed, mash herself into the corner wall with the spider webs and moldy wood, and those nights nobody slept in the loft.

Her mother has been assuring Sam for weeks that Steve is making the trip down from New Jersey, although Sam is not sure what is so different this time than, say, any Christmas or Easter or birthday for which he has never bothered. If he is coming, she is not sure what she will say to him. She does not even know whether she wants to see him. The past she thought she'd shed always seemed to slide down her neck and into the small of her back, her body tight, when she wasn't expecting it. Like when she was happy. Or when she was jogging or eating walnuts. Or when Michael proposed to her.

She knows one thing for certain: this time, Steve can have the fucking loft.

As she packs the old red cooler full of beer and iced tea she imagines him charming the women at the skunky New Jersey roadhouses where he ambles through "Nebraska" and "Born to Run" in Thunder Road, his Bruce Springsteen cover band, his voice rumbling and mucousy, his forearms shiny and sinewy and licked with sweat. Tramps like us, baby we were born to run. She thinks about his stupid Christmas and birthday cards, late, irregular, recycled. Why did he have to think about her at all? And her mother, always talking like Steve was five minutes away, down the street, ready to shovel the walk when it snowed. A perfect son. They wished. Over the years, Sam's family has wished many things about Steve.

They ranged from small wishes, like steady employment and calling more often, to larger ones such as healthy relationships with women and staying out of trouble with the law and kicking various narcotic habits he'd picked up here and there like change on the sidewalk.

But when her mother mentioned Steve might be visiting the cabin this summer, Sam sent him her book, the one she wrote about him. She sent him her words and she wondered whether he would read them, understand them, what he would say about them. It was possible that he would not show up, stupid bastard, or would be in jail, or off on "tour," or strung-out somewhere between Brooklyn and Trenton. But she had begun the last chapter, and it was up to him to decide how it ended.

2.

When Sam returns to the dock her father has placed a plate of burgers on the table, along with grilled onions and toasted buns. It makes her almost want to cry when he is capable of such normalcy. The last few months, under a new doctor and the new drug cocktail, have been a miracle for him, for her mother. But even if his stay with reality is stronger than it has ever been, Sam thinks he is only marginally more likeable—his contact with them minimal, punctuated by grunts and scowls. Trapped, by choice, in his head of shadows.

"I'm starving. These look great," Sam says automatically, sliding in next to Eve. Sam is used to saying so many light, cheery things around her father that she is worried she is becoming like her mother. And that he will begin to treat her as such. "Thanks for cooking."

"I'm giving your mother the summer off," he replies, handing her a plate. "Although her doctor ain't gonna like it. We packed a whole freezer full of meat, and her doctor's telling her she can't have none of it. What's she gonna eat this summer? Berries and twigs?"

"Same as what I always eat." Her mother appears at the picnic table, inserting her finger in the slit of a hamburger roll and popping it open. "I got blood pressure medication. And hell if I'm going to quit smoking."

Sam decides not to press the health issue any further. At least not within the first hour she's there. You're such a nag. Michael used to kid her. Just saying. But for years, she had thought it was called sanity. For years, it seemed that raising the stakes in the Pinski household was modus operandi. Everyone lived and behaved as if incapable of understanding the consequences of their actions, and she had been the one, always, to talk everyone down from the cliff.

"Did you mention to Michael we were gonna be at the cabin like I asked?" Sam's mom crushes out her cigarette and picks up her hamburger.

"No." Sam takes a long sip of beer. She does not tell them that she wanted to. "Why would I do that? To give him hope we'll get back together?"

"Give it to him."

"Yeah, Mom, but I think the point of breaking up was so that we wouldn't see each other anymore. And me getting my own place, you know? But I think he still thinks we'll get back together."

"You might—you been goin' together for a while." Sam's father stands up. "I still think you were a fool."

"Karl…" Pat Pinski holds up her hand as Sam's father shakes his head.

"What, I'm gonna lie about my feelings?" He brushes a sprinkling of crumbs off his shirt and makes his way back to the grill. "Michael was the best thing you had going for you."

"Best thing?"

"You know what I mean." He lights a cigarette, rests it on the wooden server on the side before sliding his spatula under a fresh round of burgers. "You throw away a perfectly good thing because you're unsure. It took you two years to be sure!"

"Karl, we're not going to get into this." Sam's mother rolls her paper plate into a funnel. "We both want Sam to be happy. We're going to be spending these few weeks together. We haven't all been up here together like this since Sam and Steve were teenagers. We're not gonna argue the whole time."

"All right. I promised your mother—no fighting." He inhales and exhales quickly to clear his clogged nasal passages. Then he points toward Sam's mother with the spatula. "Of course, she ain't making no promises about talking to Carol."

"Carol's family."

"And Sam ain't?"

"We're paying out the ass for them phone bills."

"I know what we're paying—I pay the bills, don't I?"

"What was this I heard about no fighting?" Sam holds her arms up as her father shoves a second plate of greasy burgers onto the table and sits down.

"Sam, I gotta tell you I've been reading your book." Her mother lights another cigarette and plays with a strand of her dark, close-cropped hair. "I try and read a chapter every night before I go to bed. It's very…interesting. It's not what I expected, but I think it's interesting."

"What she means," Sam's father interrupts, hamburger tumbling out of his mouth, "is that she wonders why you didn't write about our family instead of writing about a man having a baby."

"Why?" Sam pushes around a clot of potato salad. "I mean, I could write about what I know, but I like to write about what I don't know. It helps me to understand."

"I don't know about you, but I don't need to understand stuff that ain't real."

"It's a metaphor," Sam answers, but does not pursue.

"You only look like you're having a baby," Pat laughs at Karl. "Maybe she's writing about you, Karl. Besides, it got published. That means something."

With that, Sam's mother pats her hand, then picks it up and holds it. There is no doubt in Sam's mind her mother loves her, nor any doubt that the feeling is reciprocal. Yet, in her mother's case, Sam often feels it is akin to loving a stranger. Certainly, Sam's mother loved very specific things about her—but these things may well have been in another person, so dead were they in her. Her dislike of peas as a child, the way she danced to her Osmond records, her love of a favorite doll that peed clean, scentless water until Sam collected her own urine and poured it into the puckered spout of the doll's mouth.

And with what had Sam replaced them? Years of hiding, tunneled under her bedcovers with her Walkman, listening to New Order and The Anniversary, writing screeds about how awful it was to be a blue-collar Pole in a neighborhood full of row homes and bars pressed together and rotting like teeth. Snorting cocaine and smoking pot in college, still tunneled under her bedcovers with anemic boyfriends, wishing they were in Prague or London or Barcelona and not fourteen weeks removed from going home again to the same tumor-ridden neighborhoods. Yet her mother still loved her, and Sam did not know why; all those years of pushing her mother away and her mother still picked up her scent, still claimed her.

Her father's love, she was not so sure of. His haze of a life—the drinking, the institutionalizations, the administered drugs—had already made the plane on which he met his children slippery. Only during her twenties had they begun to interact, after her father was dulled and useless from the press of maintenance medications. Yet even then he was largely impenetrable, hidden behind the steady chatter of Sam's mother, busied with chores or fishing or some half-assed project that gave him an excuse to smoke, drink O'Douls, and be away from them.

Her father had hated—or ignored—the ratty, counterculture men Sam had dated in college and during her early twenties. He had become enamored of Michael—Michael was the opposite of every Pinski man in every way and therefore a qualified success. But respectability, security, do not always equate to happiness, Sam knows. They are vague feelings, a delicious nothingness that obscures details the same way a flash washes out a photograph. In fact, Sam cannot point to a specific incident that fueled their breakup, although it happened after her book was published, the book about the pregnant man she spent their entire relationship writing. The book about Steve, her brother.

Perhaps, she thinks, it is not necessary to speculate any longer; details will not change how she feels, or felt, or will feel. The incident remains, bacteria in her stomach that she has attempted not to agitate. But she knows she will upset it. She is about to spend, instead of a vacation with Michael in Hong Kong, which had given her father xenophobic fits for months and her mother visions of SARS, the Fourth of July weekend with her parents and Steve.

"Have another." Her father drops a second hamburger onto her plate. "You don't look healthy."

Sam is kind of touched by his gesture but nauseated by its conditions. She hides the patty in two white-flour bun halves and bites. She chews slowly, knowing that the important thing is to get it in, to keep it down. Later, she can worry about what happens next.

"Well, how did you two meet, then, if you don't teach at Hopkins?" Pat directs her attention toward Eve, who, like Sam, has eaten everything Karl Pinski has dumped on her plate without complaint. Even the deviled eggs, which Sam thought Eve hated.

"The coffee shop at Hopkins," Eve answers, pushing her plate away. "I'm Sam's barista. For months I've poured out her coffee, and in return she's poured out her troubles."

"So you're my friend, then," Sam corrects. The first one, she thinks, in a long time. If friend meant someone who you might tell your deepest, darkest secrets to, someday. Not today. And probably not tomorrow, either. But if Eve is around long enough, Sam figures, she'll break eventually.

*

Sam and Eve take the rowboat after lunch. They float out into the urine-green water, dragonflies circling them, as her parents become smaller and smaller on the dock. The sun is soft, a lamp behind a latticework of bending trees as the afternoon begins to fade. These afternoons are an illusion, Sam knows, in one small way. Conowingo Lake is not real. The 14-mile lake, where the Pinski family, along with many other steel-mill families in the 1930s and 1940s, built their fortunes amid its arteries, was created by the damming of the Lower Susquehanna River. The Conowingo Dam is ceremoniously named for the town it ironically destroyed, a town now buried under the waters created by the reservoir.

Sam and Steve used to liken the lost city of Conowingo to that of Atlantis, and they would hang over the edge of their father's fishing boat and muse about its inhabitants and origins while their father fished in silence, occasionally tossing an empty can of Schlitz into the water. Steve and Sam always added a hundred crushed Schlitz cans to the list of things a diving explorer might find when descending upon the lost city of Conowingo, those and the plastic army men that Sam and Steve used to sink into the water, old fishing line tied to their waists, to investigate the city.

Sam and Eve stay close to the shore, away from the other, faster-moving boats. Sam is not sure whether to go down the river to the old hiking trails or up to the mouth of the lake, underneath the wide basin of sky. She instead ambles along the shoreline, pushing the rowboat off the muddy flats with her oar while Eve stares at the sky in bemusement.

"You want some help?" she finally asks, stretched out in the front. She is wearing her bright blue bathing suit, the one she got at Target just for this trip, her skin pasty and rubbery and greasy.

"Are you saying I don't know what I'm doing?"

"Nope. I'm not saying that at all." Eve smiles. "Your family is the biggest bunch of self-sufficient bootstrap pullers I've ever seen."

"And what is wrong with that?"

"Nothing. A family after my own heart." She places a sunhat Sam's mother has lent her for the boat trip on her head. "So when is your brother coming?"

"Steve is coming tonight, maybe. You never know with him. That's when all the fun starts."

Sam has not told Eve much about Steve, but she figures even a little is a start. At school, both undergraduate and graduate, at work, she had always lied and said she was an only child.

"I thought the fun already started, but this is your vacation." Eve leans back in the rowboat. "I'm just the easygoing freeloader."

"Shit," Sam cusses. They have run up on the sand. She stands in the boat, planting her paddle on the ground and pushing.

"I guess this is where we stop." Eve stands up and steps over the boat and into the water. Sam watches after her as she makes her way onto the wooded shore.

"There's no path there," Sam says, still in the boat. Eve pushes some branches aside and disappears into the woods, leaving Sam alone. She struggles to moor the boat with the rope. She hopes it's lodged deep enough to be there when she gets back.

"Why are you going this way?" Sam struggles to catch up with Eve, branches whipping into her face, grabbing her hair. "There's no path here."

"Doesn't mean we won't find something."

"Yeah—cuts, bruises, bug bites."

"Don't be so uptight—you're on vacation, remember?"

"I'm not uptight. I just don't see the gain in hiking through this part of the forest. There are Boy Scout trails all over the place we could use."

"I'm not looking to gain anything. I'm just hiking."

"Well, I'm going back to the boat."

"Okay." Eve continues, quickly swallowed by the trees.

"How are you going to find your way back?" Sam hurries again to catch up with Eve. "There's no trail."

"I can make my way back to the water."

"I wish you wouldn't go this far in. You're not a hiker. People get lost in these woods. You don't even have a compass."

"I've lived in forests before. Hell, I've even lived in my car before. I can make my way around."

"What are you talking about? Why do you have to be so stubborn about everything? There are plenty of good paths already established."

"Why are you always convinced that there's a right way to do things?"

"What, are you telling me I'm not happy because I'm not a Zen master like you?"

"Who said anything." Eve rests on a small, knotty tree stump as Sam approaches. "About happiness? I thought we were talking about hiking."

"I don't know." Sam's hands find her hips. She bends over, and sweat runs down her cheeks from her temples. "It just sounded like some metaphor or something."

"You're the metaphor queen," Eve says. "I guess I should trust your judgment."

"You're getting under my skin." Sam looks up at her. Eve is sweating profusely as well, her face pink, her eyebrows blond and stark. She looks apologetic, or maybe distracted, or both.

"I'm sorry." Eve picks at the wood between her legs. "I didn't mean to upset you. Really. We can go back. I'm dying for a cold one."

"It's okay. I just…always feel like nobody worries but me."

"So what happens if you stop worrying?"

"We'll all die!" Sam laughs, but Eve does not. They walk back the way they think they came. Sam remembers roaming through the woods for hours with Steve, their youth impervious to humidity, sunburns, poison ivy, hives. Sometimes when her shorter legs would tire faster, he would carry her on his shoulders. The branches were actually thicker at that height, and she sat with her arms apart, ready to swat away the offending twigs, the soft of her bottom nestled in Steve's collarbones, his hands callous and dry on her legs. They would wander for hours, Steve assuring her that he knew the way out of the woods and back to the boat. When she'd all but given up hope, when she felt her heart shudder in her chest, her eyes wet, her thoughts of their mother worried, father angry, she'd feel a breeze, thick, resonating, and the forest would clear, the late-afternoon stillness resting on their rowboat and waters like algae.

"Row it double-time, Sam," Steve would direct her, pushing the boat into the water. Dinner would be ready soon. They couldn't afford to be late. "Go! Go!"

When he got knee-deep in the water, he'd jump into the boat. Sam would wait until the boat steadied, and then they would take turns rowing with all their might back up the river.

One summer, when Sam was eight and Steve ten, they had rowed down the river and Sam had stood up in the boat to get a clear view of an osprey she had seen dart into the forest. She was holding a pair of expensive-but-ancient binoculars with a broken strap that her Uncle Ray had lent her and Steve, with admonitions from their mother to be very, very careful with them.

Steve steadied the boat as Sam inched to the bow, cranking the heavy dials on the binoculars in an attempt to wretch the bird into focus. She was unaware of the motorboat making its way slowly past the rowboat, which Steve had begun to move with the oars out of the middle of the channel.

"Get down, Sam," she heard him warn, but ignored him. The bird and its nest were becoming crisper as she learned to steady the binoculars and focus. "Sam!"

The wave lapped against the boat like the tongue of a large dog, unaware of its own strength, pressing the binoculars against Sam's eyes and pitching her into the water, the force stunning her momentarily as she was swallowed by the creek. She let go of the binoculars, instinctively jettisoning them as far from her face as possible before she realized what she had done. Her fear of her father's belt squeezed her throat as water swam through her searching fingers.

Out of breath, she floated up to catch some air only to feel a sudden blow to her head. She had struck the bottom of the rowboat, and for a moment she could not move. She felt as if her neck had continued moving through her skull and out of her body, her ears swarming with bees and lightning racing through her appendages. She forced an arm upward, its slow-but-steady progress through the water encouraging her, as she felt the bottom of the boat. The metal ceiling loomed large and vast above her as she moved along it, searching for the surface. Little embers sprang to life in the bottom of her lungs, which spread to a full-fledged forest fire through the branches of her bronchi as she consumed the last few molecules of oxygen left in her.

Long, sinewy arms looped around her, the soft rubbery front of Steve's body against her face as he guided them to the surface.

"You dumbass." He pushed her up into the boat. "Why didn't you listen to me?"

"The binoculars," she cried from the bottom of the rowboat, where she sat in a wet heap. "I lost them."

"Shit." Steve swallowed all the air around him and drilled himself back down into the water. After several attempts, he came up empty.

"I need to get my snorkeling stuff and a flashlight," he decided, staring at the black water from the rowboat. "We're by the old Ewers property. I'll just use that as a marker."

They rowed back to the site with Steve's snorkeling set and a heavy-duty flashlight that Steve had wrapped in plastic wrap several times in an attempt to make watertight. Sam anchored the rowboat by moving the oars back and forth lightly, mimicking the treading of water, while Steve floated on his stomach, holding the mouth of the flashlight just above the water. The light made a faint beam into the first five or ten feet, but not all the way to the bottom, which was probably fifteen feet deep. Steve abandoned his gear and dove again and again, feeling the bottom a few feet at a time before coming back up for air. Sam watched the afternoon sun lazily drop into the trees for its nightly slumber. When Steve came up for the final time, shivering, his skin bluish and wrinkled, she had resigned herself to her fate.

"Let me do it." He waved her off as they rowed back to the cabin. Uncle Roy had been surprisingly lenient, acknowledging the binoculars were old and not much use to him.

"It was my fault," Steve explained, not looking at Sam. "I was standing on the bow, trying to get a good look at a bird, when the wake knocked me into the water."

"Don't worry about it," Uncle Roy laughed. "Just remind me not to lend you my fishing pole."

"Don't worry?" Their father had slammed his beer down on the picnic table. It was his sixth or twelfth; it was hard to tell by the pile of crushed aluminum littering the table where their parents and Aunt Carol and Uncle Ray had played poker all afternoon with the change from their kitchen jars. "He has to learn his lesson. You take care of someone else's property. If I had done something like that when I was little my father woulda broken my arms off. Come here, boy."

Sam's father marched Steve down to the end of the dock, where people on passing pontoon boats and motorboats looked the other way as he whipped Steve repeatedly with his belt. The thought of it still makes her skin crawl. Steve stood erect, facing the water, his face hidden, as Sam's mother and Carol and Ray busied themselves with dinner preparations inside the cabin. When Sam's father was done, Steve jumped into the lake, staying underneath the water for a long time, the only trace of his existence a rush of bubbles that exploded up to the surface, buffering, Sam imagined, his cries.

She let Steve sleep in the loft for the duration of the trip, even though it was technically her turn.

*

Sam catches a glint of the creek from the trees, the rowboat. It has been forty-five minutes since she first entered the woods with Eve. She is covered in mosquito bites, a consequence of not spraying with bug repellant like her mother told her. She is thirsty from not taking the moldy-looking canteen her father tried to press on her as they shoved off from the dock. She is ecstatic they are literally out of the woods. Her heart slows, and she sighs.

"There it is." Eve spots it also, pointing to the opening in the trees. "And you're still alive. Fancy that."

Sam punches Eve softly on the arm, pulling at the branches with her hands and easing herself through the underbrush to the lonely, cobwebbed boat.

"We used to play Huck Finn," she says to Eve as she wades to the canoe. She pulls herself in and holds it steady for Eve. "Steve used to be Huck."

"Who were you?" Eve throws a thick white leg over the lip and inches in. The boat rocks, and Sam centers her weight while it settles.

"I don't know," Sam answers. "I wasn't Tom Sawyer. Steve says I wasn't fun enough. Who else was there?"

"Jim, the runaway slave?"

"No…I guess I wasn't anybody." Sam puts the oar in the water and presses her weight against the bottom. The boat dislodges from the shore. "I guess I just watched."

"Well, you're no watcher anymore." Eve smiles demurely, batting her eyes. "Look at you, rowing a little lady like myself up the creek."

"Anything for you, miss." Sam winks. Eve holds her gaze for a second longer before Sam breaks it off. Sam wonders if Eve is flirting. She has often wondered and can never tell. She knows Eve dates men and women, flitting back and forth the same way she sometimes wore her hair up like an old movie star, her lips popping red, and the way she let her hair loose, shadowing in her face, her oversized army surplus jacket hiding her ample bosom, healthy hips.

She feels that Eve is comfortable, like a shoe, but one whose brand she has never bought, is made for another sport, whose track record is entirely unknown to her. But she has made more impulsive purchases in her life, she knows. As if she didn't have enough to worry about, Steve would be there soon. Sam digs the oars in and rows in silence while Eve trails her cupped hand in the water, trying to catch tadpoles. Sam watches as they slither into Eve's grasp underwater, only to escape when Eve jerks her hand up.

"Steve can help you do that," Sam laughs as Eve loses her fourth.

"A legend, the man." Eve lights a cigarette, tucking the match between the cellophane and back of her cigarette box. "Although I'm beginning to suspect you merely made him up to get me here."

Sam doesn't say anything, except shit when she gets bitten for the millionth time that afternoon by a mosquito.

i

How does a man become pregnant? This is the situation in which Pete Skivins finds himself.

But perhaps an even better question to start with is this: how does a man know he's pregnant?

For Pete Skivins, pregnancy is not an easy discovery. Not athletically inclined, he has always been on the thin, slouchy side. At thirty-eight, he has made no caloric adjustments or stabs at physical activity beyond what it takes to get him to his job at the Zue, the neighborhood bar and musical revue where local bands shoot to life like bright flowers and then wither. And yet he notices, as he is shaving, the way his belly begins to creep slightly over the elastic of his waistband. He attributes it to his slowing metabolism, the extra shot of whiskey when he comes home from work. He begins getting off the bus one stop farther from the bar at nights.

But then there is the sickness, a stomach-emptying retching that begins to overtake him while he is showering. He wonders whether he has an ulcer, a gastric disturbance, cancer. Antacids are useless; at the clinic, he gets a prescription for Prilosec. But, after a month, his stomach seems bigger, so much so that he hooks his jeans up under it and wears baggier t-shirts. Eventually, the vomiting stops.

It could be cancer; his liver could be pickled, or maybe his kidneys are ready to shut down for good. Pete Skivins has decided, with irritated resignation, that he will head to the clinic tomorrow and face the bad cover-band music of his life, complete with doctor who looks like Huey Lewis.

But then he feels something, just below his belly button, moving.

He's scared. The first thing he does is have a drink. And he drinks, taking in the redwhiteblue Budweiser inflated blimp and the yellowgreen YuengLing neon sign and the dusty and lighted reflection on the mirror behind the bar that gives him and his surroundings a murkiness that matches the murkiness in his head so that there is no filter and he is redwhiteblue Pete Skivins with whiskey going down his throat and then out his pores back into the bar, into the bottles, and he has another drink and observes it again, the inner circulatory system of barPeteSkivins.

She is not murky. It is not clear to him whether she is not part of his reality or he not a part of hers or whether his reality is part of the collective reality tenuously holding the redwhiteblue beer cans and browngreenclear bottle lines and mirror glass smooth bar worn in orbit around his body.

It is not even clear to Pete Skivins how long she has been here, or him, at his bar, this bar where he works and where he is not working now but where he is drinking because he does not know what to do except that he will have to kill it.

He will kill it by drinking or maybe if that doesn't work, something else. But he prefers to kill his baby the way he does himself. But he doesn't want to think about it while he does it. He calls for another whiskey and points to the girl's drink.

"Give her another one, too," he says to Drake, the other bartender who is bartender when Pete is not bartender.

"You have a lot of nerve," the girl says in response to her gin and tonic, and it is then that Pete Skivins notices her cape.

"Fuck you. I wasn't trying to pick up a girl with a fucking cape," he says, a little sloppily. "Can I bum a smoke?"

"Fuck you. Buy your own if you're going to be a jackass."

"What I was trying to say, lady, is that I wasn't trying to pick you up, you who is wearing a cape. I work here. Consider it a drink on the house."

"Well, I don't know if I should be flattered or insulted," she says, holding her soft-box dented-in foil-top-catching-the-lights-of-the-bar Camels. "But you can have a fucking cigarette."

"She's wearing a cape." Pete motions to Drake when Drake is jettisoned, connected to his rag, to their end of the bar, wiping perspiration instantaneously disappearing from the bar top. "She is wearing a cape, right? I'm not imaging things."

"Well, it is Halloween, Skiivy," Drake answers before being pivoted away by his moisture-sensing rag. Pete hates Drake's nickname for him, but mostly because Pete can beat Drake at pool and the mechanical bull and kick his ass in a fight and yet Pete always puts himself in this position, this slurry slippy pop of drunk, bubbles around his eyes and nose like a cartoon, where Drake can take advantage and call him Skiivy.

"What the hell are you, anyway?" He turns in his chair to get a good look at her. He is surprised to realize she is so small, a few ticks over five feet, with a dark, short mop of hair, like an overgrown toupee affixed to her head, big brown marble eyes and freckles. A kid-sister woman.

"I'm a superhero," she answers. "What are you?"

"I'm pregnant."

"You don't look pregnant."

"It's too early for me to show. But you, what kind of superhero are you supposed to be? And superheroes don't drink gin. When Drake comes back, I'm going to get you a real drink."

"Like what? Whiskey or something similar that you can't handle?"

"Oh, so you're a Superbitch. Got it." He realizes that all the whiskey is not leaving his body by osmosis and that some of it has collected in his bladder.

"Well, if I felt you were seriously interested in my superhero-dom, I would discuss it with you," she answers as she disappears from his sight and the urinalcoldwhite drinks from his penis.

"And another thing," he begins when he gets back, but he cannot remember because the girl is gone.

"Where did Superbitch go?" he asks Drake when Drake slings himself back to the end of Pete's bar where Pete worked but isn't working.

"Who?" Drake answers, and the umbilical synergy between Pete and the Zue bar is cut and Pete is pushed through the birth canal of sweatsobergut-clench reality. He smells the staleness of his clothes, the whiskey on the bar, notices the zit on his left cheek. And he knows that he is fucking crazy.

"You didn't see her then? The girl with the cape?"

"Oh, yeah. She was here. She left while you were in the pisser, Skivvy. She said to tell you to stop drinking now to avoid birth defects. And that she teaches Lamaze at the Women's Free Clinic downtown when you're ready.

SATURDAY

3.

Sam's parents leave early the next morning to float down to the marina and fill up the newly repaired motorboat with gas. From the screened porch Sam and Eve drink coffee after their breakfast and watch the older Pinskis take their positions on board. Sam's father turns on the motor and fiddles with the choke, a cigarette limp and unlit in his mouth. Pat and Karl Pinski seem to operate from some unspoken code, one in which the past is never mentioned, one's current desires are never articulated, and allusions to the future are always vague but predictable. The only reason Sam can think of as to why someone would want to live in a minefield after a war is that they'd know where all the remaining mines are buried.

Soon after the boat disappears down the way, where the little creek bends to the right, Sam and Eve hear a grinding sound along the trail behind the cabin. The sound settles at the base of Sam's spine and prickles upward into her stomach when she breathes. Everyone had expected Steve the night before, Sam's mother sitting in her little folding chair on the dock, where the best cell phone reception was, calling his number repeatedly while Sam and Eve ate Jiffy Pop they had baked over the grill. Steve stopped at the roadhouse a few miles before the cabin, intending to get some packaged goods, he explained, even as their mother had gone to town days ago to buy alcohol for them. Ten whiskeys later, he slept in the truck behind the roadhouse, agreeing with their mother that it wasn't a good idea to attempt the winding, tree-choked, soft-earth trail to the cabin at night.

Sam and Eve hear him make his way through the kitchen, his bags bumping against the refrigerator and sink.

"Hello?" Steve calls out. "Anybody?"

Sam waits until he steps on the enclosed porch, not moving.

"There you are." Steve stands before them, studying them both for a second before dropping his duffel bag to the floor. His other hand holds an unopened bottle of whiskey, a pack of cigarettes, and his car keys. "Can't say hi to your brother?"

"My mouth was full." Sam stands up and touches her hands lightly to his back. He smells of the staleness of last night's bourbon, underarm sweat, cigarettes, and the cheap body spray he has used in an attempt to cover it all up. His usual musk. Steve tousles her hair lightly, an unusual and affectionate gesture for him. Perhaps the alcohol has not worked its way completely through his liver yet.

"Steve." He extends his arm to Eve when Sam steps back. "I don't think I've met you. And you don't look like anybody Sam runs with."

"I'm Eve," she answers. "I'm a relatively new friend."

"Where are the folks?" He scans the lake through the porch, scratching his sandy-blond stubble and running his hands through his hair, thick and wavy, his ears and eyes red.

"Dad got the boat working. They took it down to the marina for gas."

"Sweet. The same old piece-of-shit Bayrunner he's had?"

"That one."

"I gotta get cleaned up." He turns to them. "Anybody up for a shower?"

"The lake," Sam explains to Eve, as Steve pushes each work boot off with the opposite foot. He lights a cigarette with Eve's Zippo while slipping off his socks before stretching out in a chair, wiggling his emancipated toes, his legs outstretched.

Steve has remained in shape. Sam supposes it isn't too hard when you're a bartender and musician, hauling cases of beer and amps, although the gravity of age is beginning to make up ground in his face. His eyes are still the crisp, light robin's egg that caress whomever he is viewing, his thick eyebrows quick and animated, along with the wrinkles of his forehead. He is Bon Jovi and Dennis Wilson in one, the waves of his hair dancing over his head and meeting the faint lines of his face with grace and symmetry. A discarded shirt exposes a furry chest with whitened biceps and shoulders, remnants of farmers' tans past.

"Mom told me you broke off your engagement with the wallet." He inhales his cigarette forcefully, in thought. Sam can swear that the air in the porch has been sucked up through the filter as well.

"Yes, I did. I'm sure you're pleased."

"Putting words in my mouth?" He glances at Eve and smiles. "I'm awfully sorry to hear that old Michael has fallen by the wayside, Sam." He flips the Zippo open and closed with his pointer and index fingers. "But as your brother and blood and last defender on earth, surely you can do better. And I don't mean that as a knock on Michael."

"I don't want to talk about it." Sam presses her feet into the planks of the porch. She wants to be heavier, stronger, than she is. She wants to tell Steve it's his fault she left Michael. "Go jump in the lake."

"Well, come on down, then. A man needs company." He winks at Eve.

"Don't be fooled by his charms," Sam murmurs to Eve as they lag behind his now boxer-clad form. He walks easily down the hill, his legs springy like a boy's, his feet unbothered by the exposed roots and shafts of grass and leaves and rocks that Sam carefully tests as she descends.

Eve doesn't answer. Her gaze is locked on the vertical bend of his back, which cuts through Steve's shoulder blades and disappears into his pants. Sam grabs Eve's hand, feigning a loss of balance. Or maybe Sam feels Eve is suddenly slipping away, her attention diverted. Steve drops his cigarettes on the picnic table on the dock and dives into the water, popping up a few seconds later and sending an arc of water above his head. He treads water and looks around thoughtfully. A heron snoozes on a rock across the way. The inhabitants of a boat passing toward the main lake, moving slowly to not make wakes, wave to Steve and smile at the girls.

Everything feels all right, right now. Perhaps Steve would be lighthearted and charming and teasing and they'd spend their days trying to fish and maybe they'd fish for their father's old beer cans and the lost city of Conowingo. And Steve would be the person Sam always hoped he would be, was capable of being, and maybe their family would close ranks around each other and there would be a tacit understanding that they each would rise their tide a little and all their boats would float comfortably, not mired in the muck or run ashore. If they all did their part and dammed their happiness in, here, this summer, there would be plenty to drink from, to siphon, in the lean times.

Eve jumps in the water too, warning Steve she can't swim, and when she comes up Steve helps her onto one of the floats that Sam has pushed off the dock. Sam remains. She wants to feel her feet on the warm boards of the dock. She wants to observe Steve from a distance and make sure he is the real thing, not some reflection on the water, like the moonlight, the water moon. He lies on his back, the transparent sheet of water caressing his chest and groin. His legs break the surface occasionally, to kick and propel him in a circle or out of the way of slow-moving boats on their way to the open pond. Their throttle vibrates through the tunnel of trees lining each side of the artery of the creek on which their property rests. The whole creek is electric, buzzing with tree sway and boats and the lapping of the water against the floating dock, moving gently under Sam's feet, to warm her soles.

"Sam, get me a beer, will ya?" Steve's head angles up from the supine length of his body. The water drains through his hair, leaving canals that comb through his head. He looks like he will break apart. "If you're not coming in."

Sam goes back up to the house to drag down the cooler again. She stops in the enclosed porch, where she and Eve have left their coffee, half-full, Steve his bags. She pulls the zipper of one, and a mass of boxers and socks mushroom out. She rummages carefully through the surprisingly neat duffel: his toiletry kit, one she recognizes as his mother having ordered for him from Avon for his sixteenth birthday; a pair of cheap flip-flops, still attached together and with a price tag with the name of a drugstore over in Havre de Grace; soft, worn jeans and t-shirts; a smaller flask of whiskey; and a copy of Sam's book *Water Moon*. She pulls it out and scans the pages to see whether Steve has highlighted passages, made notes. The pages are clean, except for a few small dog-ears that have since been smoothed back. The spine bears the trauma of being opened, read, the front cover perhaps pinned to the back so that the book could be read with one hand.

She has not seen Steve since before the book came out. She feels sick suddenly at the thought that he has read it. She stuffs it back in the duffel bag, rearranging its contents as she found them, and drags the cooler out to the dock, where Steve and Eve now sit, their feet dangling over the edge. They are smoking and smiling, the water running threads down their backs like translucent spider webs, their hair slicked close to their skulls.

The motorboat with Pat and Karl Pinski comes up slowly to the dock. Their mother is already standing, her smile wider than her arms, as she calls out to Steve, a mother scarecrow in her woven sunhat and red tank top and white shorts. She is already tan, but perhaps it is an illusion of condensed freckles and age spots shading her flesh. Her flesh has begun to sag a little at the knees and elbows, as if the contents of her travels have lessened, thinned, her body starved for more resonance, weight.

Steve jumps in and treads water near the dock, guiding their father, whose acknowledgment of Steve and his directions is minimal. Sam watches Steve pull himself up on the dock and walk, small-stepped, dripping, toward their mother, who acts unaware of his condition, hugging him like a favorite doll.

"You finally made it, Stevie. You had us all worried. Your father, especially." She lets him go. A large, round wet spot on their mother's tank top remains.

"Police were worried, maybe," their father mumbles, stepping off the boat with his oversized sunglasses. He looks at them, mouth slightly ajar, as if assessing them for the first time. "Your mother has some fried chicken for lunch."

They walk up large, flat stones embedded in the side of the hill to the screened porch. Steve walks to his car and joins them on the porch with a box of fireworks he bought off the side of the road for fifty dollars.

"Fourth of July party favors." Steve's eyes shine, his teeth exposed. Sam smiles back at his gesture. Everything feels all right. Or maybe she is just pretending. "I've never seen 'em this cheap. Good shit, too."

"You can't set 'em off here—you'll light the whole forest on fire," their father grumbles from the table, where he leans back in his chair like some sage in a faded black Baltimore Orioles t-shirt.

"We have plenty of room on the shore here—they'll go up a hundred feet or more," Steve says, turning around the collection of boxes shrink-wrapped together to admire its contents. "We'll be fine."

"No you ain't. And what if Roger comes down from the marina?"

"What's he gonna do—kick us off our own property?"

"Do you ever listen to me, Steven?"

"You told me to fall in front of the school when it was icy so we could sue them," Steve laughs. "I didn't listen to you then, and I haven't listened to you since."

"Well, you're listening to me now. You ain't shooting those off within 50 feet of this place."

"We'll see."

"We'll see about what?" Everyone, except maybe Sam's mother, who takes a great interest all of a sudden in her nail file, looks up at Michael, Sam's Michael, who is standing at the doorway of the cabin, his sunglasses tucked under the backs of his ears so that the frames fall over the back of his neck, a Boston Red Sox hat well broken and faded on his head, like a mold. Steve looks at Michael and smirks, his eyes darting. Michael drops his expensive survival-store backpack on the floor, and the thud of it shoots Sam out of her seat like a cannon, over to his side.

"We'll see about me and Michael sharing a bed," Steve answers finally, standing in front of Sam and slapping Michael on the back. "I mean, it would have been okay when we were younger, or even if this were the seventies..."

"Either way, I woulda chased the both of you up the road with my shotgun," their father laughs. "I woulda made them assholes even bigger, fucking queers."

"Well, I'm glad that's settled." Michael frowns, jiggling his car keys awkwardly in the air.

"Hey, we're only joking with you, Michael." Karl stands up from where he is sitting, spread-legged, at the table, to shake Michael's hand. "It's real good you're here. We were afraid we weren't going to see you again."

Steve rolls his eyes at Sam while grabbing Michael's backpack with one hand, like it is a loaf of bread.

"This all you packed, chief? Small environmental footprint for you, huh?"

"I brought some beer—it's still in the car."

"That's my man. I guess you have the living room sofa, buddy."

"Put it in my room," Sam points at the backpack. "So it's out of the way."

"Thanks." Michael watches Steve carry his luggage away before anchoring his eyes on Sam. She leans over and gives him a hug, touching his back briefly, feeling the threads of his polo shirt and shoulder blades under her fingers, before returning to her seat.

"How did you know we were here, Michael?" Sam asks finally.

"Sit down and have a drink," Sam's mother interrupts, patting Steve's vacated seat. "I know it was a hot drive."

"I have AC in the car, like most people." He steps toward the door. "But thanks. Let me unload the rest."

"Michael, do you know Sam's friend Eve?" Sam's mother intercepts him before he disappears.

"No," he answers, smiling perfunctorily at Eve as he heads to the door. "But the pleasure is mine."

"Mom, are you crazy?" Sam throws her hands in the air when he is gone. She imagines them finding their way around her mother's neck and strangling her. "You had no right to invite him."

"I wanted him to come," her mother answers, nodding at Eve like she is her ally. "He's been like a son to me."

"You already have a son, remember?" She falls back into her seat. "One that's as pure as the driven snow, according to you."

"Somebody bring coke?" Steve returns from storing Michael's back-pack. "What's that?"

"Steve." Sam's mother shakes her head. "I know you don't do that stuff anymore."

"Anymore today." He bites down on a cigarette and twiddles an imaginary mustache. "Can someone explain to me why the frat boy is here?"

Michael returns carrying a box of a stouty oatmeal microbrews from Oregon, and everyone shuts up. Steve and Eve nurse whiskey and Cokes, her father a nonalcoholic beer, and her mother lemonade. They sit at the table eating chips and dip while fried chicken from home reheats in the oven.

"So, Michael, what have you been up to?" Sam's mother asks.

"Um, not much different." He stares into the mouth of his bottle. "You and Mr. Pinski are spending the whole summer up here?"

"Yeah, if we don't kill each other." Karl sighs, looking at his potato chip. "But you know, we could do that at home, so we're trying to mix it up."

Sam's mother laughs, lighting a cigarette. "Karl's such a comedian. Actually, we've been having a real nice time, haven't we, Sam?"

Sam nods, and everyone drinks, wondering how they are going to get through the next few minutes. Then the next few hours, and the next few days after that.

"Dad, can we take the boat out after lunch?" Sam asks, figuring a motorboat slicing through the lake will give them less opportunity to talk. She can feel Michael staring at her, and she wonders if he regrets coming, if he will be able to create a moment to themselves. Whether she will sidestep it. Steve's feet rock on the floor, his elbows on the table while he lights a cigarette. He gives her a sidelong glance.

"We haven't been water-skiing in years," he agrees, exhaling and smiling at her.

"Those water skis are all broken. We bought that donut thing, inflatable inner tube at the Wal-Mart," their mother answers. "But Sam was so graceful at water-skiing, a real champion, I remember. Dorothy Hamill of the water."

"Dorothy Hamill." Her father cracks open another O'Douls. "And Stevie was the Brooks Robinson of baseball, right? Jesus, you think everybody is something they're not. Is that chicken ready yet?"

Karl burps and everyone exhales, staring at the table until Eve stands up, rubbing her hands.

"Well, that chicken isn't going to walk out here by itself, huh?" She laughs. She and Pat Pinski go into the cabin. Steve tips back his chair, shaking his head.

"You know how to clear a room, don't you, old man?" Steve looks out over the creek, where a speedboat full of the Jacobys, neighbors down the creek, wave at them. He waves back.

4.

The ashtray fills with little bent filters. They eat chicken and store-bought potato salad and baked beans from a can and plain Utz potato chips. It is the food of Sam's youth, and she almost feels fourteen or fifteen again, listening to the Saturday-afternoon Orioles game from Memorial Stadium staccato from the transistor radio Steve had tied with bungee cord to one of the beams of the porch, facing the largest swath of open space, her father down on the dock, smudged with oil from the motorboat, his mind fuzzy and brushed like a charcoal drawing after an afternoon six-pack, her mother urging Steve to go down and help him, lest he break some pivotal part or cut or burn himself or pitch over into the creek. Sam could hear their arguments from where she hid in the loft, reading the Bröntes and Austen. It wasn't until she vacationed with Michael and his friends in the Outer Banks that she experienced relatively tranquil vacations.

"You know, I had these blueberries the other day," Steve says as their mother brings out another heaping plate of chicken. "First time ever, right?" He looks at Eve. "The Pinskis weren't exactly Slim Goodbodies or anything. Mom's a great cook, but if she couldn't fry it, she didn't buy it."

"I'm sure I bought you blueberries." Their mother lights a cigarette with the intention, Sam can only guess, of clearing her palate for the chicken. "I know I got you juice. Sunny Delight, remember?"

"No blueberries, Ma. I would have remembered them." Steve lights a cigarette also. "Anyway, one of the bartenders, he brings some blueberries in one night. And I have some, thinking I know what blueberries taste like, 'cause I've had blueberry-flavored stuff, you know? Blueberries don't taste nothin' like blueberries, though. I think I like the fake blueberry flavor better than blueberries."

"That's because of all the sugar," Eve explains, lighting a cigarette too. "You just have a very developed taste for refined sugar. Which is remarkably easy, considering most of the population does."

"What did you eat, then?" he questions. "Are you one of them vegans or something?"

"Actually, I was lucky to eat at all." She looks up in the air, exhaling. "And then I wasn't so picky."

"What, you were poor? Homeless?" Steve leans forward toward Eve.

"Speaking of food, why the hell isn't anybody eating?" Sam interrupts. "Why are you all smoking?"

"Everything tastes better with cigarettes," Eve says, and the table erupts in laughter. Except for Michael and Sam, who give each other reassuring glances. *You belong with me*, his eyes seem to tell her. *Let them have each other*. Sam picks up a chicken breast and begins to eat it, grateful that a strong breeze has traveled through the porch, taking the cloud of smoke with it. The chicken is greasy and salty and Sam's more-subdued taste buds are not used to it. She makes it through one beer and then retrieves another before she finishes her chicken breast.

Everyone has another cigarette before there is a seconded motion to take out the motorboat. Sam's parents stay behind; Steve drives. They dip up and down through the narrow channel at a low speed. Steve steers with one hand while sipping his whiskey.

"Boating safety, buddy," Michael warns from the passenger seat.

"Why do you think I've got my hand on the wheel?" Steve smirks.

"No, I mean, I can drive if you're planning to drink more," Michael says, turning sideways in the seat. Sam cannot see his eyes through his sunglasses, but she can see Steve's.

"No thanks, son." Steve pats the dashboard. "You see, this is a Pinski vessel, meaning that it's unreliable and rather temperamental. It's best handled by a chip off the old block. As far as the drinking, this is my second whiskey. On a full belly of chicken and beans. You just worry about hanging onto that blow-up biscuit. It's a little different than your blow-up doll."

"I don't need a blow-up doll," Michael answers, and Sam is disappointed he has taken Steve's bait.

"Double-jointed, huh?" Steve hooks his elbow into the wheel while he lights a cigarette. "I've seen that in porn films."

"I want to go first!" Eve shouts from the backseat. Moments before, she had taken in the open mouth of the pond and the clear blue sky with something akin to reverence.

"All right, Sam," Steve concurs. "Help her get suited up."

Sam offers Eve a life vest, which Eve ties around herself. Sam marvels at Eve's fearlessness; an inability to swim would have kept Sam camped in the middle of the boat, if not rooted on the shore. Eve drops heavily into the water, and Sam pushes the inflatable tube toward her. Eve awkwardly pulls herself up, the bright blue of her bathing suit squeezing out in response to the contortions of her body in adjusting to the biscuit. Situated, she gives Sam the thumbs-up.

"She's ready!" Sam calls back to Steve, who is running his hands through his wind-blown hair. She is mesmerized momentarily by the long, tan fingers and their pinky-white undersides, like shellfish. He sticks his thumb up in the air and gently puts the boat into gear, looking back at Eve periodically. Michael has opened a new bottle of stout, apparently accepting of Steve's stewardship. Or maybe fuming. It's hard to tell in a speeding motorboat. The wind howls in the spaces between the three of them; their eyes tear and their hair gets caught in their mouths. Their bodies brace in the seats as Steve makes wide tacks in the pond, sending the round yellow tube with Eve on top skidding across the water as if it were ice. Finally the biscuit rears up on its side, like a stubborn horse, and Eve is hurled into the lake.

"She's down!" Sam shouts, and Steve idles while Eve pulls herself back up. They take a few more spins around the lake until Eve is tired, and then Sam pulls her cold-warm skin over the side.

"Wow, that was great!" Eve's eyes are glowing, soft. Sam feels more alive holding onto Eve scrambling, wet and tired on the back of the boat, than she does alone. She lets Eve go after it becomes too long and leans over the boat to corral the drifting biscuit.

"Sam—you're next," Steve says. "Eve, you're just in time to mix us more drinks."

"Au contraire. I thought you'd have refilled by the time I got back." She reaches under the seat and pulls out a half-finished bottle of Jack.

"Why don't you go, Steve?" Sam offers. "I can steer."

"I am the captain of this ship, missy. Not some dinghy sitter." Steve takes his filled glass from Eve. "Ride the donut, Mikey."

"Sam, why don't you ride? I'm fine." Michael crosses his legs in the prissy way he has when he is not entirely in control of a situation, and Sam is grateful for something, anything, to remind her of why she broke up with him in the first place.

"What, you chicken?" Steve cocks his head toward the back of the boat. "It's just a little inner tube in the water. It was fun, wasn't it, Eve?"

"It was a blast." Eve takes a large, satisfied drag from her cigarette and a generous sip of whiskey, which tumbles out of the corner of her mouth and down to her cheek. "You are missing out, Michael."

"Come on—Eve doesn't lie." Steve winks at Eve. "Sam, get this man suited up."

"I can do it myself, thanks." Michael hands Sam his beer and dives, from his seat, into the water.

"Well, la-dee-da, Mr. Greg Louganis." Steve rolls his eyes, fiddling with the gear.

"Steve, will you stop?" Sam looks at him.

"Stop what?" He looks back at her, and the coldness of his voice slaps her. "If you broke up with the ass, why the hell is he here?"

"Mom invited him, and I don't hate him," Sam answers. "Can you be civil?"

"Ready, Mikey?" Steve shouts across the water, ignoring her. Sam sees Michael give the thumbs-up, and she falls heavily next to Eve as the motorboat plunges forward. Eve lets her head rest on Sam's shoulder and shrieks with delight as Steve takes the turns sharply, flinging Michael out in wide arcs. Sam watches Michael struggle to remain on the biscuit as Steve works harder and harder to knock him off. Finally, on the third lap of the lake, Michael is catapulted from the inner tube, tumbling like a building block across the water.

"Damn, that was a good one," Steve remarks, turning back toward Eve and Sam. "Who's next on the water rodeo?"

Sam fixes on Michael, bobbing in the water against the backdrop of the cliff. The boat missiles slowly toward him. Sam pulls the biscuit in, using the rope as Michael climbs up over the back.

"Thanks for being a dick." Michael wrings out the bottom of his shorts and sits in the front, retrieving his beer.

"I was trying to make it entertaining for everybody." Steve drags on his cigarette. "If I had known you were into kiddie rides I would have suggested you'd gone to Kings Dominion for the weekend."

"Whatever. You can hurt somebody driving like that."

"Eve wasn't hurt. Were you, Eve?"

Eve shakes her head from the backseat but doesn't back him up with words.

"You want to throw somebody off?" Sam stands up in the lurching boat. "All right, carny."

She dives into the water but is unprepared for its chill, which slices up her body. She emerges quickly as both Eve and Michael make sure she is on the biscuit. She wraps her hands around the grips and tries to relax her body. She watches the boat take off and the slack of the rope in the water disappear and then she is airborne, the biscuit touching the water in fits and starts, her knees plunging into her chest, the air pushed out like a bagpipe. She cannot see where she is, only feels the wake crash against the biscuit, which she must fight with all her weight to keep from toppling over on turns. But she will not let him get the best of her. Steve can drive the boat around Conowingo Lake until it runs out of gas. She'll be on the donut, waiting for another turn.

But she hits the last wake—at least, the last one she remembers—and the biscuit flips, her body drilled underwater. The donut jars to a halt, and she struggles to reorient herself, swimming instead farther down into the lake. When she realizes her mistake, it is too late. Her lungs burn, and her eyes make out a dim lightness that she assumes is the distant surface. The light is broken by a body, and she feels arms around her, pulling her toward the surface.

"Are you all right?" a voice asks her as the murkiness dissolves, washed out by the clear sky and sharply etched trees. She coughs, breathes, and is disappointed, briefly, that the face that comes into focus before her is Michael's.

"I'm fine," she answers and they paddle together toward the boat. Eve and Steve stand at the edge. Concern contorts the relaxed whiskey shine of their faces. Sam is settled in the front bench seat, and whatever was discussed while she was underwater has been settled. They motor in silence back toward the cabin.

In the afternoon light Sam hangs her hand over the ledge, feeling the warmth of the Plexiglas beneath it, hoping the raw, doughy insides of her will bake and expand, harden back to normal.

"You want to lie down?" Michael asks her as Steve ties up the boat to the dock.

"No." She waves him off. "Thanks. I mean…for getting me out of the water."

"Sure." He nods, shrugging off his life vest. "You scared us a little."

"What did Steve do?" she asks, feels her face burning. Michael bends over to adjust his Teva sandal, pretends not to have heard her.

ii

Pete Skivins knows he is going to kill it. But he also wants to see the girl again. He thinks she must want to see him, or he can't imagine her taking word of his pregnancy at face value. Even he does not, even as he lies in bed on his back, his stubby, calloused hands lightly touching the skin between his navel and penis, skin caterpillared by hair, waiting for the faint kicking. He eats a kosher pickle and sucks on a super-sized chocolate shake while he waits, wondering if he is just imagining things and, if he isn't, whether he just is feeling an abnormally strong pulse from some main artery in his spine. Maybe there are tumor cells multiplying, growing into a form that would remain a clump of hungry, soulless cells, sucking the life out of his other ones. He wonders whether the sharp, toothless kicks are just clumps of cells springing to life, buying up more real estate in the cramped ecosystem of his body.

While he waits for the sensation, gently stroking it to life in his engorged belly, he whacks off. Really, he can't help it. Pete Skivins only touches himself for two reasons: to pee and to whack off. Otherwise, he is largely ignorant of the state of his physical girth; where moles might be hiding; how soft the skin on his belly was, once he got beyond the hairs, compared to his arm, face, feet.

He thinks of her as he strokes and tugs, the little-sister woman rubbing her cape around his cock, burying it except for the tip, which she licks slowly, thoughtfully, like a dog licks a wound. He fantasizes about lying in the cape afterward, wrapped like a burrito while she clings tightly to him and they jettison through space on the expulsion of his cock fuel.

He feels it, then, like a mouse darting into a cubbyhole. So quick, but moving through space, his guts. He presses his skin. He wants to touch it before he kills it. He wants it to know that he is here, on the other side. He wants to feel a little foot pressed against his forefinger, an acknowledgment of the rock to his hard place.

He needs to kill it but he also needs to see her before he does. He wants to lie in the cape, her clinging tightly to him, after it is finished.

He is going to see her at the Women's Free Clinic downtown. There is so much he doesn't know; there is so much he hopes she does. He takes the bus because his license got revoked, drunk driving. He sits on the blueplasticseat and reads the landscape-sized signs that span the inside of the bus. There is no shortage of advice here telling him how to be happier. How to have better teeth, better investments, a better heart. There is no advice about paternal pregnancy, except maybe in the Weekly World News on the floor. He wonders if he can tell the old bat who smells like tuna fish and mothballs that he, being several months along, doesn't have to give up his seat for her. She continues to glare at him, her tuna fish mothball aura radiating into his nostrils and stomach. She staggers up to the front of the bus and holds onto the pole, watching the township become denser and denser and poorer and poorer. He wonders whether wealth is really about space. He wonders whether happiness is loneliness.

The No. 7 tops at the intersection where he needs to be and he checks the number he has written down from the phone book. The Free Clinic is on the second floor of a three-story building that houses a martial arts studio on the first floor and a tax-preparation service on the third. He walks up the rubber-lined steps into which soft shoedirt is ground and opens the door. It is a big, brightly lit studio with crumbling walls onto which happy posters of soft laughing babies cover circuit lines that lead to the lamps on the ceiling. A class of six or seven women, mostly black and Hispanic, without accompanying men, sit cross-legged in a circle.

The girl leads them. She nods to Pete between breaths and he sits in a space made by a Hispanic woman whose fast-food uniform is stretched to its possibilities. He wonders if she gave birth now whether the child would slingshot back into the woman's gut. The girl turns out the light and the women shift positions and begin breathing. Pete lies on the floor and stares at the darkened half-moons of light on the ceiling, the smell of lotion and shampoo and relaxation tapes filling the room like a miasma of womb itself. He pretends he's in water, screaming in the floor, his gurgled frustrations erupting in small, silly bubbles at the surface. Of where? He wants to just stay here in his water but lights go on and she is standing over him, a cross between concerned and pissed. She leads him out in the hall. He can hear the women inside shifting on the mats and scattered talk but also silence, the silence of eavesdropping.

"What do you think you're doing, coming here and screaming like that? Why are you trying to do?"

"I was screaming aloud?"

"Um, yes! We were trying to practice our breathing."

"I didn't mean to scream. I thought I was screaming in my head."

"It's okay…really. I can see you're not lying." She turns toward the door. "You can come back in or wait out here until class is over. We're almost done."

"I'm going downstairs to smoke. Why don't you meet me down there?"

"You really shouldn't be smoking." She opens the door. *"It's bad for the baby."*

He sits on the curb in front of the Lamaze building. He can hear the curt yells of the martial arts students as they thrust their legs and arms into the air, into each other. He wonders whether she really believes in his baby or whether he really believes in his baby or what he is doing here. After a while, the baby brigade files out, a caterpillar of rounded maternity shirts in bright colors. They shower him with looks of disgust, an unwelcome squatter in their insular womb of serenity. Even fast-food lady seems a little less welcoming, averting her eyes to her oversized bag.

"You came during my Lamaze Without Partners class," she explains, dropping her keys into her purse. *"These women have already been let down too many times in their life by men. I don't think any of us realized you weren't fooling."*

"Their hang-ups aren't my problem," he grunts, standing up beside her. *"Bunch of bitter women with poor decision-making skills, all of them."*

She clubs him upside the head with a closed fist. He bends over, covering his ears, the bee-sting throb and hum ricocheting inside.

"First of all," her voice sounds, disembodied above him. *"If I'm going to help you, you have to lose your macho jerk shit. Considering that's essentially what you are, you've got a big homework assignment."*

"How the fuck are you going to help me? Are you still a superhero?"

"Are you still pregnant?"

They walk to a coffee shop around the corner and take a seat. She is wearing her cape as a scarf around a white cotton button-up blouse with puffy shoulders. The girl dumps several packets of sugar into her cup before looking up at him.

"So, Pete Skivins, how did you get pregnant?"

"How did you know my name? You really have superpowers?"

"If you consider asking your fellow bartender your name a superpower, then yes."

"Shouldn't you know how I got pregnant, since you're so smart?"

"I'm guessing you don't know how you got pregnant. Otherwise, I wouldn't be here."

"Are you really a superhero?"

"Are you really pregnant?"

"I don't know." He touches the back of his neck. It's damp and hot, presumably from the fire that burned in his stomach. *"I could have cancer or something. I haven't been to the doctor."*

"Why not?"

"I don't have health insurance, and waiting in the clinic all day is a bitch."

"But this mystery seems like something you'd want to resolve quickly."

"What, you want me to tell my doctor I'm feeling little kicks?"

"Those are probably psychosomatic. You're not far enough along, by the looks of you." She reaches into her purse and pulls out what looks like a plastic thermometer. *"But, to make sure nobody's made a mistake here, you do this for me and then we'll go from there, okay?"*

"What's that?"

"It's a pregnancy test. Go in the bathroom and pee on it and bring it back."

In the men's room he encloses himself in a stall and looks at the magic wand. He's seen commercials for things like these. He whizzes on it, noting the deplorable state of the stall, full of half-scrubbed shit marks in the bowl and on the toilet where some dumbfuck missed, things he never sees turned the other way around. He wraps the dampened wand in a wad of toilet paper and takes it back to her.

"Good. Now we wait." She smiles at him, like a receptionist at a doctor's office, all toothy and fake concern, he thinks.

"What's your name, since I'm not a superhero?" He takes a sip of his coffee, trying to settle his stomach.

"It's Kim Snathanapis. But you can call me Kim."

"Snathanapis. Is that Greek?"

"It's Anagrabic."

"What is that? Is that where you're from?"

"I'm from where things aren't as they seem. Like a water moon. The moon on the water looks like a moon, but it's a reflection, get it?"

"Jeez. So maybe this is a dream?"

"Or maybe everything up to this point was. Or everything after this point will be. Or maybe just a water moon. Or vice versa."

"So if this is all real…my pregnancy…how are you going to help me? What kind of superpowers am I dealing with here?"

"Well, I don't leap tall buildings in a single bound. I'm not impervious to pain or bullets or injury, and neither are you, in my presence. But I guess that's all debatable, since I may or may not be a reflection of the real situation."

"All right—enough of the Dr. Seuss shit. Have you, Kim Snathanapis, ever saved anybody from their situation? I want specific examples."

"Well, I saved a man with a brain tumor."

"How did you do that? How did he get this brain tumor?"

"He was hoarding information."

"Jesus, you're a fucking nut, aren't you? I've got cancer and I'm being humored by a fucking nut." He stands up to leave. "You're a fucking nut."

"Oh, but wait, Pete Skivins, you know what you are?" She holds up the plastic test from where she had hidden it under the table. A blue litmus paper lies in the center. "You're pregnant."

WHEN SAM AND MICHAEL MET

Five years after college, Sam was living at home. Although her mother told her she had a perfectly good reason to live at home—she was trying to finish her MA at Hopkins—Sam knew that the perfectly honest truth she was still at home was that she was not trying hard enough to leave. A six-month backpacking stint through Europe the year before with her boyfriend left her broke and brokenhearted, as he hooked up with a girl from Connecticut at a hostel in Italy, and they parted ways soon after. Sam came home and applied to school because she didn't know what else to do. She worked and went to school and had the occasional coffee or drink in Fells Point or Hampden with a school friend or writing group. Steve had been away from home for eight years, and her parents were in the early stages of retirement, although her mother worked part time at the Kmart up the street.

However, they were usually around the house, in her business, her mother at least. Instead of going home after class, Sam would sometimes read in the Homewood library, although the recent spike of muggings in the parking lots at night had begun to worry her. She often waited in front of the library until she saw someone heading in the direction of the parking lot where she was parked. Then, she would follow them. One night, she spied a tall, thin man in jogging pants and sweatshirt exit the library and took her customary ten paces behind him. Halfway across campus, he stopped. Sam also stopped, pretending to inspect the heel of her shoe, until he resumed walking. Again, twenty feet later, he stopped. Sam slowed her pace, thought about dropping back.

"Are you following me?" The man had turned. He wore wire-rimmed glasses and had a prominent nose, a Jew nose, her father would probably say, although Jewish people weren't high on the Pinski family's list of complaints, certainly not as high as blacks, Latinos, and homosexuals. Sam had stopped walking, and they stood about five feet apart.

"No. Yes." She took a step back, and he took a step toward her in a joking manner. "The muggings lately...I usually try to stay within sight of someone when I walk to the parking lot at night."

"Oh. A smart move." He held out his hand. "I'm Michael."

"Hi," she answered, not taking it.

He looked slightly offended before laughing, a high, melodic laugh. Sam wondered whether she could fold up his long arms and legs like an umbrella. "Oh, right. On your guard. I hope I don't really look like a mugger or rapist, though."

"Maybe I am," Sam answered.

"Maybe you're what?" He looked at her quizzically.

"A mugger or rapist."

"Oh. Right, right. Well, I suppose we should walk side by side, but with plenty of room in-between, so we can keep an eye on each other."

Sam positioned herself on Michael's left; her head barely made it to his shoulder. The vinyl shell of his workout pants swished with his movements, and she could hear his breath escape his slightly opened mouth.

"Are you a student here?" he asked as they walked across the courtyard of campus.

"Yes. I work here, too, though."

"As do I. I work on campus as a financial analyst, and I'm getting my MBA at night. I know that sounds so typical..."

"Of what?"

"Of every guy you meet at Hopkins. I wanted to get my history degree. I just didn't want to be a professor. And I'm not a great writer."

"I'm a writer; I could edit your papers for you."

"Heck, well, where were you last year, miss..."

"Samantha—Sam. I don't know." She shrugged, pulled her purse closer to her chest. "I've been around."

They walked in silence for a minute. In the third row into the parking lot, she had expected him to splinter from her, find his own car, but he remained beside her. Sam pointed toward an old Corolla.

"So, this is my car. It was nice talking to you. Maybe I'll see you again around campus. Thanks for the escort."

"You want to have dinner one night this week?" He remained as she fumbled with the door lock. "I mean, if you have decided for sure that I pose no threat to your safety."

"I don't know. Well, I'm just busy...maybe we can grab something at XandO on Thursday? It's my free night. Why don't you come over to my work, the JHU Press, after 5:30 and ask for Sam Pinski?"

"That I'll do, Ms. Pinski." He stood to the left of her car until she started it, then after a few long strides he stood at a late-model Saab convertible, the row in front of hers, waving. Well, that would do it, Sam thought. After a few minutes with her crazy, alcoholic father, her code-pendent mother, or her drug-addicted, shiftless brother, he'd go back to looking for dates at the Mount Washington Tavern or some other yuppie watering hole. Although Sam didn't know why she cared so much. She wasn't in the market for a boyfriend.

But Thursday evening came. Michael met her at XandO in a stiff white shirt with the sleeves rolled up, rust-colored corduroys, and tassel loafers. A tweed jacket lay folded and tidy on his seatback. Even if Michael had decided against becoming a professor, he managed to look like one. Sam looked at her work uniform, the poly-knit skirt and Payless flats with distaste, the veneer of blue collar clinging to her JC Penney blouse.

"Hey, Sam-Samantha." He stood up, presumably to help her with her seat. She slid into it before he could make his way over. "You look nice."

"Thanks. So do you."

"So." He eased himself back in his chair, his knees coming up high, almost to the bottom of the table. "I made a list of things we could talk about in case we run out of things to talk about."

"You're prepared," Sam laughed. "What are they, so I don't repeat them?"

"Number one—have you ever dreamed about being an animal? If so, which?"

"Gosh. Um, no. I guess I would want to be something with the ability to fly. But an herbivore."

"Are you vegetarian?"

"Not exactly. By the same token, I don't want to swoop down and grab a mouse or cricket for my meal."

"Oh, but crickets are quite the delicacy in some African and Asian cultures," he mused, running both his hands, sprouting with long, knuckled fingers, over his water glass.

"Have you sampled crickets in your life?"

"No, but when I was passing through the Santa Monica airport a few years back, they were on the menu at this Vietnamese place where my ex and I stopped and had lunch. Crunchy fried crickets. They were an appetizer. But the thing that stumps me is that in some Asian cultures, crickets are viewed as good luck. Does it make sense to eat something you view as good luck?"

"Excuse me." Sam dug into her purse for her vibrating phone, which she had forgotten to turn off. Her home phone flashed across the front. "Do you mind if I take this? It's my mother."

Sam stood up and positioned herself near the door so that she could keep an eye on Michael. "Mom?"

"Sam, honey, I hate to bother you on a school night, but it's your father…."

"What's wrong? Are you okay?"

"He's locked himself in the bathroom; I already hid all the knives and I've got Steve's bat here."

"Why don't you go next door to Ms. Ruth's until I get there? I'm coming home right now."

"I'm sorry, Samantha—I know you got plans tonight."

"Mom, it's okay," Sam answered. She wondered how her parents had managed during those six months she was in Europe, or the four years she was in college. She imagined the police visiting, her father spending the night in jail while he descended back into reality, her mother declining to press charges the next morning. She didn't really know—her mother never mentioned, and she never asked. The fact was, if she had let these things get to her, she wouldn't be able to do anything, go anywhere. Her father was a time bomb, on or off his medications. When he fell behind on taking them, he became violent and paranoid. When he was on them, oftentimes he was confused, a 200-pound baby, falling asleep with cigarettes in bed, leaving his wallet at the Dunkin' Donuts across the street, standing catatonic in the threshold of one room, not remembering why he'd left the previous one.

"I'm sorry, but there's an emergency at home," Sam explained to Michael back at the table. "I need to go."

"Oh, is everything all right?" He stood up, and she faced his chest.

"No…I don't know. I mean, no one is sick or going to the hospital… I think. I just…I need to take a rain check. I'm sorry."

Michael walked Sam out to the parking lot in silence. She wondered if she had blown it, if he believed her. Sam's other boyfriends, the few of them there were, knew of Sam's home life. But they were a different breed entirely, for the lot of miscreants to which Sam was usually attracted would most likely have had a similarly chaotic upbringing. Why Sam was making assumptions about Michael's upbringing she wasn't sure. She supposed it was his ease, the relaxed features of his face. His face knew not of parents dying, of poverty, of broken homes. It had received the proper attentions of both parents; the lines between familial relationships were clearly drawn, firmly enforced.

"Would you like me to drive you home?" Michael asked. They had reached Sam's car in silence. "If you're distracted...I'd hate for you to get into an accident."

"No...it's all right. How would I get back, anyway?"

"Well, I'd naturally stay with you until the situation resolved."

"No, that's not a good idea. I don't even know what the situation is." Sam shook her head. "But thank you, Michael. Really."

"Will you call me later and let me know that everything's okay?"

She nodded and fell heavily into the car. The burden of family life had a way of draining energy from equally important centers of Sam's psyche: empathy, love, excitement, kindness.

"What was question number two?" Sam asked suddenly, rolling down her window.

"Oh. Uh...who is your favorite superhero and why?" he answered haltingly. She nodded and pulled away, leaving him standing in the parking lot, hands rammed deep in his pockets, his coat curled between arm and oblique.

"She doesn't love me," her father muttered through the bathroom door. "She's been having an affair with the meter man for the past ten years. Does she think I'm blind? Right under my nose, goddamn whore."

"Dad, Mom's always been faithful to you." Sam glanced at her mother, her beginnings of a black eye. A swollen lip drooped, like a pulpy worm had fallen asleep on her face. "Dad, have you not been taking your medications again? Are we going to have to call Dr. Liss?"

"I found a watch on the bureau, Sam. It wasn't mine. I know he left it here. It wasn't mine, you see. I'm not a dummy, Sam. I've been around the block. Apparently not as much as the goddamn meter man, though."

"Karl, that's Steve's old watch," Sam's mother explained, shaking her head at the door. "Remember I told you I was cleaning out his boxes in the basement for the flea market at Our Lady of Fatima? I didn't want to get rid of it without asking him. He saved up so much money for that watch, remember, delivering the paper?"

"She's lying to you, Samantha," her father answered through the door. "I'm glad you're living at home. Now you can see how she really is, all these years while you're away."

"Dad, I don't even think the meter man comes around anymore," Sam said. "I thought we had a remote meter."

"Samantha, it's the mailman," he said, his voice curled with anger. "Why would the mailman need to check the meter?"

"Dad, can you just open up the door? You're not going to hurt anybody, and I'm not going to hurt you. I just want to give you your pills. They'll help you sleep tonight, and we can talk about what we're going to do tomorrow, okay?"

"I will not spend another minute in the house with that woman. She needs to leave. You don't understand. She tries to poison me every day. She's been putting a little bit of the rat poison in my coffee every day, trying to get me. I'm afraid in my own house, now. You gotta call the police, Samantha, and have them lock your mother up. For our safety."

"Dad, Mom's staying over at Aunt Carol's tonight." She nodded at her mother, and then nodded to Steve's old room. Her mother nodded back, in understanding, and slipped in. "I need you to come out here so I can give you your pills, calm you down. We can walk over to the Dunkin' Donuts and get coffee that nobody's tampered with. Then I want to you take your pills and watch the game and go to sleep, okay?"

The door opened, and her father appeared in a ribbed undershirt and faded boxers. He ambled past Sam and into the bedroom, where he sat on the bed, his pectorals sagging under the cotton of his undershirt. Gravity's vacuum had tugged hard at her father's body, and empty folds of skin sagged toward the earth. Sam, although dark-haired and dark-eyed like her parents, looked nothing like them. Their features were prominent and fleshy, thick and enduring, whereas hers were elfin and sharp, her skin nearly translucent, like a premature baby's. Atlases of veins appeared in the crooks of her arms and legs, her wrists and feet. And Steve, sandy-haired and blue-eyed, looked like none of them. She wondered briefly if her mother had slept with any of the local employees of the service industries over the years. From the mechanic at the garage to old Gary, the man who supplied Sam's father with a beer and barstool for many years, they certainly had much pity for her.

"Are we going to get some coffee?" she asked as her father remained motionless.

"Nah. You make me some of that Maxwell House. And turn on the game b'fore you leave."

Sam turned on the hulking, ancient television that her parents had moved upstairs when they bought their more-current Sony and found the Orioles-Tigers game. She brewed coffee in the small, cramped kitchen that her father had promised to remodel for years but never did. The walls were covered with faded, greasy, peeling wallpaper of seed packets. Watermelons, carrots, and peas, their names written in curly script on the packets. Sometimes Sam could see those seed packets in her dreams, found herself absently tracing the names on her notebook pages while waiting for the words to come.

When she got upstairs she found her father on the bed, snoring. She turned off the television and closed the door, making her way to her brother's room, where her mother sat at Steve's desk, thumbing through an old car magazine.

"I feel like I don't know Steve at all sometimes." She looked up at Sam and the two coffee mugs. "At least your father, his demons. I know them. All predictable. Even if I don't know how they're gonna end, I know they're gonna happen. And I know they ain't necessarily his fault, either. So I can forgive him. Your brother, he's like somebody else's kid. Sometimes I feel like I don't you know, either, Sam, but I know you're like me. I know how you're gonna act, most of the time. You're predict-able, too, even if I don't know all the details of your decisions. But your brother...I wonder if all parents think these things about their kids. That they grew these little plants in the ground and took care of them and then they became these huge Venus flytraps that could eat them. That they could grow like weeds and break up the yard, get into the plumbing. Or that they'd do nothing at all, dying on the vine. And you read the packet and got the fertilizer and keep them part shade, but the seeds aren't the flowers they show you on the cover."

"Well, maybe the plants aren't finished growing yet." Sam sat on the bed, watching the surface of the coffees whip and whirl with her move-ment. "You are a good mom."

"Yeah, and the moms of serial killers think they were good mothers, too."

Sam laughed. "That's funny—I had a date tonight..."

"Oh, honey, I'm so sorry." Her mother stood up partially, her hand out to comfort Sam. Sam took the opportunity to hand her a mug of coffee. "I didn't mean to mess up your plans."

"No, it's okay. It's just funny because we went on a date based on our conviction that neither of us were serial killers."

"What? That's supposed to be funny?"

"Well, yeah, kinda. I guess. I don't know. But it's just weird that you said that in light of…well, never mind."

"See, this is what I'm talking about. Who knows that their children think about things?" Sam's mother stood up. "At least I don't know what mine think."

"And you think I know what you think, or Dad?" Sam smiled. "Are you going to be all right sleeping in Steve's room? Do you need anything from the bedroom?"

"No. I'm going to go downstairs and watch *Everybody Loves Raymond*." Her mother stood up. "He'll wake up tomorrow and not remember a thing. I'll get his pills mixed in really good in his scrambled eggs. I open the pills and sprinkle them in. I learned that from giving Misty her pills all those years in her dog food, you know? As far as I can tell, he can't taste it. But who knows, maybe your father really does think I'm trying to poison him."

"You sure you're going to be all right?"

"Yeah. Goodness, Sam, how do you think I got along all those years you weren't living here?"

Sam didn't ask. Her mother left without offering. She could hear her raking the ice cubes downstairs in the freezer, gathering some for her eye and lip. Sam's father beat her mother and Steve black and blue aplenty, but he never seemed to go after Sam much. She was reduced to the role of mediator. Over the years she managed to stay out of the way and out of trouble, emerging only to talk her father into giving up the knife, the hammer, the flashlight, to take his pills, to go to sleep, to get ready for the doctor. She sat on Steve's bed, atop his pilled Baltimore Colts comforter, and dialed Michael's number.

"Is there a superhero that just solves problems quietly, behind the sidelines?" she asked, tracing the blue horseshoe on the white helmet with her finger. "Nothing flashy. Like, I could suck in a tornado and keep it from destroying a village or drink up a flood? But it wouldn't be limited to natural disasters. I mean, I could talk people down from buildings. I wouldn't have to be superhuman or immortal myself. I just have to be able to save people from themselves."

"Hmm." Michael's voice was soothing on the line. She let her back rest against Steve's headboard. "Well, most superheroes have the ability to do all these things, even if their tights and capes and mutations make them stick out like sore thumbs. I think what makes superheroes different from each other is their motivations to do these things in the first place, you know?"

"I guess."

"So maybe we should start there—Why would you save people, Samantha?" he asked. "Because you don't think they can save themselves?"

"You want to have lunch tomorrow?" she asked, her eyes racing around the corners of Steve's ceiling over and over again.

*

"Your parents won't bother me, what they talk about," Michael had assured her out in the car. Thanksgiving afternoon in Baltimore the sky was pregnant with snow, ready to cover the world, at least the brown lawn in front of the Pinski row house, with dusty tears. "Even my parents have their crazy ideas, family prejudices. I hope you won't judge me by my parents."

"Sam." Her mother stood at the door wearing a red gingham apron, the bottom right corner stained from last Christmas when her Uncle Ray dropped a plate of cranberries on her. Sam ignored the rusted, faded screen door that squeaked in the hope that Michael would, too.

"Mom, this is Michael." Sam stood aside as her mother opened the door, the air suddenly hot and fragrant with turkey and mashed potatoes.

"Michael," Sam's mother repeated, using her body as a door latch. Sam squeezed past her and shrugged off her coat. The living room had looked neat, clean this morning; now, it looked threadbare, dark, outdated. Her father sat like an old stuffed animal on the couch that no one had the heart to throw out.

"You like football, Mike?" He stood up slightly as Michael reached out his hand. Unsure of whether to pull him up or let him fall back down on the coach, Michael stood half-bent. Finally her father dropped back on the couch. "You want a beer?"

"I brought some wine." He held up the bottle, unsure.

"Oh, you didn't have to, hon." Sam's mother swept through the living room on her way to the kitchen. "You can put it over here on the table."

The table was modified to accommodate seven people which, considering the size of the Pinski kitchen, meant that no one, once seated, would be allowed entry or exit from their spot. Michael put the wine down and sat on the coach next to Sam's father.

"Who are we rooting for?" he asked, crossing his long legs.

"Skins, of course." Sam's father lit a cigarette with a match, then waved it out and dropped it in the ashtray. "You a Skins fan?"

"Actually, I'm a soccer fan."

"Soccer fan?" Sam's father sucked on his cigarette so hard his eyes seemed to cross. "What, you a foreigner or something?"

"No…I just like it." Michael scratched his head and looked at Sam, who shrugged her shoulders. "The games are low-scoring; they're more suspenseful."

"Suspenseful?" Her father frowned. "It ain't a murder mystery. It's a game."

"Look who's here." Sam's mother stood by the door.

"Is it Steve?" Sam felt the back of her neck knot, her chest fill.

"No," she answered, opening the door. "It's Carol and Ray."

A shorter, heavier version of Sam's mother squeezed past her through the door, mittened hands enclosing a glass baking dish covered with tinfoil. Behind her followed a slight man with a hooked nose and a wrinkled, sallow face. Even though the house smelled of stale cigarettes and cleaner, Sam could smell Ray's tobacco products, his nicotine-stained hands and mouth, from across the room. A smell she was convinced, even as a nonsmoker, clung to her still.

"Jesus, look what just blew in," Sam's father said.

"Happy Thanksgiving to you too, Karl," Ray laughed, handing his coat to Carol, who carried it across the room overtop her baking dish. "The game on yet?"

"Five o'clock." Sam's father squirmed and dug his behind deep into the couch. It was four o'clock.

"You want a drink?" She stood before Michael, touched his knee.

"You going to introduce us to you friend here?" Ray asked, reaching across the coffee table for a plastic bowl of chips.

"Her boyfriend, Michael," Sam's father nodded toward Michael.

"How'd you get roped into spending the holidays with these crazies?" Ray laughed, a little too loudly, a little too long, as Sam's father sat stoically, watching a commercial for men's shaving gel.

"It's his medicine," Sam explained to Michael about her father as they stood at the table and popped the cork on the wine. "It doesn't mean he isn't interested in things."

"Pat, you've got the oven up too high." Across the room Carol peered in at the turkey. "You're gonna burn it."

"It's fine." Sam's mother stood at the counter, an assembly line of canned vegetables waiting to be opened. The modern conveniences of canning had astounded the Pinski clan when they appeared in the early twentieth century, and they had never abandoned them. It was not until college that Sam tasted fresh asparagus, a sweet potato. "How do you know it's too hot? How many years have I been cooking the turkey?"

"I know these things." Carol turned the big, old-fashioned knob of the oven down exactly five degrees. "These old ovens, they overcook."

"Well, next year we'll come over and use your nice new oven," Sam's mother mumbled when Carol went into the living room. She reached over to the stove and turned the dial back.

"Mom, do you need any help?" Sam took a step toward her.

"Sit." She waved her hand, not looking at them. "We're eating in five minutes."

Sam found the wineglasses, a bunch of different pieces collected over the years, and Michael poured out two glasses before they squeezed into the middle seats by the wall.

"Are you going to be okay?" Sam asked. Michael looked like Steve's larger GI Joe doll when it came over to have dinner with one of her Barbie's, ready to slide out of its undersized Barbie chair.

"I've taken planes to Australia," Michael answered, rolling up his cuffs. "I'll be fine."

Karl, Carol, and Ray joined them. Sam's mother, whose chair was closest to the counter and oven, passed mismatched serving bowls filled with canned green beans, corn, yams, and asparagus to Michael, Sam, her father, Carol, and Ray, who wedged them into all the available space on the oblong table covered by a plastic tablecloth with a thin felt liner. Michael held up the wine bottle.

"I don't need a drink." Sam's father held up his can of Miller Lite. "Where the hell is Stevie? We're gonna need more beer."

"So Pat tells me you're a businessman." Carol leaned over the table to Michael, holding out her glass, which had, for some reason, a faded, gold dog on it. Carol's saggy, wrinkled neck, small domed head, and slightly curved spine gave her the appearance of a turtle peering out of her shell.

"Kind of," Michael answered. "I do financial stuff for the university. I like it all right. I love working for the school."

"You and Sam met there, I know," Carol nodded. It seemed to Sam that the Pinskis and their clan liked information they already knew. It was easy to remember, it didn't generally conflict with their world-view, and they could feel assured that they were never out of their league. The Pinskis, although never leaping forward in any significant way, never thought they were falling behind, either. Even if they were standing still.

"That's right." Michael turned slightly and took Sam's hand underneath the table. "She thought I was a rapist."

"He didn't mean it that way," Sam explained to her Aunt Carol, whose face drained of color faster than her husband Ray's glass of wine. "We met in the parking lot. There were some...security issues on campus at the time, so I didn't trust anybody."

"You got pepper spray?" Ray asked. He sat stuffed between Carol and the china cabinet, his body stiff like a cadaver. "You go down to Sunny's Surplus and get yourself some pepper spray. You're not going to have any trouble with nobody, you get yourself some pepper spray."

"It's better, now." Sam took a sip of her wine. "They've put little security kiosks around campus, and safety officers have been patrolling."

"What kind of world we live in, you gotta worry about people robbing you at school? What they gonna do, take your books? Creeps. And the rapists? Some people should never, ever be allowed to have children. I say we sterilize half this town."

"Well, we really don't worry about it anymore." Michael received a bowl of mashed potatoes from Sam's mother. "I drive Sam to work now."

"Comes all the way across town, he does," Sam's mother nodded her head. "Just to pick her up."

"So sweet. Pretty soon you'll be married." Carol blinked her eyes at them, shiny bluish dimes. Nothing seemed to please Carol more than weddings. Between her two daughters' three marriages, she would appear to have had enough taffeta, silk, pastel almonds, registries. But it seemed to Sam that the happiness of young people was high on her list of discussion, of details and costs and gifts, along with open bars and sirloin tips.

"We haven't even been together that long," Sam answered quickly. She wasn't sure if Michael would be offended or pleased by such talk, after only six months of dating, but it certainly bothered her. Although she wondered if she needed to be so quick to show it. She could always count on the Pinskis to embarrass the hell out of her.

"Yeah, you have to wait a little while—although Karl proposed to me nine months after we met." Sam's mother speared a large cut of turkey and put it on Michael's plate. "God, this turkey is perfect."

"What did I tell you?" Carol pointed her fork at Sam's mother.

"I cooked it at 350," she answered. "I know my oven. Been using it for fifteen years."

"Where the hell is Stevie?" Her father's head craned toward the front door and then, inching toward the television, remained in that position until Sam's mother spoke again.

"I talked to him this morning, Karl. He'll be here soon. We'll just wait a few more minutes, enjoy the delicious wine Michael brought us."

"I think we should make a toast to Sam and Michael." Carol held up her glass. "Maybe this time next year, you'll be engaged."

"You sure don't know when to keep your mouth shut," Ray said as Sam scratched her neck, studying a scab on her elbow.

"Why don't you shut the hell up?"

"Why don't you both shut the hell up?" Sam's father aimed his beer can toward his mouth. "See, you'd be a fool to marry into this family, Mike."

"His name is Michael," Sam said, but nobody paid attention. She looked at Michael, who smiled at her and sipped the wine. She could leave this town with him, she thought; they could buffer themselves against her past in some international, academic city like Boston and no one would know any better about anything.

But she would know better. She looked at the clock and at the half-empty wine bottle and at Uncle Ray sneaking bites of stuffing and the back of her father's head while he listened to some retired football star being interviewed on television.

"I'm going to make Steve a plate," Sam's mother said forty-five minutes later, when the wine was gone and the twelve-pack of Miller was precariously close to being empty. "We can't let this go cold. I'll heat his up."

"Good for nothin'." Sam's father had already retired to the living room with his beer. "Prolly wrapped hisself around a pole somewhere. Pat, bring me a plate, will ya? Game's on. Ray, you watching?"

"You stay in here and eat," Carol warned Ray. "Don't be rude."

"You like football, Mike?" Ray asked, changing the subject, winking at him. "Let's eat fast."

After dinner Sam wrapped the leftovers in the kitchen while Michael ran to the bar down the street for some packaged goods. Ray and her father sat in the darkening living room, their stomachs full under their snug sweaters, the air filled with the cacophony of their belches, Uncle Ray's glasses aglow with soft light from the television, while Carol looked over Pat's photo albums from Thanksgivings past, full of old women with perms and cat's-eye glasses and balding men with horned rims, wearing busy sweater vests or turtlenecks in the rich, warm avocadoes and golds and browns of the sixties and seventies.

"Michael's so nice, Sam." Her mother lit a cigarette and sat near the back door, cracking it open. They both watched the smoke creep out into the backyard. "He's so successful, right? More than anybody you've dated. Now don't give me a lot of crap about that. I know you loved some of those other boys, maybe, but they couldn't provide for you the way Michael can."

"Mom, it's too soon." Sam wrapped her arms around herself. "Besides, I don't need anyone to provide for me."

"Oh, it's not a women's-lib issue." Carol tapped the dregs of the wine bottle unsteadily into her glass. "My daughter's husbands have both provided for her. It means they're committed to marriage and family and God."

"He can provide, and you can stay home and write books." Sam's mother patted her on the head. "My little Stephen King. God, I wish Steve would get here. I'm getting worried."

Steve had run away to New Jersey five or six years ago. Sam could count on her fingers the times he had been back. Mostly for holidays, sometimes for money, once because he was broke and evicted. He always looked healthy, golden, beautiful, even as it made her chest hurt, her throat tighten, to see him. His address changed frequently; usually a woman's name was attached to it. Sam's mother wrote Steve dutifully, even if only a few lines on box cards she had ordered from some greeting-card wholesaler, slipping him a five or a ten or a coupon for cigarettes she'd clipped from the Baltimore Sun.

"Look out the window, Sam; is that him?" Sam's mother's ears were attuned to the slightest of her children's movements, or so she boasted. "Sounds like his old truck."

"No. It's snowing, though," she answered, hoping Michael would get back soon. It had gotten dark, and she was tired. Her family's lack of curiosity about anything, the stale conversations and preserved food, had left her grumpy. "We'll probably leave soon. The weather is getting bad."

"Well, look what the cat drug in." Sam's father stood at the front door as a shadow appeared before him. "My son."

"Sorry, Dad." Steve patted Karl Pinski on the back, a funny smirk and a day's growth of beard on his face. He wore a denim jacket that was a little too thin for the weather, jeans, and a red-and-black plaid shirt, Caterpillar boots. He looked timeless in some fashion, in his unremarkable, utilitarian wardrobe, or maybe stuck in time. "I had a little truck trouble."

"Well, we already ate, son. You bring the beer?"

"Of course, father. I would never forget that." Steve entered the kitchen and opened the fridge, looking to insert the twelve-pack with his right hand. He put it on the floor, grabbed a large plastic Tupperware bowl out of the cabinet and twisted some ice from the trays into it. He pushed a few beers into the ice, leaving one on the counter for himself.

"Anybody want one?" He glanced behind him. "Before I park this in front of father?"

"Stevie, sit down this instant." Sam's mother was already on him, her long arms wrapped around him and the ice. "I'm going to heat up your plate for you."

"Now, hold on, Mom. Have to get Dad his beer." Steve walked out in the living room and put the bowl on the table. "Happy Thanksgiving. Now, don't get greedy and ask for more for Christmas."

"What the hell's wrong with the truck, anyways?" Their father fetched a can from the bowl and fell back into the couch. "I had to send Mike out for beer. I thought you wasn't going to make it."

"Mike?" Steve frowned, taking a gulp from his can. "You got a son I don't know about, Ray?"

"Sam's boyfriend," Ray answered, peering around Steve at the television set. Steve returned to the kitchen, where a plate awaited him.

"Oh, that's right. Sam's new boyfriend I have been hearing so much about lately." He sat down next to Sam. She turned her face as his lips caught her cheek. "I finally get to meet the old man in the flesh. How come you two aren't married yet, with a thousand children? To hear Mom talk in her messages..."

"Well, at least you're getting them." Their mother stood behind Steve, her hands on his shoulders. "Would it hurt you to call back?"

"You just talked to me today." He forked a piece of turkey and shoved it into his mouth. Sam could smell the sweet-sour of whiskey lingering on his skin. "What's the score out there?"

"Skins are losing," their father answered, apparently satisfied with his situation. "You gonna watch?"

Steve returned to the living room with his plate.

"Sam's right, Pat. With the snow…we ought to hit the road." Carol stood, seemingly detecting more than one storm approaching. "Ray's a terrible driver in the conditions."

"Can't we wait until halftime?" Ray whined as Carol put on her quilted downcoat.

"You can listen to it on the radio." Carol picked up a couple of wrapped plates and prodded Ray toward the door, where they came upon Michael entering.

"I had to go another bar over," he explained, standing in the threshold of the door, shaking snow off of his expensive trail parka like a wet dog. "The other place closed early."

"The Eastern Inn? Prolly nobody gone out 'cause of the weather," Sam's father opined. "Thanks for getting them beers, Mike. You're a good man."

"An angel you are." Steve stood up and held out his hand. "The archangel."

"An archangel," Sam corrected. "There is more than one."

"I'm Steve, Sam's brother." Steve bowed toward Michael. "The antichrist."

"Steven, don't talk like that in this house," their father said, lighting a cigarette. "It upsets your mother. And you already done screwed up enough today."

"Has this man been fully vetted?" Steve studied Michael, his lips turned down at the corners. "Are you sure he's battle-tested enough for the Pinskis? Really, Michael, the popped collar is making me worry."

"Shut up, Steve." Sam moved to get her coat.

"Now, now, he has a precious commodity in you, Sam," Steve explained, grabbing her by the arm. She hadn't felt his fingers against her skin in years. She was not pained by his pressure. It was the weight of his grip that surprised her, the cliff from which he was hanging. "I'm just making sure he can handle you. I've been watching your back all these years; you think I'm just going to let anybody take over?"

"Kind of hard to do, wouldn't you say, being in New Jersey the past six years and all," Michael replied. "I'd say that Sam has survived well enough on her own."

"Really?" Steve put his beer down on the coffee table. "And who the fuck do you think you are, coming in here, passing judgment on me? I've known Sam a hell of a lot longer than you, buddy, better than you ever will. She don't need no fucking preppy wallet to come in and be all high and mighty to her family."

"He's not being high and mighty about anything, Steve." Sam pressed against Michael in the direction of the door. "You're drunk. Maybe you should leave."

"Where's he gonna go?" their mother interjected suddenly. "You're accusing him of being drunk so you're going to send him off into a snowstorm?"

"I'd rather be drunk and freeze to death than stay here." Steve grabbed his thin jacket and the Tupperware bowl full of beer and walked into the night. Sam watched him storm through the lazy snowflakes, stopping at Michael's car parked in front. He reared back and kicked the passenger door, almost losing his balance. Then he got in his truck and roared away.

"Jesus, Sam, why did you have to say that?" Her mother started out the door, up the street, her fuzzy pink slippers soggy on the moistened sidewalk. "What if he hurts himself? Why did you have to get him all riled up?"

She moved into the street, looking for signs of the truck, her slippers matted and soaked like little drowned rabbits.

"Lousy fucker. He better hope he doesn't come back here." Michael surveyed his door, squatted close to the dent, trying to push it out while Sam's mother moved aimlessly up the street, like a homeless person.

"I'll pay for it," Sam offered. "I'm so sorry."

"It's not your fault," he answered tonelessly, not looking at her, running his fingers along the indentation. She wondered if he was having second thoughts. She stood dumbly on the sidewalk, watching the snow melt into the concrete.

"Close the goddamn door," her father yelled from inside, where he was still anchored to the couch. Sam could faintly hear the crowd from the football game on television as they roared in approval. "This ain't no goddamn barn."

5.

"The kids are back." Sam's mother is sitting at the picnic table, smoking a cigarette and picking green beans, when they pull up in the motorboat. Sam wonders if her mother was ever one of the "kids," at what time she became the "adult." Although Sam loathes being the kid, she is not quite ready to be the adult, either.

"Wow." Steve sits across from her and picks up a green bean. "I've only seen these in a can."

"Well, I know Sam is trying to be healthy and all," their mother explains. "So I got these from that farmers' market down the road."

"You don't need to give in to Sam's peer pressure, Ma." Steve lights a cigarette and winks at Sam. "She's only going to live a few more years than the rest of us, anyway."

"And you're lucky you've lived as long as you have," their mother responds, pushing the picked beans into a large pile. "Between your motorcycle accident and your boozing and god knows what else."

"What can I say? I lead a charmed life." He begins to chew on one of the uncooked beans. Sam's mother watches him for a minute before putting one in her own mouth. She spits it out carefully into her hand before picking up her cigarette.

Sam follows Michael to the cabin. He has not invited her, but she imagines he will not be unhappy to see her privately. It is coolest during the day because of its few windows and dark, wooden corners, and warmest at night and winter because of the heat stove. In the main room Sam's father sits catatonically on one of the old sofas, on which Liberty Bells, muskets, and Old Glory are patterned. He cradles an O'Douls in one hand and a cigarette in the other, listening to the start of the Orioles game on the radio. Sheets of static wash out seconds of broadcast, so Sam is not sure how hard he's listening, whether it's just a planned escape from the incessant chattering of her mother. He fondles his cigarette between his fingers delicately, like a girl, and glances at her once, moving only his eyes.

"Your backpack is in my room," Sam reminds Michael. "Out of the way of everything."

She is not sure what she means by that, since everything is always about and in the way. Every unwanted item in the Pinski household was given a second reprieve in the cabin. The Pinskis were as thrifty as they were frightened; frightened that they only had the good fortune of owning something of any value just once and that to throw it away was to bar further treasures from washing up on their shores.

Michael follows her through all the rooms to where she is sleeping. She watches as he rummages through the backpack, which Steve has left on the bar, wondering whether he has bought her a card or maybe a book but instead he hands her the old mail she had left at his apartment. She glances at it and places it on the counter. He looks at her, one of those encompassing examinations, his fingers bending and moving with urging, and she looks away.

"I didn't realize Steve was coming," he says. "I wouldn't have come."

"Well, fuck, Michael." She wraps her arms around herself. "I didn't even know you were coming, so there."

"Pat said she had mentioned it to you…that you were okay with it."

"Why wouldn't I have extended you a personal invitation, then?"

"I don't know." He picks up his backpack. "Do you want me to leave?"

"Why would I want you to leave?" She lets her hand trail along the paneling of the wall. She has seen pictures of her father as a teenager, frog-legged and bare-chested on the roof, laying shingles on the original one-room cabin, his hair dark and free, splayed over his forehead and resting on his earlobes like a nest. She wonders what thoughts rested between his jug ears, how the breeze felt on his elastic skin, before everything seized in the engine of his head and illness leaked out.

"Well, you didn't want to marry me. So I'm not sure why you'd still want me around."

"My mother invited you," she says. "It's her cabin." She cannot tell him how hard it has been for her without him. Although she knows it has to be like this. At least until she figures out how to deal with Steve, herself. Fifteen years have passed and she feels she is no further along.

If it is a game of chicken Michael wants, though, she will not play, even as it stuns her that she can only examine the tactical layers of his intentions and not his emotional ones. But it is the hard pit of her heart that caused her to run from him in the first place, so he could discover waters she imagines are more amenable to him. It was a mistake for him to believe the body of her ocean was calm, comforting. Tranquil.

"Look," she sighs. "Stay for dinner, at least? Stay the night. It's impossible to get down to the main road after dark."

"Fine." Michael makes his way to the door, happy she has engineered this save-face. "I'll stay because your mother invited me. But if your brother starts anything…"

"He won't start anything. He's a grown man," Sam assures him, although she is less assured herself.

"So where'd you meet the punk rocker?" Michael says as they walk back through the cabin. "She seems like a blast from your past."

"Yes—I'm regressing back to college," Sam laughs, picking up a dishtowel off the floor in the kitchen. "You wouldn't believe it to look at her, and I didn't at first, but Eve is one of the smartest people I've ever met."

"Well, maybe that wisdom comes after a few more whiskey and Cokes for her," Michael comments, looking through the window of the front room. Sam joins him. They watch Eve and Steve try to throw their boots up into the pine tree near the dock. "Or me."

She was just a girl, Sam first thought, if she thought of her at all. The girl who worked the late shift at the coffee shop at 31st and Charles Street, where Sam got her muffin and tea, had made no impression on Sam at first other than the fact that she belonged to the legions of urban service-industry workers who filled the coffee shops of the city, seemingly cast from the same disaffected dye: slightly unkempt shoulder-length blond hair, tattoos, a blank expression, rings and jewelry of all vintages on all digits and appendages, an affinity for black and brown and gray fabrics.

Although it wasn't rocket science, the girl quickly remembered Sam's order, a large Chai tea with milk and a cranberry oat bran muffin, and would have it ready the nights she usually stopped by.

"What would you do if I don't show up?" Sam laughed one evening as she counted out $4.20. "With my order, I mean?"

"You'll show up," the girl answered and smiled. "We've built this subconscious system of trust and dependence on each other. And, if not, I guess I'd give it to the homeless guy outside my building."

"Well, that's nice of you, ma'am." She put the money in the girl's outstretched hand. "I hope you don't have to pay for my waste. I feel like I should pay in advance or something."

"Don't worry about it."

The girl held Sam's eyes for a second or two, causing Sam to wonder briefly what the girl thought beyond all this, this being quite vague, of course. What the girl thought about anything, Sam supposed.

"I'm Eve Christmas," the girl said finally. "If you want to thank me, you can call me by my name and not ma'am. You make me feel old."

"I'm sorry," Sam laughed. "I'm Sam Pinski—I don't like being called ma'am, either. That's quite a name you have—there's a story behind it?"

"Maybe." Eve wiped some poppy seeds off the counter with her rag. "See you Thursday."

Their acquaintance began, although Sam did not think much about it. Mostly she thought about starting over again after Michael. As an adult, she wanted her life to be the exact opposite of the one she had as a child, and Michael, of course, was just that. His parents lived in New Hampshire. He graduated from Syracuse, then Hopkins, stayed on as a financial analyst for the university. He cycled on the weekends. He ate hamburgers and tofu with equal vigor and did not mind attending a play or poetry reading with her. Like a smooth, well-rounded stone, one, Sam sometimes thought, that didn't leave much of an impression in the palm. But they had built so much together in two years, a striking, shiny house, albeit on a rotten foundation. Her own. She wondered whether that pair of her shoes still waited optimistically for a reunion in the closet of his apartment, a Lady Bic between the toilet and the bathroom sink. Somehow, she wanted these things, the safety a relationship offered without actually partaking in its strange-yet-formal rituals.

She began to find gifts from Eve in her Tuesday and Thursday muffin bags—a Gumby pin, a Holly Hobby handkerchief, collages of strange-looking characters culled from magazine clippings. Sam delighted in these presents, a contamination of kindness inserted in her somewhat-sterile life. She reveled in her and Eve's secret alliance, the secret workings of which, to Sam, were dim at best. Sam fancied that she and Eve both knew the deep, jaded mysteries of life, of relationships, of people, that they were just passive observers who winked at each other because they knew what the world was in for. It became a game, a harmless one, their banter at the register. To counter her gifts, sometimes Sam would slip something thin between the four one-dollar bills she presented—a bookmark, a quote from a book she was reading, a photograph she found on the street.

One Thursday bag contained a note, not unusual but for its content: *Club Charles. Midnight. I don't expect you to disappoint me.*

It had been so long since she had been out with anyone—what did one do at bars? Perhaps some man would engage her in conversation. What would she tell him? She was just shy of the altar and hopelessly lost?

Sam found Eve sitting in the back. She hated to have to walk through all the people, peering at their faces in the dimness to find Eve while Eve was able to observe her remotely, safely from a hidden space. But Eve had not been looking at her, Sam discovered; she was leaning over the bar from her stool, reading. She wore a dark cardigan and vintage skirt a little tight for her large bone structure, nursing a glass of whiskey and a pack of cigarettes. Sam watched Eve push a chunk of hair behind her ear and swallow the contents of her glass without grimace, her sad features soft and yearning underneath the soft red light of the bar.

"Waiting long?" Sam slid down quickly beside her. Eve turned her head and smiled.

"Nope." Eve touched Sam's arm and then withdrew to her box of cigarettes. "I hope I'm not keeping you from anything."

"No...just work."

"Work for your classes?"

"Yep—student class assignments."

Eve signaled the bartender. "What are you drinking?"

"Um, a seltzer with lime would be fine."

"Come on—you didn't come all the way out here for a seltzer, did you?"

"I'm not a big drinker. My father was an alcoholic."

"Both of my parents were—all it did was make me an expensive date."

"All right, just one. But not straight like that."

"What would you like?"

"A glass of red wine."

"All righty—another whiskey, no chaser, and a glass of house red." She opened her wallet and pulled out some bills. "So what do I get in exchange for a drink, Sam Pinski?"

"I don't know—what do you want?" Sam folded her hands in her lap and looked around the bar, where the young and old hipsters of Baltimore sat on fifties-era leather furniture in the smoky dim and drank strong liquors and cheap beer.

"Hmm, you're a generous person, letting me choose." Eve held up her shot. "To...wherever the night takes us."

"To friendship," Sam added.

"Here, here." Eve drank quickly and lit a cigarette. "So, the real reason I lured you here—how does it feel to be a wunderkind literary sensation? Don't think I haven't been doing my research on you, Samantha Pinski. How does it feel to be 33, have a novel published, and teach writing classes at Hopkins?"

"I don't feel any different, to be honest. I guess you read the article in the paper, huh? But don't worry; I'm nobody. But what about you? You're attending Hopkins?"

"No, but I attend to most of Hopkins," Eve laughed. "What you see is what you get. I work at a coffee shop. And that's it. If I'm lucky I get to have a drink with those on the up and up."

"You're not from around here." Sam noted her accent. "How'd you get here?"

"Now that's an interesting story. Or not. As the book review might read, promising but not fully realized."

"A Southern state—South Carolina?"

"Close—Georgia. As I mentioned, my folks were alcoholics. I lived with my grandmother in a trailer with occasional visits from them, not noted for their creativity but sometimes for their scariness. When I was thirteen my grandmother died and I went to live outside Atlanta with my mother and her new boyfriend, who thought part of raising me meant fucking me while my mother was at the department of social services getting our welfare checks. When I was sixteen I ran away and moved in with a woman who encouraged me to get my GED. Then she got jealous and became a possessive piece of shit who liked to humiliate me in public. So I met this guy who attended Hopkins and was home for summer vacation. We got kind of close, so I thought, so when he went back to school I saved my money and drove up to be with him. Well, his girlfriend didn't like that so much, so I lived in my car for six months and talked him into letting me use his PO box at school as an address so I could get a job. For the past ten years I've worked at a glue factory, as a secretary for a construction firm, as a temp, and I've been at the coffee shop for three years. Yet they made some Hopkins student who's been there six months the assistant manager. I guess they figure all that education from Hopkins makes her more qualified to clean the espresso machine than me, I don't know."

"I'm sorry."

"Don't be sorry." Eve patted Sam's hand again. "It's not your fault. I didn't come here to wallow in the past. I came here to look forward to the future. Besides, I just want you to know now, so you don't think I'm something I'm not. And I don't have to pretend to be something I'm not."

"I like who you are just fine." Sam stared in her wineglass. "So what's the story behind your name?"

"Hmm, you writers are all the same." Eve stirred the ice cubes in her empty glass. "Always looking for material. It's not much of a story, really. My mom didn't want me to take my father's name because at the time he skipped out on her. But she didn't like her last name, so she told the hospital my father's last name was Christmas. She said at the time that my birth was like the feeling she used to get on Christmas Eve. It never felt like Christmas Eve living with her, that's for sure."

"Well, at least you're always Eve Christmas, right? The best is yet to come, so to speak."

Sam didn't know why she split a cab home with Eve. Perhaps she wanted to see a bit of herself in her. Or perhaps she felt that Eve, whiskey-drinking, thick-skinned, half-cocked, and world-weary, was the rightful family heir, not herself.

"So do I get a signed copy of your book?" Eve asked as they pulled up to Sam's three-story row home in Bolton Hill. "You know, something I can sell online for megabucks when you're rich and famous?"

"Yeah, sure." Sam unlocked the door. She'd gotten the house gutted, cheap, literally a walls and roof with outdated plumbing and kitchen, but hadn't gotten around to looking for contractors. Her tabula rasa, she'd joked to her father, who'd threatened to come over and hammer nails into something. She bent and looked through a stack of boxes in what would be the living room and found a copy of her book. She pulled a pen from her purse. "How did you like it?"

"You're a great writer. I think that…you still need to find your voice, though."

"What do you…" Sam snapped but kept silent, handing the book over.

"What do I know?" Eve laughed. "I'm just a high-school dropout with pickled genes—is that what you're thinking?"

"No—I'm sorry." Sam wrapped her arms around herself. She wondered, for a moment, whether Eve could have written the story of her life better than Sam herself. "I think your criticism is very valid. Thank you for thinking you can share it with me."

"I've been reading all my life." Eve took the book without examining the inscription. "It's the only way I've been able to convince myself that things are better out there than what I've seen so far."

"Eve, please." Sam took Eve's forearm. She could smell the heaviness of alcohol on Eve's breath, the space between them sour and sweet and wet. She smelled like the boys she knew, her father, her brother. And also of a musky, oil scent, like sandalwood or patchouli. Something dark, rich, and aged, to be savored.

"No harm." Eve twisted the book back and forth in her hand. "I was rude. It got good reviews, and they know a lot more than I do. I've just forgotten my manners."

"No, Eve. It's okay. I want to hear the truth, from somebody."

"Well, no charge this time." Eve winked and walked out the door. Sam watched her amble up the street to continue her night of drinking a few blocks over at the Mount Royal Tavern. Eve had told Sam earlier about a man she was sort of seeing, sorta, who would be hanging out there, maybe. When Eve reached the end of the street she turned and gave Sam a paramilitary salute, and Sam smiled, waved back.

Maybe it wasn't such a great book, Sam thought as she let herself back inside, but she had needed to write it, even if its truths were cloaked in metaphor, in surrealism. But maybe if she heard the truth enough she could learn to speak it herself, loud and clear.

She began to ask Eve to places: museums, free concerts, readings. She watched how Eve sat, what she wore, the way she spoke to ushers and other patrons, how her eyes moved over paintings and sketches, her fingers over book spines at secondhand stores. It was not a new tactic on Sam's part. She had spent the better part of college and her twenties observing, like a field anthropologist, her friends and lovers. How her friend Jackie tied her scarf that lay so carelessly across her clavicles to the way her roommate Rebecca slung her straw purse with the leather straps over her shoulder, stuffed with dog-eared copies of Tess Gallagher and Carolyn Forché. The way Tom, her boyfriend sophomore and junior year, smoked a cigarette, the way it hung out of his mouth while he packed a bowl.

She asked Eve places and she began to think of what Eve would say to things, how she would answer questions. It was not that she wanted to be Eve necessarily but perhaps someone more like Eve and less like herself. She wanted to be single correctly, and she wanted to fall in love correctly. She didn't want to leave another boyfriend with an engagement ring he needed to sell. She wanted to be an adult. She was tired of guessing what might work. Eve was the antithesis of Sam, and since nothing Sam had done had worked, it only seemed logical to try something different.

"I think I'm going to die." Sam sat on the curb outside Fraziers bar in Hampden as Eve smoked a cigarette. Like the Club Charles, it was a dark basement of a place, albeit much dingier, although it had the advantage of having two rooms, a large space for live music and a second room/bar in which to escape the band. The outside, however, was even worse—the sidewalk stained with beer, puke, bubble gum, and old butts that collected on the pavement around the ashtray instead of in it.

"You only had four beers; you'll survive," Eve answered, smashing the butt into in a flowerpot that was missing its plant. "Besides, you wanted to taste the single life again, see how the hipsters live"

"I guess I can die happy now." Sam stood up, the alcohol making her light, wobbly. "But I need coffee first."

They walked down 36th Street, past the boutique stores and antique shops and tacky five-and-dimes that sold things like Baltimore Ravens beer cozies and beach towels, the cherry of Eve's cigarette igniting and receding as if it were breathing on its own. Sam wondered if she had chosen the wrong person to study. Eve did not do anything in moderation, at least what Sam believed was moderation. They saw the loudest bands at the Ottobar and went to the most obtuse performance art pieces and the most crowded student parties at the Institute, where strobe lights swam over everyone's heads while they bobbed, fish in the dark sea.

They made it to the 7-11, where Sam bought the biggest coffee and Eve bought another pack of cigarettes. Outside a man in a jean jacket sat on a motorcycle and looked at a map. He rubbed the tanned, five o'clock shadow of his face with the heel of his hand while he chewed down a toothpick.

"Evening, ladies." He nodded to them. "Can one of you tell me how to get back onto 83?"

"It's easy," Sam answered, taking a sip of her coffee. "Make a right here, a left on Northern Parkway about a half-mile up, then it's a right exit."

"Thanks." He tucked his map back into his jacket and grabbed his helmet. "I appreciate it."

"Where are you going?" Eve asked, running her hand through her hair.

"Pennsylvania, biker bar outside York." He patted the gas tank of the Triumph. "Would one of you ladies like to come? Or is it rude to choose?"

"No choosing necessary; I'm going home." Sam answered, trying to remember where she had parked her car.

"You're not driving anywhere." Eve grabbed Sam's arm as she began to drift through the parking lot. "Thanks for offer, mysterious biker man; it would have been a blast."

"I don't know how you can get involved with strangers like that," Sam said once they were back on the avenue. "You don't know if he was really going to York."

"I have a good sense about people," Eve answered. "But, you're right. Maybe a few drinks ago I would've had a better sense of people. You got to admit, though, that guy was gorgeous."

"He was okay." Sam shrugged, taking the lid off her coffee. She felt angry at Eve but didn't know why. She wanted Eve only to look at her, care about her, listen to her, even though it was entirely unfair. The steam danced off the top of the coffee cup and disappeared into the warm April night. "He looked like my brother Steve."

"Wow, I guess I need to meet your brother, then." Eve lit a cigarette. They passed the bar they had left, a beer banner dangling precariously on one side, the ropes used to anchor it to the awning dragging along the sidewalk.

"No, you don't."

"Why not?"

"He lives in New Jersey. We don't see each other anymore. He's kind of a jerk."

"Define jerk."

"I don't know." Sam put the lid back on her coffee. It was cool enough, but she felt too sick to drink it. "He dropped out of high school. Has drug problems, flits from job to job, anger-management issues. That stuff."

"I thought you said you adored him, growing up."

"We grew up." Sam dug her free hand into her purse for her keys, which she could not find. Deeper and deeper she probed, and she wondered whether she left them on the bar, whether they fell on the floor under the table, out of her jeans and onto the bathroom floor. It was so hard to keep track of things when she was drinking, which is why she didn't do it very often. She was wondering how much a replacement key would cost, how much time it would take to go to the dealer, how she would get in her house tonight when she felt the sliver of metal and the adjoining key-rings.

"I do drugs, didn't finish high school, have worked a bunch of jobs." Eve stomped out her cigarette by the passenger door of Sam's car. "Does that make me a jerk, too?"

"Of course not. You're trying to make a better life for yourself. Steve ran away and he'll never own up to anything. That's why he's a jerk."

"I like your brand of crazy." Eve arched her eyebrow and smiled. "I can't imagine why Steve would want to miss out."

"We've seen him three times in eight years." Sam leaned against the driver side of her Jetta. "But I guess it's been better that way, for all of us. I'm sorry—I can't drive yet. I need to sober up."

Sam put her coffee cup on top of her car and wedged her keys tightly in her front pants pocket. They walked around the streets that circled the avenue, past the quiet residential homes of varying upkeep and colors, past stray cats that slinked across the streets toward women with frowning faces and over-colored hair and soft doughy breasts in tight shirts.

"Well, look who's come back," Eve said. They had heard the roar of the motorcycle a block over, were surprised when it turned out to be the man on the Triumph. He crept along beside them, his eyes smiling from behind his helmet visor.

"There you are—been looking all over this place for you." He leaned back in his seat.

"Well, you found us, Romeo," Eve answered, a smile forming on her lips.

"I'm sorry, ladies. I can't get you off my mind." he grinned. "Why go to York when there are so many beautiful women here in Baltimore?"

"Charmed, really," Eve laughed. "But you can tell us more over a drink at Fraziers."

"Can tell you more," Sam whispered. She grabbed Eve's arm and turned her away from him. "Look, I don't condone this, but I'm sober now if you want to go back to the bar. I'll go home."

"Are you sure?" Eve looked at her, and Sam saw the traces of disappointment hovering on her face. She felt like she had failed some test on how to be fun, spontaneous, interesting.

"Yes—this is what you want, right?"

"Sure." Eve nodded. She looked at Sam for a second, as if waiting for something, then hurried toward the bike. It whined away up the street, boring Sam's ears in its wake, belching smoke. She held her keys through her pocket, retracing her steps back to the car. When she passed the bar again the motorcycle wasn't parked in front, and she felt her heart throb in her throat. But Eve was her own keeper

She saw the figure huddled on her steps when she got home and figured it was a bum. She wished Eve had come home with her; she was better at handling the various beggars and addicts than Sam was. Sam parked the car a block over and held her keys in her fist on the walk to the house, the strongest stem sticking out between her fingers, ready to stab anybody who came up on her. But as she neared the step she recognized the combat boots, the pale, thick thighs, dirty-blond hair.

"I had him take me here," Eve explained, standing up as Sam fiddled with the door locks. "I hope you don't mind."

"No." Sam shook her head as they entered the dark halfway. "I'm just glad you're safe."

"I just would rather . . ." Eve's eyes searched for the elusive word. "You want to play Scrabble? Best of ten?"

"Best of one—I'm tired." Sam flicked on the lights. She dragged some boxes and crates together in the high-ceilinged living room for chairs and furniture and found the Scrabble game in a box marked *misc*. It was almost new, not like the ones her friends in college had owned with broken box lids and oily, smooth tiles rubbed down by many fingers. She had received her game for her twelfth birthday, her only request. And only her mother had played with her, and not well.

"Best of three." Eve smiled and cracked her knuckles. "Believe me, you'll be begging for three after I kick your ass."

"I like when you're cocky." Sam smiled, bringing out a few cans of tepid soda and chips from the kitchen. "You'll be easier to beat."

They settled under the single hanging chandelier in the living room, the one missing various prisms and light bulbs. Gradually the room brightened; the air was warmer with April daybreak. Sam opened one of the window sashes and they listened to random cars on Mount Royal Avenue. It was nearly six-thirty when, deadlocked at six games, Sam fell asleep. When she woke up, huddled with Eve under a quilt that Eve had brought down from her bedroom, Sam felt like she had made the right decision, moving here, alone in the old house, hardwood floors, lots of light. She felt her strongest here, with Eve beside her.

"Eve?" But she was alone. She sat up in a sweat, tears in her eyes that Eve had slipped away from her, onto a louder bike, a stronger drink, a more interesting person. But Eve stood at the window, watching the parishioners head to Mass at Corpus Christi Church.

"Sorry it got so late." Eve turned to Sam's voice, met her face where it peered out from the quilt. "I hope you don't mind that I stayed."

"No." Sam shook her head, wrapped her arms around herself. "It was nice having someone here. I haven't lived alone in a long time."

"You'll get used to it easier than you think." Eve bent down, her hand moving along the floor for her cigarettes.

"Should I be afraid of that?" She watched Eve open the window. The smell of cherry blossoms wafted into the room, the quick chatter of birds, the random song of church bells.

"What, that you'll be a lonely, bitter old gal like me, unable to commit to a fella?" Eve smirked, shrugging her fatigue jacket over her shoulders and placing a cigarette on her bottom lip. "Don't worry; you need people. You're a people person."

"What about you? You're a people person, too," Sam said. "What about the guy on the motorcycle? What about me?"

"I guess you got me there." Eve stretched her arms.

"I'm glad you didn't go with him."

"Well, I've been doing things my way, all crazy and stupid, so I thought I'd try yours," Eve answered. "You always seem so centered."

Sam laughed aloud. It was not her own laugh. It couldn't be; its force, authority, startled her. She felt the muscles in her stomach move, her lip crack in the middle from the smile that grew so big, quickly, on her face.

"What's so funny?" Eve arched an eyebrow.

"Nothing," she answered, stretching too. "You want to get breakfast?"

"Gotta work." Eve waved a little with her hand. "Thanks, though."

"Will you come back? I'll wait."

Eve studied her for a moment, her eyes moving back and forth across Sam's face, looking for something. Sam smiled; she did not look away. She concentrated on burning the feeling of home into Eve, the delicious hurt of safety after a perilous journey. What she felt just now.

"We do have some unfinished business." Eve smiled back, nodding at the Scrabble board. She crouched by the box and searched through the tiles, picking out four. She pressed them into Sam's palm and curled Sam's fingers over them.

"No peeking." Eve nodded at Sam's fist.

From the window Sam watched Eve go up the street, watched her hand moving along the seam of her jacket pocket in search of her sunglasses.

In her own hand the cool wooden tiles grew warm. When they felt so warm she thought they would burn into her palm, scarring her forever, she opened her fingers to look. There was an H, an M, an O, and an E.

*

Sam is not sure how she envisioned Eve would act at the cabin, but she hadn't planned on her acquiescing to her brother's moves. Steve and Eve stand by the grill, prodding the dull lumps of black to life, Steve brushing his elbow against Eve's as he adds some old paper to the coal bed, cigarette reclining lazily out of his mouth. He laughs easily, the tautness of his bare back muscles relaxed. Michael sits at the picnic table, trying to get reception for his cell phone as Sam's father tries to pick up reception for the Orioles game. Sam watches her mother, who basks openly in the perceived courtship of Eve and Steve, eyeing Sam and nodding toward Michael, eager to have Sam enter this Shakespearian comedy of love.

"Did you bring your guitar, Steve?" Pat Pinski asks, wrapping the freshly shucked corn on the cob in aluminum foil for cooking on the grill. "Maybe you can play us something later?"

"Nope, sorry Ma." Steve glances back at her. "Didn't want to torture you with my cat-scratching."

"Springsteen is hardly cat-scratching," Sam pouts, and feels her face redden. She opens one of Michael's microbrews in an attempt to placate him and numb herself in the process.

"I remember—what did you used to say, Karl?" Sam's mother walks the tray of corn to the grill, where Eve intercepts it and makes room for it among the plates of steak. "If it ain't Johnny Cash, don't bother playing it?"

"Musical genius, that man," Sam's father agrees, lighting a cigarette. "Man is a god, better than Elvis. Way better than Springsteen, that jackass."

"You know some Johnny Cash, don't you, Stevie?" Pat Pinski presses. "You and your father have a lot in common."

"Well, it don't matter, Ma, because I didn't bring any guitars." Steve throws the slabs of steak onto the grill. They hiss and he moves them around roughly with the grill fork.

"You could sing," she suggests.

"How about everybody just shut up?" Sam's father turns up the radio. "Can't a man get any peace around here?"

Everyone is quiet. Sam can see the muscles in Steve's back tense once again and, for the first time, she can feel the two halves of her jaw press together. She had taken to wearing a mouthguard at night after she began clenching her teeth in her sleep a few years back. Her doctor had prescribed her some valium, but she did not like the untethered feeling it gave her. She preferred buckling down, whether by body or by teeth, to brace any sudden storms that might blow through.

"Reno, Chicago, Fargo, Minnesota," Steve begins singing loudly the Johnny Cash song about traveling, and Eve joins him. They both have good voices, which is unsurprising to Sam. Steve twirls the fork in the air and dances a little jig while Eve claps her hands and keeps time with her feet. And there it is, Sam thinks: the hard-luck losers of the Pinski clan and its honorary members whooping it up and enjoying themselves while the "success" stories sit glumly in the circle. Michael stands up and mumbles something about work e-mails before heading into the cabin.

"Come on, Sam!" Eve skips her way over to Sam, an elbow extended.

"I don't know the words," Sam apologies, and that much is true. Although she doubts she can join them. She wants to, but she doesn't know how. She feels submerged in herself. She doesn't feel as if she's drowning, so maybe she's already drowned. Eve makes her way to Sam's mother, who dances a gentle polka with Eve, her feet hitting the dirt by the fire softly, displacing only the smallest bit of dust.

"Ah, the good old days," Sam's mother says, although Sam is not sure to which days she is referring. "Remember when we used to go to dances, Karl?"

"At the American Legion," Karl Pinski answers, but offers no clarification.

"Were you a vet?" Eve asks, making her way to the picnic table, cigarette and Jack and Coke in hand. She is a little drunk; Sam can see it in the loose way her limbs work, the half-buttoned shirt over her bathing suit. She plops down in front of Sam's father.

"Naw—my brother went to Vietnam. I got a deferment."

Sam's mother, behind Sam's father, points her finger briefly toward her head to elucidate for Eve the type of deferment.

"Did he make it through okay?"

"Tet offensive." Sam's father shrugs, inhaling cigarette smoke. "He didn't talk about it much. So I didn't ask him much."

"It was rough," Pat Pinski confirms. "He was in the VA hospital for a long time."

"That's terrible." Eve nods.

"Yeah, he was a good brother." Karl Pinski stares at the darkening creek. He sighs, and Sam can feel the pulpy, velvet softness of his thoughts disperse through them. "He used to come get me out of the hospital on the weekends when I was younger and take me up here fishing. We caught some bass like you wouldn't believe. He always wanted to be buried here. Damn wife of his had him buried with her family up in Pennsylvania."

"I'm sure the Conowingo community is better for it," Steve quips.

"Well, you laugh now, buddy, but I put it in my will that I'm gonna be buried here. My ashes. You can throw half in the creek and scatter the rest in front of the cabin."

"What about you, Ma? You want us to scatter your ashes up here next to Pop's?" Steve asks, taking a sip of his whiskey.

"I would like a proper Catholic burial," she replies. "And I bought your father a plot, too, so don't listen to him."

"Proper Catholic burial. Pfft," Sam's father laughs. "Like you are a proper Catholic."

"Living with you should qualify me for sainthood," she mutters, taking a sip of her Coors. Everyone is quiet for a moment, watching Karl Pinski. He drags slowly on his cigarette, his black-button eyes moving evenly across a point on the horizon, before smiling.

"That's a good one, Patty," he says. "You got me. But you kids make sure to throw some dummy in the box and bring my ashes up here. It's the least you could do."

Karl Pinski stands, sighs. He clears his throat and makes his way up the hill. Everyone watches him slip through the screened porch into the house.

"Is he going to bed?" Eve asks as Steve takes their father's vacated spot.

"He did a lot today," Sam's mother says. She rubs her chest, clearing her throat. She looks slightly damp, although it is not that hot. "Me too. I better get a good night's sleep for tomorrow."

"What's tomorrow?" Eve opens her mouth and a limp ring of smoke floats out.

"Fourth of July parade," her mother answers, standing up with her cigarettes in one hand, plastic tumbler of beer in the other. "Your father is bringing the old pontoon boat up from the marina tomorrow morning."

"What, for the parade?" Steve chortles. "That thing'll sink before it even gets there."

"Well, I know he wanted to surprise you tomorrow, but he had the guys at the marina patch it up a few weeks ago so we could be in the parade. So make sure you're all up and ready to go after breakfast."

"Where'd he get the money for that?" Sam asks. Her mother looks back toward the house.

"The money we were saving for your wedding," she whispers, as if Michael could hear her from up in the cabin.

"Money well spent," Steve answers, and Eve hits him on the forearm. He grabs it playfully. In the dark Sam can see the glint of teeth through his grin. She can see it through the tears filling her eyes.

"Mom, I'm sorry," she blurts, letting her face rest in her hands. Her mother's body presses against her back, her arms around her. "I wish you didn't save the money…for me."

"It's okay, honey." Her mother's voice hums into her neck. "We can save it again. We just knew we didn't need it right now. Don't worry about it."

With that, she kisses Sam's head and releases her, making her way up the hill.

"Don't cry, Sam," Steve slurs, patting the table. "Come over here and have a drink."

"Shut up," she says, and she can see them, the muscles in Steve's jaw, slacken. She is happy she has hurt him, that she still can. He sinks the rest of the whiskey in his glass and wipes his mouth with the back of his hand.

"I know what'll make everybody feel better." He smiles, standing up. "Sam, go get Michael. We got fireworks to set off."

"Are you crazy?" Sam stands up, too. She can hear the night birds, fish jumping out of the creek. "What did Dad say?"

"Sam, I'm thirty-five years old. I ain't heard what Dad's said in almost twenty years." He hangs a cigarette out of the corner of his mouth and moves quickly to the porch, where he has left the fireworks. Sam and Eve watch him disappear into the house and reappear a few minutes later with Michael. They each have hold of one end of the box as they slowly retreat down the hill, finding footholds among the roots, depressions.

"Eve, grab the drinks," Steve whispers.

"Et tu, Michael?" Sam says, and he smiles thinly at her. They climb back into the motorboat. Steve opens the clutch and they drift down the creek, out of site of the cabin, before Steve turns the motor over. They slowly thread the tree-lined creek before the lake opens up on them, the moon sliced like a hard-boiled egg on the chop of the water. Most of the boats are in for the night.

"I figure we can go to the cliff rocks, set 'em off over the lake," Steve yells over the engine.

"And what happens when someone calls the police?" Sam says.

"By the time the police get up here, we'll be long gone," he answers, making a wide turn before cutting off the motor and waiting for the boat to float close to the woody shore. "We shoot a few right off in the middle, we enjoy, and then we beat it out of here."

"You men like to shoot things off," Eve replies, pulling her hair away from her face. "Your mouths, your dicks, your fireworks."

Steve grabs his crotch through his shorts, a pair of jeans he has cut to mid-thigh, and climbs on the front of the boat with the rope, looking for something to anchor. Michael lifts the box of fireworks on his lap to protect them from the cascades of water that have spilled over the sides of the boat and onto the bottom where Sam can feel its coldness, its warmth, between her toes.

"Michael, why are you going along with this?" she whispers.

"This is your freak show," he shrugs, not looking at her. "I'm just along for the ride."

Eve touches her forearm. Sam recoils slightly, more from surprise than revulsion. She smiles at Eve apologetically.

"Don't worry. It's not your fault if someone goes wrong."

"What do you mean?" Sam reaches down, rescues her sandals from the rising water on the floor. "I'm here, aren't I?"

"Yes." In the moonlight Eve's face is kind, her chin and cheeks rounded, gentle, like a nun's. "And you're going to have fun."

Steve has tied the boat to a tree. Michael leans over and passes the box to him before jumping out. The water is up to his knees. He holds out his arms to Eve, who inches to the front of the boat before falling in. Michael moves closer to the boat, holding out his arms. Sam grabs his hands and jumps. He stays back, holding onto her arms, when she wants him to come closer, pull her into his body. She needs to feel close to something, something. She's afraid she doesn't know how. On the shore she crouches behind a boulder that rises to her waist, wrapping her arms around it while Steve and Michael dig holes for the launchers.

"Eve, get back there with Sam," Steve instructs. "I don't want you to get hurt."

Sam eases up on the rock as Eve positions herself close. She can smell the whiskey, the cigarettes, the dried creek on Eve's skin. Eve takes her hand in the dark, smiles at her. Sam watches Steve and Michael light the fuses of a line of launchers before running toward them.

Sam hears the thonk-thonk-thonk-thonk-thonk as the rockets leave the launchers, and then the sky lights up: a red-and-white snowball, white streamers, a green dragon that zigzags across the sky. A small blue flower that disintegrates into hundreds of small detonations. She can't help but smile. Whatever the cost, they are beautiful.

Steve and Michael scan the water. The cabins dotting the lake remain dark, so they hurriedly work toward setting off another round. The sky lights up again, purple, white, green, red, but the second round of screaming missiles comes and goes with a few lighted windows.

"Let's pull out." Steve jerks his head toward the boat.

"We have to wait for these to cool off," Michael says, standing over the smoldering launchers. "So the woods don't catch fire."

"Here." Steve makes a bowl with his hands in the water, scooping some out and flinging it in the direction of the launchers. Michael finds a discarded can and holds it under the water until it's full and then pours it as well. Eve and Sam wade quickly back to the boat. Michael brings the half-empty box to the boat, and Eve and Sam slide it on the bench seat between them. Steve is the last, untying the rope and then pushing the boat out in the water before climbing aboard. They float under the cover of darkness, engine off, while they see if any other boats enter the lake.

"They probably expect a lot of this stuff," Eve says, lighting a cigarette. "I mean, it is the Fourth tomorrow."

"Yeah, I think we'll be all right." Michael takes a swig of his beer, stretching his legs in the little available space. "That was pretty fun."

"You see, my man." Steve points his whiskey glass at him from the driver's seat. "I am going to turn you into a Pinski yet."

Everyone is quiet. The moon follows them back to the cabin.

THE PROPOSAL

The night they pulled to the house on Narragansett Bay, it was raining, the air humid, hot like the breath of a dog. Not an hour and a half earlier, when they had left Baltimore on the 10:00 p.m. flight to Providence, the sky was cloudless, miles of black felt paper, its ceiling high, topped with stars.

"It'll clear up tomorrow," Michael assured her, heaving their duffel bags over both of his flat, broad shoulders and moving toward the house. Sam stayed by the rental car, pretending to refold the map. The word "cottage" was used by Michael to describe his parents' summer home in Newport, but the only thing humble about the large, peaked house on the cliff with three garage doors was the gray aluminum siding encasing it, which, Sam guessed, was a better protector from the elements than wood.

She crushed some gum wrappers and the waxy sleeve of a muffin into her hand and followed. It had been a surprise to her, the trip, known only to her that morning. His parents were guestless that weekend, a sudden cancellation, and wanted to know whether he and Sam wanted to come up. She had thrown a few things and her bathing suit in a bag before her classes, and when she got home they drove to the airport. Although the house was dark, she could see the shell of a room begin to form around her as she walked down the vestibule past Michael. In the living room, white walls and blond wood floors covered by oriental rugs in happy, pastel colors outlined a room with beige settees and armless chairs. She imagined she might have more in common with the weekly help than with the owners of this palatial house.

But the room was only the placemat for the stunning view of Narragansett Bay, which undulated darkly beyond the west wall, composed entirely of four ceiling-to-floor windows and two French doors. She could faintly see the bridge into Newport they had just crossed forty-five minutes earlier, serenaded by Styx's "Come Sail Away" on the region's classic rock station and strongest radio signal.

"Looks even better in the morning," Michael whispered behind her. "Come on, everybody's asleep."

She followed his lumbering, luggage-laden frame up the stairs and down the hall, where they passed three bedrooms, one of which was alight behind a closed door, before heading into the fourth. It was a small room, as white and airy as the spaces downstairs, with a queen bed sporting nautical-themed sheets, a stuffed pelican doll resting above its shams.

"I'm going to say hi to Winona." Michael cocked his head toward the door and, presumably, the lighted room. "I'll be back in a minute."

"I'm going to take a shower," she answered, rummaging through one of the bags. She slipped into the adjoining bathroom, which was decorated in a similar, simple theme of anchors and seashells. She hit the water in the shower and eased her shoulders in. Sam still had a stack of revised student stories to read, grades to be decided before the end of summer classes. She brought her briefcase stuffed with papers and was prepared to dive into them at any sign of awkwardness, boredom, discord—citing a need to get grades to the bursar first thing that next week.

She wondered about Michael's relationship with his younger sister Winona, whether there were any similarities between them like between her and Steve. She hoped not. Winona had been away at Vassar most of the time Sam had known Michael, studying abroad the rest, and Sam had only known a smiling, freckled face cloaked in a ski cap or hidden behind a visor and sunglasses from the three-by-fives tacked to the refrigerator in Michael's apartment. At least he had these mementos, proof of familial functionality.

She was half-asleep when Michael came back, forty-five minutes later, but she did not hold it against him. She sensed that her time alone that weekend would comprise precious few minutes, and she had climbed into the cool, nondescript sheets in the cool, nondescript room of the big, nondescript house and deliciously absorbed the quiet and dark.

She listened to his shower, felt his warm, slightly damp body slide next to hers, his erection in her back. She turned over and opened herself up as he climbed on top of her, kissed her breasts and neck, framed her hips with his hands. She reached between them, found his penis with her hands, felt it bob between her fingers as she stroked it. He quietly entered her, and she could count, almost to the second, how long it would last. She closed her eyes, thought of going to the beach tomorrow, the sun making her skin hot and tight.

She felt his body arch and stiffen, and she stroked his shoulder after he rolled to the side of her, breathing heavily. She felt guilty that she was able to give him so little sexually; she had blamed it on a female illness, endometriosis, that she didn't even have. It seemed easier than trying to explain her complicated history with the men in her life, even if he deserved to know. She wondered if this would be the night he would say something—she always wondered after their anemic sex whether he would pull a leather harness or a dildo out of the night table or ask to be spanked or bring up the name of a woman who was interested in a three-way. But then she heard him begin to snore, and she knew she was safe for another night.

*

The light woke her the next day, bouncing off the walls of the white room at six-thirty in the morning. She squirmed out of Michael's grasp and went to the window, watching the blue wake lines rippling through the water, an occasional white triangle from an early bird sailboat. Beyond the window cattails waved in the narrow strip of dune below, separating the house from the bay, but she could not hear them. She longed to be outside, to have a cup of lemon tea and begin writing, but she could not explore the house, the porch, unannounced until Michael woke up.

That could be hours. She sat on the wicker rocker by the window, balancing her laptop on her bare knees, and began to type. Next door the fabled Winona's shower turned on; groans and creaks occurred from other areas of the house, and she felt braver. She closed the laptop and dressed, wondering if she could slip outside without anyone knowing, explore the property, find a place to write near the shore.

Sam slid her laptop into her tote bag, fetched her sunglasses from her purse, looped the thongs of her sandals through her middle finger, and retraced her steps down the stairs and into the living room. She was surprised to find a slightly overweight man sitting on the settee and reading the *Boston Herald*.

"Oh," she said, louder than she had intended. The top half of the paper fell forward to reveal a graying bald head the shape of a light bulb, Michael's hazel eyes screwed into it like buttons. The man's large expanse of forehead wrinkled, perplexed, before relaxing.

"Oh," he mimicked her and laughed, setting the paper down. "You must be Samantha."

"Yes." She nodded, taking a step toward him.

"At least, I should hope so," he continued, folding the paper and moving toward her while tightening the belt of his robe. "Or I would have to think my daughter Winona has really changed."

She shook his big, dry, calloused hand. For some reason, she had expected it to be soft, slightly damp, the hand of a banker. But she remembered that the Smiths had a thirty-footer and probably other outdoor toys, things that rubbed and calloused them.

"You want some orange juice, bagels?" He swung a meaty arm, like the boom of a sailboat, toward a glass-and-steel kitchen. "My wife forgot the capers for the salmon and cream cheese, but she should be back from the corner store soon."

"No, thanks." She shook her head. The family vocabulary was quaint, charming—cottage, corner store—but she wondered how much was affected. Or for the benefit of people like her. At home in Baltimore, the corner store was the 7-11, which had just as much of a chance of carrying capers as it did moon rocks.

"You sure?" He blinked his right eye. "You're a pigeon of a thing, but you have to eat sometime."

"The thing is," she explained, glancing back toward the front door. "Is that Michael sleeps late, and I always try to sneak a little writing in before he gets up. That way it doesn't…interfere with our time. So I thought I'd write a little until he came down. And then eat. Do you mind if I set myself up on your porch?"

"Oh, yes, you're a writer." He moved toward the French doors. "I'm sure my wife will love you. You can talk all about the latest Nora Roberts book."

She smiled thinly, squeezed past him onto the deck. The smell of seaweed and orchids rested heavy in her nostrils, along with the last night's humidity. She settled in a deck chair and tilted her laptop screen to the best outdoor angle, but she found she could not write, a combination of the daylight and the foreign surroundings, smells, including cigarette smoke. She leaned over the edge of the rail at the steep descent to the shore. She leaned further and caught the source of the smoke: a mass of dark, tight, unkempt curls. Sam walked along the length of the deck, past the living room where it flanked the two west-south corners of the kitchen, and found the gate, which she let herself through and onto the path straight down to the bay. And her.

"Hey." Sam gave a small wave when the girl, about twenty-five, turned to face her. "Are you Winona?"

"Yes, you psychic woman." The girl crushed her cigarette at the bottom of her sport sandal and rose. Unlike Sam, she kept her hair long and wild, past her shoulders. Her eyes were green and her skin nearly olive. She was smaller than Sam but more muscular, tanned. "And you're Samantha?"

"Sam," she answered, gripping the straps of her tote bag. "I use my full name only to establish that I'm a woman."

"That's not always necessary," Winona said. "And brevity is important. I'm sorry I didn't say hello last night. It was late and..."

"I was tired, anyway." Sam shrugged her shoulders. "Needed to get settled."

"Well, you're everything and all that." Winona clicked her teeth, her eyes starting at Sam's feet and ending at her eyes.

"You haven't even met me," Sam laughed.

"Are you calling Michael a liar?" Winona looked over Sam's shoulder. "Where is my brother? Still sleeping like a fucking slug? You smoke?"

"No." Sam watched Winona light another cigarette without waiting for her answer. "But it's fine. My family smokes."

"My family hates it. Which is why I will be hiding from them all weekend." Winona blew a cloud of gray-white smoke toward the bay.

"They can smell it, I'm sure."

"Shh." Winona sat back down on the step, patted it with her hand. "They can't prove what they can't see. Come, sit with me. Conspire with me."

"Sam?" She heard Michael's deep voice cut across the bushes, cattails. "I'd better see what he wants," she apologized to Winona, walking back up the steps, somewhat relieved. After last night, she hadn't expected to find anything of authenticity in the Smith household, anything that she'd have to guard against. She met him at the top of the steps. He wore a white Syracuse t-shirt and plaid shorts. She curled her arms around his long, lean midsection like a snake and squeezed.

"I thought you ran away," he joked, kissing the top of her head. "Want some breakfast?"

"Yeah—I was just chatting with Winona." He took her tote from her, slung it over his shoulder.

"What, work already?" He peeked in the opening of the bag at her laptop.

"Writing," she answered. "The next Nora Roberts bestseller, you know."

She was immediately ashamed for saying it, but Michael didn't seem to notice. They went into the dining room, where a spread of bagels, lox, salmon, cream cheese and capers, fruit awaited, along with a short, dark-haired woman wearing white Capri pants and a soft, wrinkled blue button-up. Bangles of silver poked out from her upturned cuffs, and meticulous nails curved off the ends of her fingers. Sam had expected a family of tall, thin Europeans, but whatever their height, Sam couldn't help but be overwhelmed by their competence. Matching tableware, all white, flatware, napkins cut the table symmetrically like the eighths of an orange. Sam's mother could make a mean omelet, but chances were she'd serve it on a plastic McDonaldland plate scarred by twenty years of knives and forks.

"Mimosa or Bloody Mary?" Michael's mother, the consummate hostess, asked her first. "I'm Esme, but everyone calls me Em."

"Bloody Mary, please, uh, Em," Sam stuttered. Michael's father stood by the bar, blending ice for drinks, and the request seemed fitter for him. His big pink light-bulb head nodded as the whirr of the blender drowned out any thoughts he may have had on the matter. Michael handed her a plate, to which she modestly adorned half a bagel, a sliver of salmon, a spoonful of cream cheese.

"Oh, dear, Michael, she eats like a bird." Em shook her head, and Sam knew she had failed the first test. Em took Sam's plate from her hand and immediately doubled her serving, also adding a cantaloupe slice and half a deviled egg. "Here you go, dear. No need to be polite."

"And please, no sipping at this." Michael's father pointed to her Bloody Mary in process. "Spicy?"

"Yes, please."

"A girl after my own heart." He held out her beverage. "Winona, would you like a Bloody Mary?"

"How about a tall glass of rum?" Winona had entered a few minutes behind them, but surprisingly she was already sitting, a bagel moving toward her mouth.

"How about after lunch?" their father answered.

"I don't see what difference it makes," Winona complained between bites. "Alcohol's alcohol."

"Michael and Sam, we're so glad you could join us." Em held up her glass. "And it's certainly a pleasure to finally meet you, Sam. How about a toast to good futures?"

"Michael only invites girls up that he's sure about," Winona laughed, letting her butter knife clang against the plate.

Sam took a large gulp of her drink. She nodded and smiled weakly at Michael's stories of their two-year relationship between sips of her continuously filled Bloody Mary. She wondered where he got the idea he was sure about them, since they only saw each other a few times a week, lived separately. Sure, Michael had met her parents, but so did many boys she wound up not living with, not seeing more than a few times a week, and not marrying.

"Who's up for sailing?" Michael's father asked, and she had no choice but to say yes, no matter how dizzy, to any Smith suggestion, whether it be sailing, raping and pillaging, or snorting crack. She tucked herself into a small ball in the base of the Catalina 30 sailboat, feeling her suntan lotion squiggle down her cheeks and behind her knees, while the Smith family coordinated a complex dance of line pulling and weight shifting. They tacked across the bay, and then back. Then they did it again. Everyone smiled, commenting on the fortuitous breezes, the low chop. Sam worked every muscle in her face until it froze into perpetual grin. It might have burned into her face, so high and fierce the sun on her skin.

"You like lobster, Sam?" Michael's father inquired when they were back on land, refreshing their drinks on the porch. She almost thought he was making fun of her impending sunburn, but no one laughed, and she realized he was inquiring about dinner. "We up for Pier 49?"

"Of course." Em rose, leaving her glass of white zinfandel full, moving toward the door. "We always treat our guests to Pier 49."

"It's at the marina," Michael explained, both helpfully and unhelpfully.

"I thought you Southerners ate those bottom-dwellers—crabs?" Winona sipped from a can of Miller Light, alcohol, Sam assumed, she'd brought on her own.

"We do," Sam nodded, "although, respectfully speaking, lobsters are bottom-dwellers as well."

"Respectfully speaking," Michael laughed, kissing Sam's red cheek. "You can throw your shoe at her, Sam. Really—it's encouraged."

Winona looked at her and smiled in a no-hard-feelings sort of way, her freckled, dimpled face inviting. Everyone showered and Michael drove them in his father's Cadillac into town. Sam watched the old money in summer outfits walking up and down the cozy streets, pretending the heat wasn't suffocating, eating ice cream, waiting outside restaurants for dinner. At the pier Sam dined with the Smiths on steamed lobster, mussels, corn on the cob, white zinfandel. Sam tried to eat one-quarter of the plate more than she normally would have; she could not risk Em's admonishment again. She pushed a blob of mashed potatoes into the empty lobster shell when no one was looking.

"Newport's a wonderful place to get married," Em said at dessert. "St. Mary's Church is here. You're Catholic, right, Sam?"

Sam felt her heart stop in her chest, her fears from this morning revisited. But the possibility that his parents also were somehow privy to his plans horrified her, angered her.

"The Kennedys married there," Winona added. "If you like that kind of star-fucker stuff."

"I'm sure my mom would be pleased," Sam answered. Would-be, in a hypothetically speaking sort of way, she thought. Everyone would be happy, certainly. Everyone but her. It had happened so fast, arriving at this point. Was two years too fast? She should probably be sure by now. After all, Michael had been an open book during their two years together—the only mystery to Sam had been his parents, to whom he was not close. Yet she should have realized, regardless of his relationship with them, that they were the final frontier before marriage, commitment, and that was why Michael and Sam were here: the official blessing.

She threw up in the parking lot. She blamed it on mixing liquors. Michael had never shown a proclivity for drinking, and his family's gluttony had surprised her. She failed miserably to keep up with them.

"You need to get Sam some practice," Michael's father joked from the front seat as Sam leaned her head out the back window, Winona holding onto her waist from the middle seat. "There's always weekends like these."

"All this can be yours," Winona laughed, stroking the soft wavy tufts of Sam's hair. "Choose wisely, young jedi."

At the house, Sam refused bed. She knew if she passed out the hangover would come that much sooner.

"Why don't we go down to the beach?" Winona suggested. "Michael, get my beer and meet us down there."

"Sam's not drinking anything else tonight," Michael said

"I don't mean her, stupid." Winona took Sam's hand and guided her from the porch. Winona pulled them in a patch of cattails almost to their heads. There was no path, and Sam struggled between consciousness and the whip of cattails following her.

She felt better at the beach. The air, while not cool, was cooler than during the day, and it was soothing against her hot cheeks.

"Here." Winona handed her what Sam thought was a cigarette but turned out to be a joint. "This will take the hangover away."

Sam took a puff and held it. She had not smoked since college, more than five years ago. Way before she met Michael. Long before she began purchasing her weekend clothes from outdoor-wear catalogs and not the t-shirt rack at the local record store. She smelled the sweet herbal fragrance, felt her lungs burn. Winona cupped her hands over the joint against the wind while Sam inhaled again. Then Sam laid on her back, looking at the purple eating the yellow and mauve of the sky.

"I'm happy for you guys," Winona said, crossing her legs and lighting a cigarette. "At least my parents will get one marriage out of this."

"You're not getting married?" Sam forced her eyes open as the pot pressed like a brick against her forehead. She suddenly felt very conventional, wondered if Winona thought she'd been in a sorority or something.

"Well, it looks like Michael will have to ask you another time," Winona answered. "Unless you sober up enough for a walk down the beach."

"I don't want him to ask me at all," Sam said. "I think...well, I think it's a waste of money. That's why. I don't believe in it."

"My parents have money to waste," Winona answered. "But, to answer your question, about one wedding, I'm a lesbian. My family doesn't know that."

"Michael either?" Sam sat up to get a good look at Winona, if she missed something, like a secret pinky ring, a birthmark, that identified her as a lesbian. The only thing unusual about Winona was not so unusual—a pair of tattered sky-blue Converse chucks, bay-soaked, then dried, which she had worn to the pier, much to her mother's dismay.

"No one," Winona answered, offering Sam more of the joint. She shook her head. "I just needed to tell somebody."

"I won't tell," Sam responded, sifting her hands through the sand for something. "But your family, they seem okay. At least your brother."

"They subscribe more to the church of the NIMBY," Winona explained, dragging on the joint. "You know it? Not In My Back Yard. It's okay for daddy's friends to smoke cigars and cigarettes, and it's okay for mommy's gay friends to take her to New York for culture, but not for me. Michael, I'll tell him sometime. I just know he's really into you and I didn't want to take any of his thunder this weekend."

"I like your brother, but…" Sam said. She handed Winona a piece of sea glass, a buffed green shard that was once a beer bottle. "There's something I need to tell him."

"It's none of my business," Winona laughed, taking the glass and pocketing it without examination. "And I had no right to tell you anything, either."

"Sometimes it's easier to talk to strangers than people you know," Sam said, tracing her fingers through the hard sand. "It's just that I…I don't know."

"Here." She handed Sam her empty beer bottle. "I've got a piece of paper and pen. Just write down all your deep, dark secrets and we'll send it out to sea in my bottle, let someone else find them."

Winona gave Sam the paper and pen, but Sam did not write. She watched the dark waves rushing toward them in coordinated rows, a flanked attack. She listened to the bugs, a dog barking in the distance. She felt the half-moon of red, raw burn on her neck, the weight of feet in the sand behind them.

"Ladies." Michael's voice was behind Sam, his hands on her shoulders.

"What took you so fucking long?" Winona asked, moving over so he could sit between them.

"The Bermans' dog got out, that little shit terrier," he answered, handing Winona a cold six-pack. It was the Guinness he had bought last night outside Providence. "Took me forever to catch him and bring him back."

"Fan-cy," Winona commented on the choice of beer, plucking out a bottle. "Got an opener?"

Michael produced his key ring, which had a little plastic snowboard bottle opener from Vail on it. "I come prepared, dear sister."

"Did I ever tell you how much I love you?" Winona smiled at him as she pulled the bulk of her curls away from her face and into a ponytail.

"Always when you're drunk, sometimes when you're sober," he answered, popping off their bottlecaps. "How are you doing, honey? You hanging in there?"

"Yep," Sam answered, now confident that she could put pen to paper.

"What are you writing?" he asked, taking a puff off Winona's joint, which had whittled to a roach.

"It's nothing," Sam answered, stuffing the paper into the bottle and walking toward the bay.

"Don't throw that in there." Michael began to stand up. "Don't litter."

Sam stuffed the bottle into her pants pocket and ambled along the little rocky shore toward the docks. She wondered whether Winona would be too drunk to remember this night. She wondered whether she would be. Michael grabbed her hand and they stumbled along in the dark, a shell occasionally pressing into the meat of her foot, back to the light of the house.

"You have a good time?" he asked.

"Sure," she answered. Her hand tightened in his as she stumbled over a piece of driftwood. "Next time, I won't try to keep up with your family."

"It's always tough meeting somebody's family," he answered. "I was worried for months that your father thought I was a snob."

Sam's father always thanked Michael for the single-malt scotch he brought over for the first Christmas, even though he no longer drank alcohol. It sat like a trophy alongside a bottle of wine Sam's mother had received from a coworker in the kitchen, both yearning for guests who would not bypass them on their way to the refrigerator for a beer or a wine cooler.

"Do your parents like me?"

"Of course," he answered. "Why wouldn't they?"

Sam broke free when they reached the front door, claiming she'd left something in the rental car. She ambled along the pebbled driveway barefoot until she came to Winona's silver Saab convertible at the end of the driveway. The top was down. Perhaps Winona felt the worst of the storms were over. Sam dropped the bottle in the footwell behind the driver's side. When she came back in Michael's father was sitting on the same settee in the living room, trying to finish that morning's *Herald*.

"Everything all right?" He raised his eyebrows.

"Yes, of course." She curtsied for no reason, and went upstairs. In the shower she turned the water on cold, tried to soothe the rawness all over her, wash the drunk away. She felt fat and bloated, that lobster juice and zinfandel were dripping out of her ears, nostrils. She rubbed the soap against her skin as if she were scouring a pan.

"You want to go for a walk tomorrow morning, before breakfast?" Michael asked from inside the bathroom. She heard the faint scrub of his toothbrush against his teeth.

"I might need to sleep in," she said.

"I'm setting the alarm," he answered.

"I might be hungover," she insisted.

She turned off the shower and waited until he left the bathroom. Then, she sat on the toilet seat and listened for him to begin snoring before slipping between the covers. She should say yes, she thought, as the room spun and dipped and she grasped the side of the bed, fought her eyes open. But she would have to tell him about her and Steve. She wondered when it was a good time to convince someone that a person was defective. On the first date? When the person was crying in the bed in the middle of the night? Before she gets married or breaks up with him?

It had been two years—she should already have told Michael that for the first three years at the University of Richmond she contemplated suicide every morning in the dorm showers. That the only thing that kept her from it was the thought of her parents using their retirement money for her funeral. That she became convinced her unhappiness was linked to certain foods, which she then avoided: first chocolate, then eggs, bagels, green beans, pudding, cheese, bacon, tomatoes, strawberry jam, hot dogs, cantaloupe, French fries, roast beef, ravioli, grape soda, limes, fried chicken, popcorn, pizza, baked beans, buffalo wings, and oranges added over time.

How did she get this far, so close to normal? Was it because she knew if she smiled long enough, worked hard enough, if she got up every day and made it through the five things she wrote on her to-do list—brush her teeth, go to work, smile, remember to eat, sleep—she would pass?

She had made it this far because marriage was one item too many. She could not make it through every day and have to attend to Michael, attend to their children. She could spend two four-hour evenings during the week, every weekend, with him, but she could not spend every day with him. It was too much time to account for, too much time during which she'd rather sit in the dark and wish she were dead.

She decided to sleep on it. When she awoke, if he asked her, whatever she said, that would be the answer. And she would have to live with it. She was used to living with things.

*

The next morning Sam felt as if she had sprung a leak. It took her a few minutes of crusty eye opening, lip licking, and reorientation to the nautical room to realize that that was exactly what had happened. The wet spot under her was cold, massive. It hadn't even woken her up.

"Shit, Michael." She pushed at his still back. "Michael, get up."

"What?" he murmured, rolling over onto his back, toward her. She stood up and he rolled into the puddle.

"I've fucking peed the bed," she said. "We need to get these sheets off."

"Jesus." He groggily sat up, touched a palm to the mattress. "Were you that drunk? Or was it the weed?"

"Come on." She began pulling the sheet off around him. He stood and watched her strip the bed, half-asleep and half in disbelief. She was relieved, holding the massive damp collection of top sheet, fitted sheet, and mattress pad that it had not stained the mattress. She then pressed the soiled linens onto him. "Here."

"What am I supposed to do with these?" He dropped them on the floor and added his dampened boxer shirts to the pile.

"You know where the laundry room is. And the spare sheets."

"Spare sheets?"

"Ask Winona."

Michael threw on a t-shirt and shorts and left the room, going into Winona's room, and Sam slipped into the shower. His parents would find out. What would they think of her? She could lie and say she got her period. Either way, it was not a conversation she was looking forward to having. She heard Michael come back into the room and re-exit, presumably with the sheets. She dressed quickly and packed her suitcase.

"How is everyone feeling?" Michael's father asked the table at brunch. The spread was a reissue of what had not been eaten the day before, sans alcohol.

Sam smiled to no one in particular. She felt Em look at her. Sam took Em's lack of greeting that morning as a tacit acknowledgement, disapproval of her behavior the night before, the subsequent sheet soiling. Had Michael told? Had Winona? She suddenly did not know where her trust lay. When Sam stole a glance at Em, she was studying her from over her water glass. Their gazes locked, and Sam felt her face burn. Em smiled, a perfunctory smile, Sam thought. Sam wondered whether she could get an earlier flight home.

"You want to take a walk?" Michael asked. They excused themselves from the table and went through the screened porch, down the steps and to the beach. At the base of the steps he took her hand and yawned.

"I'm sorry for waking you up early," Sam said.

That's okay." He shook his head. "I preferred not to sleep in pee all morning, anyway."

"I'm sorry for ruining everything."

"No." He squeezed her hand. "It was a joke. Or something. It was a bad joke. I didn't mean to make you feel bad."

"Michael, I can't marry you now. I've embarrassed you and your parents."

"What are you talking about?" He stopped and pinned her with her arms.

"Isn't that what this is all about? The weekend? And I couldn't even behave myself—I got drunk and high and peed in your parents' guest bed. You think they want you to marry me now?"

"It doesn't matter what they think." He stroked the side of her face. "I don't even really care about them. But they would pay for a wedding if your parents couldn't. I mean...if...that's something you want to do, get married."

"Can we talk about this when we get home?"

"Is that your way of saying no?" He pulled a black velvet box from his pocket and threw it into a wall of cattails between them and the house.

She looked at his feet as he walked back to the house. She wondered how long it would take her to forget them, the bulbous big toes on either foot, the hair, curly hairs on each, the manicured nails, the layers of sandal-strap tans accumulated over the years. The feet disappeared from her sightline, and nothing but the shore remained. She searched the patch of cattails for the box, scratching one foot on the other in response to the sand flea bites and dried seaweed bits squeezing between her sandals and her feet, and when she found it she put it in her pocket to return to him, not opening it, too afraid to see what she would miss. She only remembered the bottle in Winona's car when they were on the way to the airport, and she chided herself for thinking, briefly, that she had forgotten the more important thing.

"Are you all right?" Michael asked from the other side of the bathroom door in his apartment. She had been in it for hours since returning from Rhode Island, sitting in the empty tub in the dark. It was the only thing that protected her on most sides, sort of like crawling under the bed. She should have just gone home to her parents' house, but the only thing worse than sharing a bed with her now ex-boyfriend would be explaining to her mother that night what had happened.

"I can sleep on the couch," he continued. "You don't have to sleep with me."

"No…don't. I think it's just hormones," she cried, picking up the soap from the soap dish. She contemplated putting it into her mouth, biting down, swallowing, moving on to the shampoo, her body wash. And then, when she was clogged, the drain cleaner. After that, if she was lucky, she would slide down the drain with all other unwanted hair and skin cells from her body.

"Do you think you're…pregnant?" he asked.

"No." She knew that much was true. In addition to being on the pill, she made Michael wear a condom during her ovulation times and bought pregnancy tests every few months. She told Michael she was just being careful, that she didn't want a child before they were ready. Surprises, change of any kind, scared her.

"What, then?"

She wished he would just go to bed, forget about her. Forget about his crying soon-to-be ex-girlfriend who was hiding in his tub, who had panic attacks, bad dreams, obsessive-compulsive reproductive tendencies. A past. Because if he really wanted to ask her to marry him, he couldn't possibly know her, see how vile she truly was.

"I'm fine," she said. "Just go to bed. I'll be in soon."

She twisted a dry facecloth as tightly as she could and bit on the stubby terrycloth rope, breathing and choking in the filaments. In the quiet she heard him lean toward the door and, after a few minutes, away, heard the end of the bed groan. A soft snore. She was angry at him for staying up, angry at him for going to sleep. Angry at him for reading her book and not getting what she meant by it. Angry at him for not knowing about her when it was her responsibility to tell him everything he needed to know. Angry at everything. Just angry.

iii.

He really knows now he is going to kill it. There is no turning back. The evidence is, while not foolproof, proof enough. But he doesn't know how. He doesn't know anything. How does a man have an abortion without killing himself?

"You're not going to have it?" Kim stares at him incredulously. She has signaled for more coffee and has begun pulling pamphlets with soft colors and fonts and smiling baby faces out of her oversized bag and placing them on the table. "It's your responsibility as a human being to see this pregnancy through. Don't you understand, Pete? You're going to be a father-mother."

"I'm not going to be anything. He lights a cigarette and inhales so quickly he begins to cough. "I just want to go back to my life."

"Pete, you're a medical miracle. And you're going to give birth."

"I don't want to be a fucking sideshow. And how am I supposed to have a baby? Squirt it out my penis?"

"A C-section, most likely," Kim muses, twirling a lock of her hair. "But at least you're thinking about delivery—that's good."

"I'm not thinking about delivering it. I'm thinking about how the hell I'm supposed to get it out of me without killing myself."

"I think you're making a mistake. This is not what I was sent to do."

"Who sent you here? What the hell are you, anyway? We never did figure that out, did we?"

"I'm not at liberty to discuss these things." She takes a sip from her coffee.

"I think you're fucking mental, and I don't know why I'm even here." He stabs out his cigarette and stands to leave. She grabs his wrist. He likes the fact she is touching him, so he tugs away a little harder, but not too hard, in order to feel her grip tighten.

"Considering I'm the only one who will even entertain the fact that you're pregnant, I don't see you having a lot of choices," she says, and he feels like he has disappointed her in some big way. He sits down and attends to his coffee. He wishes they had not met under these circumstances. Why could she not have come to the bar on a night he was working? Why could he not have met her when he wasn't pregnant?

"Well, then...what do you think we should do?" he asks in the quietest voice he can muster.

"I'm thinking, maybe, even though what's done is done, maybe we should figure out how you became pregnant in the first place. The circumstances, the girl. Maybe she or the situation can offer us some insight."

"Well, the thing is," he begins, rubbing his hands through his hair. He was blowing his only chance, if he ever had one, with Kim, because she would surely lose interest in what he had to tell her next. "I haven't slept with a girl in ten years."

"Oh." She sweeps the baby brochures together in a neat stack. "No one told me this was going to be some immaculate birth kind of thing."

"You don't think there's any connection?"

"Ten years...is a long time. But the baby could have been dormant. Maybe something sparked it. Or maybe there's no connection at all. Do you have access to this girl? Was she a girlfriend, a one-night stand?"

"She wasn't any of those things," he answers. "Look, it probably doesn't mean anything, right? We were just kids then, she and I. So we should just forget it."

He stands up and drops some bills on the table. He thinks maybe he could look up on the Internet how to kill it, but maybe the government would be monitoring computers and see that he was researching it. Maybe he could just keep drinking and smoking and poison it. Surely it could not stomach the levels of toxins he was used to ingesting on a regular basis.

"Where are you going?" Kim stands up with him. Somehow, she looks a little taller, but he figures it is her sneakers.

"I'm going home. It's late."

"You're not going to do anything you're going to regret, are you?"

"It's none of your business, now, is it?"

"Fine." She slings her bag over one of her small, rounded shoulders. "I'm going with you. To make sure."

"I don't remember inviting you to spend the night with me," he answers, although the thought of her, possibly in his bed as he had imagined, makes him feel hot and tingly. She doesn't say anything, following him out of the coffee shop. And he doesn't say anything, either, as they walk back to his place.

There she sits on his sofa and he brings her a glass of water. She holds the water and he sits at the other end, putting his feet up. The extra weight hurts him. She puts the glass on the edge of the coffee table and takes one of his stockinged feet in her hands. She rubs.

"So this girl from ten years ago, tell me about her," she says. He closes his eyes, comfortable, the pain leaving his feet and going into her or into the air, he is not sure. He wonders if the pain will hide in the room, behind the couch, under the table, and return to him when she leaves.

He is comfortable and he does not speak. He thinks about the girl from ten years ago. He thinks about the girl and he feels Kim nodding her head, as if she can see him thinking. He thinks about the girl from ten years ago. She was not a girlfriend-girl but she was not just a girl. He loved her like his sister but not as a girlfriend. But he slept with her like a girlfriend. But she was not his girlfriend and she did not want him to be her boyfriend and she did not want to sleep with him but he wanted to sleep with her. He wanted this thing and he was stronger and he got it. He thought that she would be okay getting it once she got it, once she discovered how wonderful it was and how wonderful he was, but she did not think it was wonderful. She did not think he was wonderful, and she did not think she was wonderful, either. She took her life away from herself and she took a lot of his life away, too. But he was still alive, ten years later, so she did not take all of it.

He moved away from where they lived ten years ago. He moved away because she took her life away and he still had his. He was not worried that he would take his life away or that she would take his life away but he could not stay where life was taken away. He still had his life and he took it away and now he was growing again. Maybe the life she took away from him was growing back.

When he opens his eyes Kim's are closed. He does not know if she is sleeping. He sits up and takes a drink of the water and finds a blanket for her. If she is not sleeping, she does not argue. He covers her and then gets on the floor next to the sofa. He listens to her breathing, his breathing, her breathing, his breathing

her breathing, his breathing, her breathing, his breathing

Their breathing.

O

When Pete Skivins awakes the next day Kim has made breakfast, even though the cupboards were empty when he went to bed the night before. He pretends she has always made breakfast and he has always eaten it. He likes how this feels.

"Will you marry me?" he asks.

"You don't even know who I am." She hands him a plate of eggs and waffles. *"We have a lot to do today. You need to call in to work."*

"What are we doing?"

"We're paying our respects to the past," she answers, sipping a glass of orange juice. Pete gets in the shower and watches the water curl over the arc of his stomach. He wonders when it will come out, when it will be ready. If it is a boy or a girl. If it is a superhero. If it is only his or if it is his and someone else's. If it's Kim's. If it's all in his mind. If it's all just a dream.

In the shower he pulls the razor across the whiskers on his face, knocking them into the drain. He pulls the razor over the long curly hairs that anchor his belly button to his groin. The skin is smooth underneath, and he pets his pale fleshdome cancerbaby. If it is really a baby, he will die. If it's cancer, he will die, too.

If it's ust a dream, all he needs to do is wake up.

"What are you doing?" She is in the bathroom, the shower curtain balled in her fist. Leaning against the shower tile, he slaps his face, hot and cold and hot and cold wet. With her other hand she grabs his wrist, the wrist he has pulled the razor across, where there is now his blood, baby blood, everywhere blood. Blood on the tiles, in the tub basin, on the hair of his toes, between them. She wraps a towel around his wrist and pulls him out of the shower. He sits on the toilet seat, feels the wet between his ass and the plastic cover. Soon he will not be able to see his penis under his stomach. This is the least of his worries, he knows.

"Are you all right?" She squats in front of him, holding his wrists. He closes his legs, wishes he could get dressed. The cut is not deep, but he still feels lightheaded, nauseous.

"I don't want to do this," he says.

"Do what?"

"Any of this."

"You put these events in motion." She peels the towel off his wrist. The blood still beads there. She wraps it again. "It's too late to stop them now."

"What events?

"Your pregnancy—me. You put all these things in motion, in your belly, here in front of you. Hold this."

He puts pressure on his wrist as she riffles through his medicine cabinet looking for gauze and tape. Her arms are meaty—rope wrapped over bone— and maybe he has not noticed before.

"I still don't understand what you mean," he says as she turns back toward him with an old cotton ball and a Band-Aid.

"It's simple—things we don't let go of stay with us, grow with us. Sometimes they grow in a bad way, like cancer, and sometimes they grow in a good way. And sometimes…men get pregnant, if there are women involved."

"Other men have gotten pregnant?" He stands up, involuntarily. He should have searched the Internet better.

"I don't know of any personally, but I am only assigned to certain people. I know men who have gotten cancer in their testicles and warts on their penises, but I've never known anybody who's gotten pregnant after so long." She presses the cotton ball on his wrist and affixes it with the Band-Aid. "Maybe you had a tumor that turned into a baby. But don't you see? You have good growth. That must mean you're sorry."

"Sorry? I'm sorry I'm pregnant," he mumbles, following her into the bedroom. He suddenly remembers he's naked and pulls a quilt from the bed. It smells like cum. Everything in his room smells like cum, and he reasons it's possible, literally swimming in it, that he impregnated himself.

"We really need to get to the store, get you some proper medical supplies," she muses as he pulls on a pair of sweatpants. "You should really have a bottle of isopropyl alcohol, Betadine, you know?"

"Who are you?" He grabs her arms. "Why were you sent here?"

"I already told you—you're getting ready to have a baby. Now get ready."

"No—tell me who you are." He continues to hold onto her arms but she shrugs him off. She opens his closet and pulls a t-shirt off the hanger, tossing it to him.

"It doesn't matter. You don't need to know everything."

"I'm already suspending disbelief to swallow the little I know." He pulls the t-shirt over himself. It is smug around the belly and also across his chest. Are his pecs getting bigger, or saggier? He wades through the clothes on his floor and emerges with a mustard-stained hoodie, which he pulls over himself.

"Ready, fashionista?" She smiles.

"I guess I'm driving," he answers. He grabs a few CDs from where they lie near the bed. He knows this will be a long trip. He wonders if she knows, too.

SUNDAY

6.

The giggles, murmurs in the room, stir Sam awake. She was too tired to concern herself with where everyone slept last night, only making sure Michael had clean sheets. Now, she can hear a female voice, certainly Eve's, and her brother Steve, next door, in the loft room. She feels cold and hot and sick at the thought they slept together, forces herself to think that they only shared the room. It is possible. Steve could be a gentleman. He wouldn't force himself on a stranger. At least not a total stranger. She sits up, reaches for her towel, and knocks loudly on the door. She must walk through their room and her parents' room to get to the bathroom, so she gives them plenty of time to separate if they are together.

"Who is it?" Steve's voice sings out.

"Who do you think it is?" Sam is in no mood for kidding. She flings open the door to find Steve standing in the middle of the room in his briefs, legs spread, pulling an undershirt over his head. She holds her breath, trying not to inhale the poisonous, sweet and sour scent of alcohol, cigarettes, and who knows what else.

"Sammy mammy, nice pajammies," he laughs at the oversized Baltimore Colts t-shirt she'd found in a trunk in her room. She did not risk wearing Michael's old shirts and boxers, her preferred sleepwear, with him around to take note, to wonder whether she changed her mind.

"You're such a child," she mumbles, scanning the room for Eve. She is leaning over the loft, sandy strands of hair pasted to her forehead, her eyes swollen, small. She no longer looks wise, sagely, but rather someone who has lined up for atonement.

"Sounds like someone woke up on the wrong side of the bed," Steve smirks. As Sam tries to walk past him, he grabs her in a bear hug and wrestles her to the bed. She can feel his weight, on top of her, his arms, the kinked blond hairs on his chest, the line of his stomach down to his genitals. She wriggles against him as he presses down harder, and all of a sudden she is sixteen again and he is eighteen and they are in her bedroom at home.

"Stop it, fucking stop it." She claws at his back, feeling the air leak out of her lungs, blackness at the edges of her eyes, the panic lock her body into a series of jerks and convulsions. She wonders if she will have a seizure, if this is what it feels like. Steve releases her and she scrambles from the bed to the door.

"I was only teasing you." He frowns and scratches the back of his hand with his head. "Hey, I'm sorry, Sam."

"We're not six," she mumbles. We're not sixteen, she thinks. She breathes deeply, feeling her heart begin to settle in her chest like a coin that has stopped spinning, before she fumbles for the door that leads to her parents' room, not bothering to check whether they are awake. She sees the lump of her mother rolled against the wall, huddled under a quilt, the air conditioning on full blast.

"Mom?" She sits on the edge of the bed, careful not to roll into the sag that her father has created over the years. She puts her hand on her mother's back. "Are you all right?'

"I'm fine, sweetie," she answers, turning slightly. Sam can see the strands of gray-white hair on the top of her mother's head where the color is growing out. "That fried chicken gave me heartburn something awful."

"Are you sure you're all right?" Sam tries to remember the last time she's seen her mother sick. "You want some antacids?"

"I took some a few hours ago. I'll get up." She makes a move but Sam presses her against the bed, hand on her back. "Somebody's got to make breakfast."

"I'll make it, Mom—don't worry." Sam stands up. "You just get up when you're feeling better."

"Just give me a few minutes." She rolls back toward the wall, pulling the blankets tightly over her body.

"And no more chicken for you today," Sam jokes. There is a knock at the door, and Steve peeks his head in.

"Just coming through to the bathroom." He is wearing his undershirt, a pair of jeans now. "Ma, you sleepyhead, get up."

"She's not feeling well," Sam whispers/scolds as she follows Steve through the opposite door into the hallway. "I need to take a shower."

"I'm just taking a piss." He goes into the bathroom and shuts the door behind him. "I'll only be a second, grumpy."

Sam goes to the kitchen, a cramped, six-by-twelve space off the living room. Michael stands by the stove, watching pancakes on the griddle.

He is dressed and showered; she can smell his aftershave, Drakkar Noir, from the doorway.

"Need some help?" she asks and, without waiting for him to answer, finds the bacon in the fridge.

"Your father woke me up," Michael says, almost in apology. "Came through the living room, couldn't figure out the coffee machine. So I made him some of that instant stuff and he went down to the dock."

"That instant stuff sucks," Sam says, digging in her grocery bags from Wegman's and emerging with a bag of gourmet coffee. "Especially when we have this."

"Wegman's hazelnut, my favorite," he says, sliding a spatula under one of the pancakes and flipping it over. "And to think I make myself a cup of your father's crap."

"Let's get rid of this." Sam takes Michael's mug and dumps it in the sink. She is comfortable, safe. She can imagine Michael spending his summers here with her. She knows it is only she who judges herself, not him. But it is necessary. She thinks.

"All yours, Sam." Steve appears in the doorway of the kitchen. Sam grips the empty coffee mug, directing it under the spout of the sink and rinsing it out. She thinks she sees a stain of brown, faint and filmy, and she rubs the cup under the water until Michael reaches over and turns off the faucet. "Smells good in here."

"The pancakes are almost ready," Michael says, not looking at Steve. "If you want them."

"Really? Thanks, buddy." Steve picks up the silver bag of coffee and sniffs at the opening. "This coffee looks good, too."

"Can you see if Dad needs any help?" Sam asks, turning toward the counter and opening the bacon. "We need to make sure we're ready for the parade."

"Shit, that's right," Steve says, but lingers. She wonders if he wants to apologize to her about earlier. He doesn't. "Well, I'll come back and grab some grub. Dad's liable to blow up that fucker."

Sam hears the door to the porch slam closed, then the porch door to the dock slam a few seconds later.

"He certainly knows how to make an exit." Michael piles a few fluffy medallions on a plate.

"Thanks for being so nice to him." Sam drops the fatty white and pink strips onto the griddle in the spot of a recently vacated pancake.

"Well, he was nice to me last night," he answers, measuring out another cup of pancake batter.

"What did he say to you?"

"I was checking my e-mail in the living room and he comes in and says, like a cowboy, 'Michael, I know we ain't close, but I'd appreciate your help in setting off some fucking sweet fireworks that are gonna make the girls really happy. And if we can't make the girls happy, then we ain't got no reason being here.' And I was ready to say that it seemed obvious that I couldn't make you happy when I thought, fuck it, it's my last night here, anyway, ever. Might as well go out with a bang."

Sam is silent, watching the bacon squirm and spit on the griddle. She pokes at it with a fork.

"Where does he get that twang, anyway?" Michael laughs. "Fucking East Baltimore cowboy."

"From his friend Brian," Sam answers, scooping up the bacon and dropping it on a napkin-soaked plate. "Brian went out to Wyoming one summer and Steve made fun of him when he got back. He talked like that all the time, making fun, and now it's almost natural for him."

"Like if you cross your eyes enough they'll stay that way?"

"I don't know." Sam shrugs. They work in silence for the remainder of the pancakes and bacon. Sam dices some cantaloupe, adds a few grapes.

"Can I help?" Eve appears, freshly showered, wearing a faded Clash t-shirt over her bathing suit.

"You can help eat these." Sam hands her a plate of pancakes, bacon, and fruit.

"Your mom is in the shower," Eve says, before making her way to the sun porch.

"You eat, too." Sam hands Steve a fresh cup of Wegman's coffee. "I'm going to clean up in here."

"Sam," he says, and she waits for him to connect her name with something, some request or declaration, but he finally pulls his lips thin and long into a smile and takes the coffee cup. "Thanks."

Everyone has eaten and Sam and Eve have washed the dishes, set them on the drainer to dry. Sam's mother stands on the middle of the dock while Steve envelopes her in a cloud of bug repellent. Sam's father sits in the driver's seat of the pontoon boat, unmoving, like a piece of scrimshaw, cigarette hanging out of his mouth. Michael stands at the foot of the deck, holding a cooler of drinks and waiting for Steve to finish spraying Pat Pinski.

"Are you okay?" Eve asks as she advances the film on the disposable camera she has brought. She sits at the table in the screened porch, waiting for Sam to finish her coffee.

"Did you sleep with Steve?" Sam asks, passing the mug on the table between her hands.

"Is this what this is all about?" Eve puts the camera in her shoulder bag and meets Sam's eyes.

"Is this all what what's about?" Sam shrugs. "I was just asking a question."

"I'm not sure how you want me to answer."

"You did, didn't you?" Sam drinks the coffee too fast, begins to choke. Eve leans over to help as Sam sits back in her chair.

"No." She stands up after Sam has recovered. "I didn't."

"My mistake." Sam stands up as well, leaving the coffee behind. She moves toward the screen door but is blocked by Eve. "Look, I'm sorry I accused you. You just asked me if something was wrong and...I assumed the worst."

"It's just that...it seemed like there was some greater issue this morning between you two. I don't know." She shook her head. "Do you want to talk about it?"

"There's nothing to discuss." Sam waves her hand flippantly, and Eve steps out of her way. "You're both adults. At least you are, anyway."

When Sam gets to the deck her mother has brought out streamers of red, white, and blue and has busied herself taping them all over the pontoon boat.

"I got some sprinklers, too," she says when she spots Sam. "I know they ain't fireworks, but we just can't have those here."

Steve shoots Sam a secret smile from the front of the boat, where he is tying a piñata resembling Uncle Sam to the railing. Sam, ignoring him, positions herself on the bench, behind her father, hoping that Eve and Steve will sit in front. Michael pushes the cooler against the wall of the boat and offers Sam a microbrew, which she takes. She looks away as Eve climbs on the boat and makes her way to the front. Michael grabs the other end of the bench where Sam rests, and Sam's mother squeezes in between them.

"Are we all on?" her father grunts, turning the key in the ignition before the door of the pontoon even comes to a rest. "Jesus."

He waits for an opening in the parade of boats passing and then backs carefully out of the dock into the tree-lined creek. Most of the boats, other pontoons of various years and conditions, have decorations on par with those Sam's mother picked up, presumably at a dollar store: cardboard placards depicting fireworks or Uncle Sam or red, white, and blue motifs. Families without boats or who just got up or who are too lazy to join in wave from their decks, children hollering from donuts tied to the decks. One family has a floating trampoline on which three young boys take turns bouncing. Just for the occasion, one is wearing white trunks, the second red, and the third blue. Sam watches Eve take a picture of them. Sam's mother trains her lighter on the end of a sparkler until it detonates, and then she holds it out over the creek.

"Here, Sam." She gives Sam the one burning while she turns to light another. Sam watches the sparks fly off the gunpowder and into the water. It seems so sudden, the spark of intense, white heat, electricity, before it dies. Quick and brilliant. "Michael, you want one?"

"Sure." Michael takes a sparkler from her and waves it in the air, writing his name.

"Your parents have plans today?" Sam's mother asks him.

"No, Ma," Steve laughs from the other end of the boat. "They're hiding under their beds. Of course they have plans."

"They're probably at the marina in Newport, getting the yacht ready," he answers. "They usually sail and eat and drink. The same as you."

"I remember Sam had a real nice time when she was up in Newport with your folks in the spring," she says. She omits the obvious details of the breakup. "You should ask your folks up to the cabin sometime. We don't have a yacht, but we've got this and the motorboat and the lake."

Sam sighs audibly, but it's swallowed by the chug-chug of the pontoon boat. She doesn't know why her mother has to beat a dead horse, but she does not have the energy to argue. Even if they were still together, Michael's parents would never come down to Darlington, driving down I-95 past the small towns and guns and tackle shops that shadow Northeastern Maryland like sun spots, to the last foothold of lower middle-class leisure. Surely, Sam thinks, her mother must know this.

"Thanks for the invitation, Mrs. Pinski," Michael says noncommittally. "You've always been so nice to me,"

"It's Mom to you." She pats Michael's cheek.

"Pat, get me a soda," Sam's father grumbles. Michael reaches over into the cooler and fishes one out for him.

"So what happens at the end of the parade?" Eve asks.

"What, has the excitement been too much for you?" Steve asks. "Everyone parks at the marina and there's a crab feast."

"I'm a crab virgin," Eve confesses, lighting a cigarette.

"What, you ain't never had no crabs?" Sam's father repeats.

"What, are you deaf, man?" Steve smiles, holds out his hands toward Michael, who's opened the cooler again.

"Shaddup, Steve. I'm getting real sick of your mouth." Sam's father sets his can in the beverage holder on the dash.

"What are you going to do, ground me?" Steve shoots back. Sam watches Eve grab Steve's arm, Steve take a breath.

"Look, he was just teasing," Sam's mother says. "Man can't take a joke if a gun was pointed at his head. Don't worry, honey—the Pinskis are expert crab pickers."

"And nose pickers," Steve laughs.

"Shaddup, Steve," their mother says. "Now you're plucking my last good nerve."

"What's all this about taking a joke, Ma?" Steve smiles.

"You're right, Stevie." Sam's mom adjusts her hat, scratches her knee. "I oughta just be happy yous are all here, healthy and in one piece. The Lord's been really good to us."

"To the Fourth of July," Steve lifts his bottle just as the boat lurches and sinks to the right. "And the hope that we're not under water soon."

"What was that?" Sam's father half-stands and looks over the edge.

"It was probably that pile of beer cans from you and Uncle Ray piled up on the bottom," Steve says, standing up and looking over the edge himself. "Or a dead body. No, look—you snagged an old rope or some-thing—see it trailing behind the boat?"

"Yeah." Sam's father sits back down. "But now you just reminded me we ain't gone fishing yet."

"I'll get that rope off at the marina," Steve says. "And we'll talk about fishing then."

"What the heck can you find in these waters?" Eve asks, pulling off her t-shirt and spreading her white arms across the front railing of the boat.

"All sorta stuff," Sam's father answers. They are on the lake now, angling toward the marina, which is three deep in boats. "Rockfish, blue-fish, croaker, flounder."

"No crabs?"

"You don't fish for crabs, silly." Steve pats the top of her head. "They have to trap them. They're bottom-dwellers."

"Like lobster," Sam answers, but she doesn't know why. She wonders whether Winona ever found her beer bottle in her car, the message inside. She never saw Winona after the spring. Word from Michael was that she came out as a lesbian and then made herself scarce, moving to Philadelphia to accept an assistant teaching job in the anthropology department at UPenn.

"Lobsters are much better than crabs," Michael says, "But I like them both very much and may be a little bit biased."

"Well, after you've had these crabs you ain't gonna be biased no more," Sam's father answers. A man wearing a green polo whose stomach lops over the waist of his shorts guides their pontoon into an available space. He is wearing a hat that says *Aberdeen Proving Ground*, the Army base northeast of here.

"Hey Roger," Sam's father addresses him. "Got 'er runnin' again."

"And you got it filled full of folk, too," Roger observes. Sam's father takes out his wallet and fishes out a couple of fifties. Roger then gives each of them, as they deboat, a red ticket for the crab feast.

"Is this all-you-can-drink?" Steve asks as his passes Roger.

"We got some beer," Roger answers. "You can drink it until it's gone."

"Leave our stuff on the boat, Michael," Steve calls back to him.

"You don't have to pay for my ticket," Michael, taking out his own wallet, says to Karl Pinski.

"It's on me." Karl Pinski shakes his head. "I ain't got much money to be throwing around, but I spend what I got wisely."

"Thanks, Mr. Pinski," Eve concurs. "You're a generous man."

Sam's father doesn't answer, doesn't object when Sam's mother kisses him on the cheek.

"My little softie," she laughs, hooking her arm through his. They take a picnic table, the wood grayed from exposure, far from the front of the marina. Steve waves his arms empathetically to one of the teenage girls whose job it is to bus trays of one-dozen crabs to each table. The girls are long and willowy, tan, their legs sticks of caramel scissoring in their high-cut shorts.

"Keep waving." He touches Eve's shoulder as he steps over the bench of the picnic table. "I'm going to get a couple of pitchers."

Eve stands and begins to move her arms in the shape of the letters C-R-A-B. For the "B," she bends her leg at the knee, resting her foot on her shin while she bends her arm at the elbow, resting her hand on her stomach.

"She's too much," Pat Pinski says of Eve, almost as if she's not there. Karl Pinski stares at Eve, mouth slightly open, cigarette hanging out, as if she were an alien. Finally one of the girls brings a tray, which she tips toward the center of their table. Blue crabs, now orange that they've been steamed, with clumps of Old Bay Seasoning so thick it looks like they've been rolled in dirt, tumble over each other into a pile, pinchers and fins moving in futility after death. Karl Pinski digs a meaty, hairy hand into the pile and emerges with a steaming crab from the bottom. He pulls the pinchers from the body and sets them aside, followed by the smaller legs, and then wedges his finger under the shell and pulls it off, revealing a skeleton of lungs, that he pulls away. Then he breaks the crab in half, like he's shuffling a deck of cards.

"Sweet." Steve has returned with the beer and is excited at the latest developments at their table. He puts a pitcher on either end, takes a plastic cup from the tower he's holding, and passes the rest to Eve, who does the same. Sam pulls the crab closest to her into her area of table. Sam's mom, holding her own crab in her hand, leans over Eve.

"All right, honey." She winks at her, a little rogue makeup running into a crease on the top of her cheek, near her eye. Sam is amazed that her mother has not gotten any color yet. She browned so easily when they were kids. "Let me show you how to do this."

Eve picks up her crab and studies Pat Pinski's motions before mimicking them. Steve has disassembled his crab as quickly as her father. His fingers are specked with Old Bay, which is smeared on the plastic cup when he grabs it and takes a long drink. She wants to pretend that this is how they've always known each other, that they have always had crab feasts in summer. She doesn't know why she just can't pretend. After all, they are having a crab feast now. They don't even have to pretend.

Sam nibbles on a claw. She realizes everyone else is on their second, third crab and that another tray will come soon. Steve hops up and grabs refills on the pitchers. Her mom leans back, lights a cigarette, and does a sweep of the area.

"Look, there are the Kowalskis," she says to Karl, whose hands are moving from crab to mouth and back like an assembly line. "And the Pritchards."

"Who cares about them?" he manages to say, little slivers of crab meat oozing out onto his lips. "Don't be a busybody."

"I'm not being a busybody, Karl—they're our friends. We should say hi to them."

"Well, let's get a little food in us first." He wipes his nose with the top of his index finger, being careful not to get Old Bay in his nostrils. "We just sat down."

Sam looks at Michael who, if he's bored or unhappy, is careful not to show it. He scrapes the insides of his crab halves intently, making sure he extracts all the meat. She wishes her mother hadn't invited him to the cabin, given him any hope. She figures she must tell him the truth about why she broke it off, even if it means he'll never speak to her again.

"Hey, Eve, you going to marry me?" Steve asks after he returns with the fifth and sixth pitchers in his hands. "Let's get married."

"Here?" she snorts, a piece of crab meat clinging to the edge of her lip. "Who's going to marry us, your event planner Roger over there?"

"We can have my father marry us," Steve answers, putting his arm around Eve's shoulder. "He has a personal relationship with our savior."

"Why do you say that?" Pat questions, putting her cigarette out in a crab shell. Sam groans.

"Well, he talks about him all the time—Jesus Christ this, Jesus Christ that," Steve laughs loudly. Sam pulls a pincher off her second crab so forcefully she almost flings it over her shoulder.

"Ha, ha, you're such a comedian," Karl Pinski says. "Maybe you oughta tell a few jokes onstage and get pelted with fruit instead of playing that guitar."

"Everybody should get married. It's the best thing ever." Steve winks at Sam, who looks at Eve.

"How about you shut up?" Eve, taking the hint from Sam, says to Steve. "It's not like you've even asked me on a date or anything."

"Oh, is that how these modern romances work?" Steve asks. "Well, little lady, how's about an ice cream? There's a Dairy Queen down the road."

"I don't know." Eve shakes her head, tossing her crab skeleton to the top of the pile. She sucks the grime and spices off her pinky finger. "I'll have to check my schedule."

"When do you need me to take you to Fallston?" Sam asks.

"Geez, is the weekend over already?" Eve frowns. "Marcie is leaving from work around noon, so I guess before then?"

"You just got here, Eve," Sam's mom says. "Well, you know Mr. Pinski and I are up here all summer—we got plenty of food—so come back the next time you're off, okay?"

"How long are you staying, Sam?" Michael asks.

"I don't know," she answers, and she wonders whether he will stay longer as well. "For a little while yet."

"You're welcome to stay, too, Michael," Sam's mother adds, and everyone is silent.

"Jeez, Ma, you oughta start renting rooms," Steve says, draining his beer. "Then everybody can stay at Chez Pinski and you make the big bucks."

"I don't want anybody's money," Sam's mother says. "We got all we need. I don't see why we can't share the cabin."

"Steve is just pulling your leg," Sam explains, sighing. She is so tired, suddenly, of them. She wants to get away from all of them and lie on a raft in the creek. "He doesn't really mean that."

"Sure. Why not?" He smiles. "We can set up a little wedding chapel. Marriages and honeymoons. The Conowingo Cabin, House of Love."

"I don't want to talk about weddings," Sam says, placing her cup of beer forcefully on the table. "Can't we talk about something else?"

"Everybody read Sam's book?" Eve asks. Sam shoots her another look, and Eve bites her lip. "The critics liked it. I liked it. I guess that's all that matters. Next subject."

"The pregnant-man book," Steve says. "Whatever happened to your stories about baseball players? She wrote a story about me once, Eve. She was my biggest fan. My only fan. It's not like my father ever came to see me play."

"Steve, your father had to work," Sam's mother interrupts. "He had to put bread on the table. I came to your games, didn't I, Steve? Our neighbor, Annie Wisecki, her son was on the team, too. Anne and I used to sit on our lawn chairs and pick on the coffee cakes I brought and cheer the boys on. Remember?"

"Yeah, my father was busy working," Steve continues, ignoring her. "Busy getting drunk."

"Let's go see the Kowalskis," Sam's mother nudges her father. "Hurry up—before they leave."

"Will you stop it?" Sam says to Steve when they are out of earshot. "This is not the time or the place."

"When is the time and the place?" he asks. "And you have a lot of room to talk."

"At least I'm not acting like a baby. Really, how old are you and you're whining about this?"

"Like I said, you've got a lot of room to be harping on about the past." He stares at her. She wonders if he's referring to the book. She's afraid to ask.

"So, how's your holiday weekend been?" Michael turns to Eve. "These Pinskis are just a bundle of fun, aren't they?"

"They sure are." Eve lights a cigarette. "You'd think they were brother and sister or something."

"I don't know why you're even here," Steve says suddenly to Michael. "Nobody wants you here. My sister doesn't want to marry you. So maybe you should get a clue."

"Maybe you should get fucked." Michael stands up. Eve, who is between them, stands up as well.

"Michael, no," Eve says, holding her arms out. "It's not worth it."

"It's not worth it because he's going to get his ass kicked." Steve stands up behind her. But instead of going after Michael, he takes the half-filled pitcher of beer. "I'm going back to the boat."

"Hope you drown," Michael mutters under his breath. Sam begins to roll the layers of newspaper that line the picnic table over the eaten crabs, watching pinchers and fins and shells press together in impossible configurations.

"What a fucking baby," Michael continues. "I wouldn't be a strung-out loser if my pa had come to see me play baseball?"

"We all have our shitty childhoods," Eve says, taking a sip of beer. "But, yeah, it's good to let go of things."

"We have a lot to be angry about," Sam defends. "You don't think I'm still angry at the way things have turned out for us?"

"Yes, I do think you have a lot of anger about a lot of things," Michael says. "And it's insulting to the rest of us when you won't deal with it."

"What are you trying to say?" she cries, picking up a stray leg and flinging it in his direction.

"I have to hit the head." He stands, jiggles the drawstring on his swimming trunks, and walks through the crowd of picnic tables to the marina.

"Well, beer makes everything better, right?" Eve says wryly. "I'm sure they'll both feel better when they sober up."

"I can't believe he just ran away from me like that." Sam shakes her head, pressing down on the wadded mound of wet and spice-smeared newsprint with her hands.

"Why not?" Eve stands up to help her carry it to the trash can. "You did."

When they return Sam's parents have also returned to the table, wearing the expressions of people who have had their home broken into; shock that has not quite crossed over to anger.

"We're ready to go," Sam explains to her mother.

"I should say so. Where's Steve?"

"Waiting on the boat."

"Oh, I didn't think we were that long," Sam's mother says, threading her purse over her shoulder.

"You weren't," Michael, who has just returned, answers. "But I have to get going tonight."

"You got hours still," Sam's mother fights but moves toward the docks. "Sam, did you know Amy Kowalski moved to Iowa? What the heck's in Iowa?"

7.

On the boat Steve is asleep on the front bench. Eve nudges him to a sitting position and squeezes next to him. He lets his hand rest in her lap. After a few minutes, she touches the thick, golden curls of his hair. Michael opens his phone and begins to type while Sam's mother dabs at her face underneath her wide-brimmed straw hat.

"It sure is humid," she says to Sam. "You oughta go swimming. I bet the water's real nice."

"Why don't you go swimming, Mom?" Sam asks. She feels the urge to dive into a good book, into others' dramas for a while.

"I got to get dinner ready."

"We just ate. I'll help you cook dinner. Why don't you take one of the rafts on the river?"

"We'll see, hon." Sam's mother wraps her napkin around the dripping can of soda she has brought from the cookout.

Back at the cabin Michael disappears inside, presumably to pack. Sam hangs out by the picnic table in her bathing suit as Eve helps Steve into the hammock on the hill between the cabin and dock. She places an old Orioles baseball cap over his face so it doesn't burn.

"They never grow up, do they?" Eve shakes her head and smiles.

"You want to go for a walk or something?"

"Actually, I'm just as happy to relax on the shore here."

"It's important, kind of." Sam watches her fingers whiten over the bottle of suntan lotion she brought from the boat. It was under her seat, Coppertone SPF 4, coverage that one would be a fool to use now, the bottle bleached by the sun and time. "Why don't we take a couple of the raft chairs out on the creek?"

Sam and Eve take a couple of floating pool chairs from where they are stacked on the dock and lay them in the water by the edge of the dock. Sam dives into the creek and is surprised at how cold it is, considering the heat of the day. She emerges, paddles over to her chair, and pulls herself atop.

"You make it look so easy," Eve says from the dock. She turns around, squatting, trying to fall backwards into the chair. Her body overshoots the chair so that she is only half on it. She tumbles into the creek as the chair shoots out of the water and back onto the dock, where Karl Pinski, the last off the boat, picks it up and patiently waits for her to resurface.

"You lose somethin'?" He smiles, dangling the chair over the dock toward her. Eve grabs for it as she goes under the water.

"Shit, Dad—Eve can't swim," Sam says, letting herself fall off the raft. But Sam's father has already kicked off his sandals and jumped into the water feet first, splashing the dock and the side of the pontoon boat. He disappears under the water as Sam paddles over with the empty chair. He and Eve re-emerge instantly, shot up from the water like a cannon.

"There you are." Sam's father treads water, his arms around Eve, as Sam positions the chair before her. "No worse for wear."

Eve struggles to hoist herself up, and Sam's father pushes her by the butt onto the chair, where she clumsily rights herself. Sam opens her mouth but closes it.

"Karl, you didn't tell me you were going to go swimming," Sam's mom calls from the screened porch. "Did you put suntan lotion on?"

"I think I'll stay out here—away from her screaming and yakking for a few hours," Sam's father smiles. He treads water, observing both of them, his smile crooked, his eyes soft. Sam supposes he doesn't know any more what they are thinking than they do him. "Me and my brothers used to swim up and down this creek back in the days. I was younger then—thinner, too. I used to take you kids out, too."

Sam doesn't mention to her father that he paid them so little attention once he left Sam at the marina when he went to buy worms for fishing. For hours she looked at night crawlers and Kit Kat bars while Roger eyed her nervously, assuring her that her father would be back any minute. Roger had boys, Len and Doug, two and five years older than her; sometimes they played with Steve. They never played with Sam and Steve together. Sam always wondered if they didn't like her or girls in general, but by the way Roger looked at her that day, like she had fallen out of the sky, she wondered if they just didn't know much about them. Later Sam's mother told her that Len and Doug's mother had moved away.

"I always thought I'd own the cabin—I was gonna live here when I grew up," her father continues, looking up the creek at a pontoon boat creeping toward them. "Damn if I didn't outlive all my brothers. But your mother would never want to stay up here. Not in the winter, and not with the plumbing all fussy."

"I could live here," Eve says from the chair, eyes closed. "I suppose I would have to learn to swim, though."

"Everybody should know how to swim." Sam's father makes his way back to the dock, pulling himself up heavily, step by step on the ladder. "And everybody should know CPR."

"That's the most I've heard your father speak all weekend," Eve says when Sam's father is out of earshot, ambling toward the cabin, knocking the water out of his ear. "Does he really know CPR?"

"Yeah, he learned it when he was the union leader at his old job," Sam answers. "Thankfully, he's never had to use it."

"Did you want to talk?" Eve asks.

"No, forget it—enjoy your last day." Sam closes her eyes. "Not that you're not welcome back here."

"For what's it's worth, and I don't know that it's worth anything, but if you have issues with Steve, maybe it's best to just do what you do…and let him do what he does."

"What does that mean?" Sam sits up slightly in her chair. "Did Steve talk to you?"

"No," Eve answers. "But it's not hard to tell you've got lots of past."

Sam watches Steve emerge from the hammock. He's wearing his cut-off shorts, holding a beer can, cigarette behind his ear, whistling. When he spots them he does a little wave, tears down the hill. They watch Steve hit the dock in his bare feet. He tosses the cigarette onto Eve's stomach before cannonballing into the water. Sam feels the cold droplets of displaced water pelt her shoulders.

"Got a light?" Steve grins at Eve as he emerges, water tears running down his cheeks and onto his chest.

Michael appears, ready to leave. He stands outside the cabin, on the hill, backpack on and his leftover microbrews in hand. Seeing him there, maybe for the last time in her life, makes her hurt. Sam climbs out of the creek and slips on her flip-flops, making her way up the hill.

"Are you sure you want to leave now?" she asks, following him to his car.

"I have to work tomorrow," he answers, sliding his backpack and beer into the trunk of his Saab. "And it's not like you were terribly accommodating or anything."

"What are you talking about?" Sam crosses her arms.

"You didn't spend any time with me."

"Well, I didn't even invite you, Michael."

"Yeah, but I didn't come up here for anyone else." He slams the trunk. Sam leans against it to keep him from leaving.

"Michael." She looks at her feet. "We aren't together anymore. I don't want to get back together with you."

"That's not what Pat told me."

"What did she tell you?"

"That you told her you wanted to get back together, that you were just confused. Needed time. Encouragement."

"What?" Her right leg moves so involuntarily hard that her sandal is flipped through the air, landing feet away. As she goes to retrieve it, she wonders why her mother has taken it upon herself to patch things up between them. Does she think Sam is desperate, or is she?

She watches Michael open the passenger-side door, rummage through his glove compartment. He emerges with the bottle, the bottle Sam left in Winona's car earlier that spring in Newport.

"Winona is convinced you're going to hate her for the rest of your life for giving this to me, but I told her it wouldn't matter, since you and I are apart," Michael says. He hands her the bottle. "No one has opened this. If you need to keep your secrets, maybe you should have this back."

Sam takes the bottle from him, satisfies herself with the fact that no one can see the contents of the paper inside. Before she has time to think about it, stop herself, she takes the bottle and breaks it against the sycamore tree a few feet from Michael's car. She pulls the paper from the glass and holds it out to Michael.

"Here—if we're together or not, you should know this about me."

He takes the paper almost greedily. Sam busies herself collecting the glass shards while he reads it. She cradles them carefully in her palm, large and small pieces, determined not to cut herself.

"This is why you won't marry me?" He looks at her, holding the paper between his hands, like a scroll or treasure map. "This is true, about you and Steve? What you did together?"

She nods. She is crying. She doesn't know whether Michael will leave or stay. It doesn't even matter, she thinks. She will still cry, still be hurt. Still not know what happens to her next.

"Sam, I..." His lips are parted, but no sound emerges. He folds the note carefully. "That son of a bitch has been up here the whole time and I never knew a fucking thing."

"I'm sorry, Michael. I just wanted you to know." She closes her hand around the shards and feels them scratch her palm. "I broke up with you so you wouldn't have to break up with me later."

"Sam, do you love me?"

"Of course I love you, Michael. It's me I'm not so fond of."

Michael wraps his arms around her. She does not fight him. The weight that had been pressing on her, at least part of it, is gone, somewhere through the trees, up the creek to the lake. She wonders whether the dreams, the anxiety, will go with them. Michael pulls away and opens Sam's palm and turns it over. The glass leaves her hand and rests in his, the folded paper cupped in his other hand.

"I'm not sure what I think about this. I don't know what it means for us." He looks at his hand holding the glass. "This is all very fucking weird. Like somebody died and I don't feel anything yet. But I'll tell you something about me. I know it's not the same, but once when I was twelve and Winona was ten, I beat the crap out of her. She told the girl I liked that I had a crush on her, and all the kids in my class teased me for months. Anyway, I was so mad at her and I actually broke her nose. My parents made me go to a psychiatrist and learn anger-management stuff. I feel guilty about it to this day, and I still worry about my temper. But I can't take it back. There. I was content to keep that from you forever. I even made Winona promise not to spill the beans."

"Michael, you were a child then."

"Maybe we could make the same case for you." He touches her face with his free hand. "I have to get rid of this glass."

He scrambles down the hill toward the all-purpose trash can by the grill. Sam watches Steve pull himself up on the dock, shaking the water from his head like a wet dog. Michael suddenly runs to the dock, tackling Steve. They fall back into the water.

"Michael, stop it!" Sam gets to the dock's edge as Michael pushes Steve under the water. Eve paddles over on her chair and leans over, punching Michael in the back. Michael pushes at Eve's chair, and tips it over. Sam shrugs off her sandals and dives into the water to collect Eve. She threads her arms around Eve's waist and kicks with her legs toward the dock. Steve reemerges, spraying them with water, and curses. He struggles with Michael again above the surface before getting the upper hand and pushing Michael below.

"What the shit is going on out here?" Sam's father has come back on the dock, followed by Sam's mother. Her father dives in again and paddles over to the grunting, gurgling bodies of Steve and Michael and becomes entangled in the flesh octopus that is thrashing in the creek in front of their house.

"Get your father out of there." Sam's mother bends over the dock. "He's gonna have a heart attack."

"Lousy motherfuckers." Sam's father spits a lot of water, a little bit of blood, after Michael and Steve are separated. They breathe heavily, treading water a few feet apart. "What, are you trying to kill each other?"

"Ask Michael," Steve answers, swimming toward the dock. "He started it."

"Maybe if you weren't such a slimy pervert I wouldn't have," Michael answers as Sam's mother grabs onto Steve's arm to keep him stationary. She then waves to the pontoon boat full of the family a few cabins down. They move painfully slowly past the Pinski dock, having witnessed the entire event coming up the creek toward the lake.

"Happy Fourth of July!" Sam's mother yells, and the family members smile and wave tepidly back. Sam's father grabs his chest as he struggles to get to the dock. Michael swims up behind him and locks his arms around his chest.

"Not too tight," her father grumbles, the tight, Brylcreemed whorls of his hair opening like flower petals and falling onto his forehead, the greasy product veining down his face.

"Oh, Jesus Christ—what did I tell you?" Sam's mother is twitchy, agitated, as Steve touches her on the back. "Hurry, hurry, get him up here."

"I'm fine, Pat." Her father's feet find the rungs of the ladder on the side of the dock and he comes up unsteadily. "Somebody elbowed me in the chest underwater."

"Are you sure?" She hovers over him as he falls heavily onto the picnic bench, gulping breaths and rubbing his white chest.

"Yeah, yeah." He makes his lips into a whistle, smoothing his displaced hair back. "Jesus, that stung."

"You sure you don't want to go to the hospital?" Sam's mother clenches her cigarette pack so tightly Sam can hear the cellophane covering buckle.

"I told you I got hit in the chest, Pat. If I was having a heart attack, I'd tell you." He squints the remaining water out of his eyes and looks over at Michael, who has slipped out of the water unnoticed. "Michael, I thought you was leaving."

"I am." He pulls off his wet shirt and wrings out the corners of his shorts. "I'm sorry if I made any trouble for you."

"You do that again, motherfucker pussyboy, and I'll be ready for you."
Steve spits off the dock into the water. "Figures you'd have to sneak up
on me."

"Steve, shut up." Sam's mother lights a cigarette, inhaling deeply, pulling the back of her shorts out of her butt. "I'm sure you did something
to deserve it."

"That's right, Ma—it's always my fucking fault." Steve shoots her a
look. Sam wants to touch his shoulder but she doesn't. She feels his pain,
it is palpable, not any less than hers. Maybe even greater.

"Well, I'm leaving for real now." Michael makes his way up the hill to
his Saab. "Please—go back to being a happy fucking family."

"Michael, you want to change in the house?" Sam's mother asks. "Put
on some dry clothes?"

Sam jogs up the hill after him. She grabs his wrist but he shakes her
off.

"I'm sorry, Sam," he says. "I don't know if I can be around that guy.
Knowing that."

"You don't have to be around him," she says. He opens his trunk and
rummages through his backpack, emerging with a dry shirt and pants.
"You only saw him once the whole time we were together."

"Once again will be one time too many." He leans against the side
of the car, away from the water, and slips off his wet shorts, pulling the
dry ones on. "Listen, I just need time to be alone right now. I know this
hasn't been fun for you, either, but if I'm here a minute longer I'm going
to kill that guy."

"I understand." She nods her head. She can already feel him pulling
away. "Just remember—you're not obligated to do anything…for me."

"I'll call you tomorrow, okay?" He smiles a little smile and starts the
engine. "I'm sorry, Sam—I have to go right now."

"You deserve better, you know," she says.

"So you do," he answers, nodding back toward the dock.

She watches him back the Saab slowly down the hill. He gives a little
wave, not looking at her, before concentrating completely on the hill. She
wonders if he will call her like he has promised. She decides to turn off
her phone so that she is not disappointed either way. She glances toward
the dock, at Steve and Eve and her mother standing around her father,
who is waving them away. She sighs and heads back down to the dock.
The last thing they need is for him to have a heart attack.

iv.

They were returning to the place he left, where she died and he lived, even though she took some of his life. But now there was life growing in him, and he wondered whether it was hers, not his, and whether when the baby came the life in him would be gone again. He wondered whether Kim would be gone. He hoped she would stay.

"Are you hungry?" he asks her when she pops a third stick of gum in her mouth.

"Maybe a little. Can you pull into a drive-thru when you see one?"

"That stuff will kill you."

"Really, mister whiskey and smokes?"

"I'm not eating that stuff," he says as he pulls into a burger joint. "I've got the baby to worry about."

"What am I hearing?" she smiles, leaning over him to get a look at the drive-thru menu. "Pete Skivins actually cares about something?"

He doesn't answer, smelling her neck, the faintness of perfume and soap. He is happy he is pregnant because the baby pushes his erection down, keeps it hidden.

"Get the double cheeseburger and a vanilla milkshake." She slumps back in her seat. "I've been binging since I gave up smoking."

"Why'd you give up smoking?" he asks after repeating her order into the metal menu box.

"Well, like you said, I have the baby to think about," she answers, and he smiles a little, wondering if she means she is staying around. He is afraid to ask. His hand is shaking as he holds it out for her money.

"Any strange cravings?" she asks, and takes a long sip of her milkshake.

"No," he answers. "Not yet. Have you ever been pregnant?"

She continues to suck on the straw of her milkshake. It seems like forever and when she bites into her double cheeseburger, he doesn't ask again. He turns up the volume on the CD and drums his fingers against the steering wheel.

"Not now." She turns it back down. "What is her name?"

"Sissy," he answers. "We've got a few hours to go yet, you know. In case you want to turn around."

"Absolutely not." She bites into the burger again. The smell of it is making him sick. He rolls open the window. "So tell me about Sissy."

"I'm surprised you don't already know—you know so many other things I don't know. It's really fucking annoying, you know, you holding all the cards."

"How does it feel?" she laughs, and he swears it sounds like Sissy, but it can't be Sissy, because Sissy is dead and Kim is alive and does not look like Sissy. And Sissy was in no way a superhero—at least not that he knew of. She was small and scrawny like a boy, like someone's little sister. But one day she stopped looking like a boy even though she still looked like a boy. She just stopped looking like a boy to him. She looked like someone who needed to be protected from the other boys who treated her like a little boy and knocked her around, teased her. But she was a girl and would be a woman and Pete knew that. And he was proud of knowing that because he became less of a boy and more of a man.

He would tell the other boys to stop when they tossed her backpack around. He would keep them from taking her lunch money to buy Slurpees and Hostess Cakes at the 7-11. He would push their hands away from her boy tits, their lips away from her boy mouth, when they were drinking and skunky on the back of the bus in the afternoons.

And Sissy had always been nice to him, and he had brushed it off when she was still a boy. But when she became a girl to Pete, he wanted more than nice because he was becoming a man.

All the kids hung out at the Skateland, only the "e" was burned out in the sign so it said Skat land. The other boys laughed and Pete Skivins laughed too but it was years until he laughed, really, about Skat-land. They were outside smoking when Sissy pulled up with her mother. She never went to Skat-land, at least not since Pete had been going. She wore a tight, glittery shirt and her boy tits were becoming girl tits.

Inside he watched her lace up her rental skates and wade her way out to the side rail. She strode three or four times to accelerate, decelerated, and then did it again, like she was on a skateboard.

Goddamn, Sissy, that's not how you skate, he said, rolling up to her in the pair of skates he bought at Sears. He replaced the original laces with skulls and crossbones laces and scuffed up the heels. Here, you have to glide, nice and easy.

He skated backwards in front of her, holding her hands, getting her to mimic his movements. She slipped and fell into him, and he wrapped his *arms around her and felt the entire weight of her body, heavier than he imagined but still light, and he smelled her bubble gum and some kind of perfume, different than his sister's.*

I'm sorry, *she said. They'd gone the circle of the rink and Sissy had fallen three times.* I don't skate much.

S'okay, *he shrugged as she hugged the wall, away from him.* You just need to practice. You want to get some fries?

She waded, clomp, clomp, clomp in front of him to the snack bar, and boomeranged herself into a booth while he skated across the slick floor to the counter. He wondered if she would let him kiss her before she went home. He wondered if he was getting ahead of himself.

Why'd you come to Skat-land? *he asked.* You never came before.

I don't know, *she shrugged. She carefully pulled a fry from the pile—Pete had drowned them in ketchup without even asking*

Sorry about all the ketchup. *He felt his face get hot.*

I love ketchup. *She held the fry above her head and moved her mouth up toward it.* Thanks for getting fries, Pete.

He felt his face stay hot. He watched some of the other girls in the grade above them glide by toward the counter. They were the girls that got his dick hard at school, and he'd think about them at home at night. He probably wouldn't talk to them the way he was talking to Sissy. He would talk to them the way other boys talked to them—baby this, baby this. But he talked to Sissy like she was his sister. And he felt almost like she was a sister, but more.

He wondered what love felt like. He wondered if he was getting ahead of himself.

You want to skate some more? *They had eaten all the fries and all that remained was the boat with the grease spot and streaks of ketchup on the bottom. She cradled the paper boat in her hand and he wondered whether she would take it like a souvenir but then she handed it to him and he threw it away.*

It was open skate and he always showed off because he had played roller-hockey for years up at the tennis courts with the other boys but today he just skated backwards in front of Sissy, making her move her legs with his. Like a zipper back and forth they jerked, and when she began to get the hang of it a little he fell in beside her. He felt the buffed floor roll to and away from his feet, the saturated purple and orange and blue lights moving through his body, and he felt his heart living, beating so high in his neck he thought he would throw it up if he opened his mouth.

He caught her staring at Brian Dawkins in the dark well of lockers. All the girls liked Brian, so it wasn't a surprise in one way to Pete but it was a surprise in the other that Sissy did, too. And that she probably braved the trip to Skateland to see Brian, not Pete.

Where are you going? *she asked as he glided toward the opening in the rink. His heart was hot and hurt in his chest, and he said nothing. He could have danced with Kelly; Kelly had girl tits and was sexy. Sissy was a stupid boy-girl and he didn't need to waste time with stupid boy-girls.*

Outside behind Skateland he bummed a cigarette from Cole.

Whattaya all into Sissy for? *Cole smirked, brandishing his Zippo with the snake on it he'd stolen from a friend's father.* She's fugly. You see Kelly today; she was fucking hot.

She's all into me, *Pete shrugged.* I was being nice. Plus, she lets me fuck her.

Really? *Cole nodded.* Maybe I oughta be nice to Sissy.

Find your own piece. *Pete punched Cole's arm.*

There's your whore now, *Cole said. Sissy was standing in front of the Skateland entrance. He felt sprinklers on his skin, his dick, when he thought that maybe she was looking for him, but then he saw the big Buick driven by her mom pull up and Sissy was ferried away.*

Looks like Cinderella had to leave before she turned into a pumpkin. *Cole threw his butt in the tall littered grass.* A rotten pumpkin.

He sat with her on the bus.

You coming back to Skat-land? he asked, scanning the cover of her binder. WHITESNAKE. MOTLEY CRUE. BD. Brian Dawkins. *No PS. I could teach you some real sweet moves.*

Maybe, she answered. If you promise not to leave me next time.

Although perhaps it was not the right context, he took it as a request for him to stay. So he did. On the bus. At lunch.

People kept asking me if we're going out, she told him. They skated side by side now, slow, but steady. Sometimes Pete cut the curve sharply to bump into her, run his hand against the length of hers.

Maybe you should say yes, he answered.

We haven't even been on a date. She was wearing the glittery shirt again, and he liked how she twinkled like he felt.

Let's go to the movies Friday, okay?

"Where are you?" He feels Kim's hand on his and he jumps and shakes. He is driving and he is pregnant and he is crying. "Pete, you have to tell me about the girl."

"If you promise not to hate me," he answers.

"If I hated, you, I wouldn't be here," she answers, and perhaps it is not the right context, but he takes it as she feels for him like he feels for her.

He is ravenous now, and he stuffs the sponge-soggy hamburger bun in his mouth, ripping it with his teeth and moving it around in his mouth until it dissolves and he is still hungry, hungry, hungry.

WHEN SAM WAS FIFTEEN, STEVEN SEVENTEEN

The night her father tried to hit her it started. It was late, and she had been studying for a French exam up in her room. Je croîs, tu croîs, il croît, ne croissons, vs croissez, ils croissant. Her textbook, *Mes Amies*, spine broken, its pages resting against her desk, flat, along with her notebooks and copybook and coffee. She had recently started drinking it, at fifteen, since she started the college track that year at school. Suddenly, the weight of the house around her had lifted, along with the oppressive blocks of row homes on either side of theirs, pinching her in. The streets had lengthened, the air swirling through them, tentatively, like a dog in search of an elusive smell. These streets, which seemed to lock and grid around the same four destinations—school, work, the library, her maternal grandmother's—opened, their paths long and welcoming.

Don't you want to go to school here? her mother had asked as Sam folded the pages of the *Best Colleges Guide*. Berkeley. Washington State. Bennington. Pennsylvania, but only for Bryn Mawr and Swarthmore. *You could live at home.*

Sam flipped the pages. Je crus, tu crus, il crût, ns crûmes, vs crûtes, ils current. She didn't like the taste of coffee, at first. It reminded her of her parents, the acrid ghost of death that lingered about them, the bubbling blackness like an acid. But it helped her to study that extra hour, to make honors. To apply for scholarships. She sweetened it with a little vanilla ice cream. She bought her own mug from a novelty store in the mall. It had a picture of Hemingway on it, and when she wasn't drinking coffee from it, she kept her change and loose bills inside it in her room.

She had returned to the kitchen, past the inert form of her father on the couch, a litter of beer cans like kittens in his lap, the light of the television projecting *M*A*S*H* onto the glass of the picture frames on the end table. She had walked past him lightly, feeling the decrease in her blood sugar and needing another hour's worth of consciousness. But somehow, she miscalculated the weight of the coffee pot in the kitchen, it slipping through her hand and onto the floor, the hot daggers and slivers pelting her legs like a miniature army. She gasped and grabbed about her ankles.

"Jesus Christ, what the fuck are you doing in here?"

Sam's father filled the doorway, a blur of booze and sleep and cough. "I gotta fucking work tomorrow, and you fucking broke the coffee pot? How am I going to drink my coffee tomorrow, Samantha? Am I supposed to brew it in my hands?"

"You act like I did it on purpose," she murmured, still smarting from the impact.

Her father's strength was quick from its heavy slumber, his fingers boring deep into her shoulder. Once his momentum began to roll, from a great, stationary mass, it was powerless to stop. She'd seen the succession of slaps and blows that could erupt from her father like the spirit of a dead prizefighter.

Sam felt herself lift up, and she raised her hands to her face. But before her father could reach her, Steve stumbled in through the kitchen door. For once, his carousing on a school night had been fortuitous.

"Get the fuck off her, you dirty piece of shit." Steve wrapped his arms around the barrel of their father's chest and bent him backward awkwardly, tying up his arms with his own. "You want me to break your back, you old crazy fuck? You are never, ever to touch her, you understand me? Or I will break your fucking back and then I'll kill you."

"Get off me, you no-good bastard piece of shit." Her father's face was like a coiled sausage link, raw and flecked white and red under the strain. He drooled slightly at the corners of his thin lips. "I'm gonna have a heart attack."

"Good." Steve's face grimaced in delight, his forehead pretzeled and ugly but somehow beautiful in its viciousness.

"I ain't kidding, Steven." Her father paused, unable to squeeze out another hyphenated insult. "Sam, get your mother down here."

"Steve, let him go," Sam pleaded. It would have been easier, she reasoned, to take the blows. It would have been easier to absorb the minor weather system her father blew through the house. She understood why her mother let herself be tenderized. It would have been all over, no escalation. No more trouble for Steve other than what he brought on himself, his own. "Steve, please. It's over."

Steve hitched their father back a little more. The drooling turned into snorting and grunting. "Steve, please."

"Steve!" Their mother appeared in the doorway, drawing her robe tightly. "Let your father go!" And Steve, perhaps wanting to let go but not wanting to concede, did finally release him after a few more seconds.

"Your little bastard is trying to kill me," their father explained, after a few gasps. He turned his head halfway toward Steve but did not look him in the eye. "You get out of my house."

"You get out of our house, you stupid fuck," Steve answered. "He was down here trying to smack Sam. Had her on the floor and everything, the coffee pot broken."

"Karl, what on earth are you doing?" Sam's mother bent down over him. "Go to bed."

"Fuck you, Pat."

"Go to bed, Karl. You gotta work tomorrow. You can't miss any more days and you know it. Steve, help me get your father upstairs."

"Nobody touch me." Their father's arms shot out, making sure that the space around him was free of familial interference. He stood up unsteadily, his face regaining its normal pallor, and surveyed them. How far to take things, once they started, had always lain heavily in everyone's minds, especially his. In order to establish his dominance, to ensure their fear and subservience, he needed to raise the stakes. Become a little less predictable, a little more violent. Make good on his outlandish promises to break every fucking bone in their bodies, slap the lips off their faces. But the dynamic had already begun to shift, now that Steve was seventeen and could neutralize him physically.

"Fuck all of you." He swabbed his mouth with the back of his hand. "Bunch of shits."

With that, he went upstairs. And everyone felt the plates shifting underneath their feet, the flags on the battlefield changing positions, a sigh of collective relief that the opposition could be handled, cracked, driven to defeat. Even if their alliance was unsteady and prone to betrayal.

"What the hell are you kids doing up?" Their mother sat on a kitchen chair, the adrenalin passing, the blood and gravity returning to her heart and knees. "And what happened to the coffee pot?"

"I was studying," Sam explained. "I came down to get more coffee and…it just slipped."

"Here your father thinks we got burglars or something, I bet, you making all that noise when you're supposed to be in bed, and you scare him half to death, breaking coffee pots. How am I going to make him his coffee tomorrow? You know he can't miss any more days. You want your father to get fired and we're all out on the street? Is that what you want?"

"Ma, that's no excuse." Steve's hands, which had momentarily slackened and wandered towards their mother's shoulders, to grasp them, fisted. "That's no fucking excuse to beat anybody."

"And what are you doing up? You been out? I smell the beer on you, Steven Pinski. You're grounded. You're both grounded. You need to be in bed by eleven on school nights. What's wrong with your kids? Can't you see how you drive your father crazy?"

"Ma, just stop it and go to bed, okay?" Sam turned toward the sink, aware again of her wounds, of the cleanup that still remained. And the studying. "I'll get some coffee from the 7-11 tomorrow and leave it for him. I'll just get up early."

"You'll do no such thing." Steve stood beside her. She could smell the beer and pot on him and wondered how he could drink and smoke and throw his chances away. "Dad is capable of going down to the 7-11 on his way to work tomorrow."

"You shut up," his mother barked, teary. "Don't you cause enough trouble already?"

"Don't you not cause enough? Christ, you'd let him kill me and Sam in our sleep if you thought it would cure him."

"Steven Pinski!" Their mother shook her head violently, as if she meant to exorcise his words from her ears. "You are not my son. You are not my son."

"Mom, he didn't mean it." Sam turned and drew her mother off the chair. "We're all tired. Let's just go to bed, okay? I'll get some coffee and buy a new pot tomorrow. Everything will be fine—I'll take care of it."

"You'll do no such thing," Steve said again after their mother went back upstairs.

"So principle is going to change things?" Sam answered, throwing the plastic handle of the pot into the trash.

"What?"

"Nothing. It's just easier this way." She busied herself with wetting paper towels to pick up the slivers of glass that lay about the floor like confetti. "You go to bed, too."

"It ain't right. He gets away with murder, practically, and everybody wants to treat him like a fucking baby."

"He's not going to change. We just have to wait it out and get out. That's what I'm doing. That's what you should be doing, instead of messing up your life."

"Jesus—thanks, 'Ma'. Here I save your ass and you're giving me shit."

"Steve, I'm happy you were here. It's probably the only time I'm glad you were out late with Brian."

"So I'm still your hero, huh?" Steve's eyes shone suddenly as he found the Bactine in the cabinet. "You still adore me? Gimme your hands."

"I wouldn't say that." Sam stepped away from him as his body collided with hers.

"I'm serious." He held out a paper towel dampened with Bactine. "I'm not letting that bastard hit you. You'll be safe here. You and Mom don't have to worry. I'll kill the bastard and not lose a second of sleep over it."

Sam didn't have to worry, much. After that night, that morning, after she had left two large coffees on the counter before school and returned after school with a new glass pot, nobody spoke of the incident again. Not that the others were mentioned, but there seemed to be a truce, a tacit acknowledgment that Karl Pinski could no longer throw his weight around. His words, maybe, and other objects, but no longer could he make sense of the pathos in his soul by attacking his family. At least while Steve was still around. And by the time Steve left, their father's latest pharmacological cocktail pushed him deeper into the padding of his own skin, his arms and mouth unable, seemingly, to fight out of the chemical cloud of mind.

It started then, when their father's tyranny ended. Steve started to check in on Sam at night, to make sure she was okay, that their father hadn't reneged on his unspoken word. Steve would slip into Sam's room, after slipping in from wherever he went after work with his friends.

"Everything okay?" He'd lie on the edge of the bed. She'd turn the light on, and he'd read the gatefolds of the cassette tapes littering her bed. "Echo and the Bunnymen? That's a fag-sounding name. Are they any good?"

"You might like them."

"They sound like Aerosmith?"

Sam tried to stay up as long as she could, her light on, waiting for him. He wasn't always drunk, but he was always quiet, friendly. Her hero of old, protective and chivalrous. He'd lie on her bed and reach across what seemed to her a cavern of space to flick open the bottom window shutter so he could smoke. He talked about a guitar he'd fallen in love with at Bill's Music House and was saving up to purchase, an ash Fender telecaster, how he'd learned to play "Thunder Road" on his old one the other day. He'd ask her what she was studying in the tenth grade, pushing off his worn, stained Nikes and wriggling his toes in his tube socks.

Suddenly, Sam had a friend, a confidante, a brother. As long as his services were required against the waning threat of the lumbering man two rooms down. But Steve began to stay out later, sometimes drunk. Instead of sharing his struggle with his thoughts, he began to recede from her again, moody in the waking hours, quiet in the bed at night while she filled up the increasing pauses with the French club and the summer writing workshop she had applied to for that summer.

It started then. Perhaps it was her fear of losing him. Of losing each other, their childhood, the bonds that would strain and break as their paths became more and more diverging.

Steve was coming home later and Sam had given up on waiting for him. Although she would often wake up to find him next to her in the morning, in various states of dress and hangover, it seemed their intimacy was over. Perhaps he felt guilty, leaving her to sleep alone after keeping vigil with her for so many months, so he remained, waiting for her word. The next night, she waited for him in the dark. It was after three when she saw him slip into her room and gently let himself into bed.

"You don't have to sleep here anymore, Steve," she whispered, pushing his body away from where it pressed into hers. "I think I'm okay now."

"What, you don't want me here with you? Am I stinky and gross or something?" He grabbed her wrists, and she could feel his bare arms against hers. In a saucer of moonlight that bathed the room, she could see the bleached white of his underwear.

"No, it's just..."

"You don't enjoy my company anymore?"

"I do. I like you here. It's just...you don't have to feel obligated."

"I'm not." He put his arm on her stomach.

It started then. An arm across her stomach, on her thigh. She had never been so close to a boy, close enough to feel the scratch of chest hairs on her back, the rough, warm pressure of fingers cinching her waist. She knew Steve had girls—more than he knew what to do with—she figured, by the gossip around school, and the warmness, the nearness of him surrounded her, his breath constant on her neck. And she knew she liked it to this point and wouldn't go further. She knew she liked it to this point.

She did not think about any other point until it happened, the swell of him against her back one night. She had wondered how it would feel, the blood-engorged muscle, and was surprised that it was springy and playful, teasing. She turned around and he guided her hand to it. She gasped and laughed at the warmth and softness of the shaft and testicles, the nest of hair in which it presumably lay dormant.

She held him in her hand, the baby bird between his pale, strong legs, and she thought of the other soft things of Steve's she had touched and shared. The inside of his oiled, broken-in baseball glove. The soft wool of his skullcap, on which she had heaped handful after handful of snow when they were younger until his large, crooked teeth emerged from his mouth like a walrus and he pushed her in the snow, laughing and rubbing snow on her cheeks. The stuffed bunny named Bugs, which their mother still had tucked away somewhere.

She lay in the softness of all those things and the softness of this, the soft, insides of Steve, offered to her in this patient, elaborate ceremony, this initiation of trust. She felt his heartbeat in it, in her hands, and then the sticky wet and flaccidness, Steve's voice wounded, his hand in her hair. The little visitor went away, back in its nest but Sam held onto it, even after Steve rolled over. She wasn't going to let go, where she could feel it, his heart.

It started then that she just stopped thinking about it. It was an itch scratched, acknowledged only when it needed scratching. How far to take things, once they started, hadn't weighed heavily on Sam's mind, since she had stopped thinking about it.

*

Most things Sam learned about boys were from Steve; their smells, their fears, their anger, their shyness. The strange codes and rituals they adhered to, all to project those things most precious to them: their identity, their turf, their loves. She wasn't sure if she could learn anything else useful about them. But she was only sixteen and still years away from learning anything useful about herself. Even so, Steve's friend Brian was the quietest, dullest person she'd ever known. Steve's friends, after he had drifted away from his baseball teammates, had filled very specific roles in his life: drug and booze supply, knowledge of cars, and brawn to have his back in the event that he bit off more than he could chew, which was often.

Brian filled the brawn variable of Steve's equation of living, and he filled it with little room to spare. He was still growing at 6'2", as evidenced by the baby fat rounding his cheeks and chin like a half-donut. He wore sweatshirts that hid the softness of his abs and jeans with grease stains on the back pockets from repeatedly wiping his hands on them. But Brian could knock anyone unconscious if riled, and he could trick out a car like a professional. Brian lived life through his hands—his feelings, his moods, were molded by the dexterity, the strength, the quickness of his fingers, his fists, his biceps. But Sam hadn't had much use for Brian. He was too quiet, like her. If Steve left them alone, he may as well have turned off the light in the room.

Brian's existence depended, to a large degree, on Steve's schemes. He reaped the fruits, although maybe only the smaller, spoiled pieces, of Steve's ideas. Girls that Steve tired of, who dated Brian in the hope of making Steve jealous, the last can of a twelve-pack that Steve was too drunk to finish, the bulk of Steve's weight when carrying him home from an ill-fated excursions. But when Brian went away the summer of his seventeenth birthday to Wyoming to spend time on his uncle's ranch, cleaning cow shit and barns and trying to break horses, Steve pouted. He was resigned to spending quality time with his girlfriend of two months, Nikki, who aspired to be a hairdresser to the stars. Or at least own a salon in the Essex suburbs.

At least Nikki had aspirations, which was more than Sam could say about Steve. Without Brian, Steve seemed lost, a boat without an anchor. He was without transportation, Brian's '78 white Trans Am with the blue racing stripe dormant in the driveway of his parents' home, the spare key hidden. He was without his ID, as Brian's size belied his age and they had been able to get into some of the seedier roadhouses down on North Point Road, where everyone's money looked the same. Now, when Steve took on two, three men at a time in drunken bravado, he usually came home with a split lip and black eye.

"That stupid sack of shit is never coming back," he bemoaned loudly to Sam one summer evening as he got ready to hang out with Nikki. Sam sat on Steve's bed, listening to the hairdryer as Steve curled and coiffed his hair the way Nikki had taught him. "He's gonna get in good on that farm and marry the first thing that looks at him, even if it's a fucking cow."

"Hmm," Sam responded, scribbling in her notebook. She was writing a story about a werewolf and a girl. She wasn't sure whether the werewolf would fall in love with the cheerleader or eat her.

"Did you hear what I said?" He turned to look at her. She nodded, not looking up at him. He wasn't the only one blown off-course that summer. As soon as Steve had started dating Nikki, he had stopped his visiting of Sam. Although Sam was mostly relieved that this part of their relationship was perhaps in the past, she assumed the guilt and problems that had polluted her thoughts, her body, would also dissipate with its retreat. The past, like her stories, she thought, could be created and ended, tossed into a cardboard box with the rest of her spiral notebooks, revisited and revised only when she was ready.

But the feelings did not leave. The shame and anger lay dormant, her chest a clogged sink. And their absence in Steve only seemed to magnify them in her, as if she, like Brian, had to carry the burden of their indiscretions.

"You need to get some friends, Sam." Steve put his comb in his pocket after flicking off the hairdryer. "Get some dates or something. You're all shut in here with your notebooks."

"And you're a stupid bastard," she answered, running out of his room before he could do anything.

She had learned from Steve one important thing about boys: they would always betray you.

Contrary to Steve's predictions, Brian came back that fall, tan and leaner and, although not exactly handsome, well-proportioned and well-made, like one of his souped-up junkers. When he pulled up in the Trans Am, Steve was at work, an internship of sorts at a local garage that Brian's father had arranged for Brian before he decided to spend a summer punching cows. Gone was the sweatshirt, replaced by a t-shirt so tight it looked like a mesolayer of skin, trapping the bulbous pectorals and deltoids that had sprouted off Brian's chest.

"Come take a ride with me over there." Brian nodded his head toward the Trans Am when Sam explained to him the reason for Steve's absence. It was the most he'd ever said to her at once, and she felt compelled to obey. He closed her into the dark car, full of red pleather and pulsating stereo woofers pummeling her with speed metal. He turned down the radio upon entering his side and absently rattled the car into gear.

"How was your summer?" she asked, watching the veins roll and pop in the fist of his gear hand. "Don't tell him I said it, but Steve missed you."

"Yeah?" Brian replied, and Sam was disappointed that, despite his refined physique and quiet confidence, he hadn't developed into a brilliant conversationalist during his time away. She picked at her fingernails and noted his recent decision to begin using cologne. "You miss me, too?"

"I miss you?" she repeated, unused to having her opinion solicited for anything. She had been convinced that their knowledge and interest in each other was tangential and passing, Steve the main body around which they orbited. "It was quiet without you around."

A stupid thing to say, since Brian filled a room no better than she did, even given their disparities in size. But she often said stupid things when she opened her mouth. Sam also lived by her hands, her pen capturing the complexity and eloquence of her thoughts better than her voice.

"I'm glad you're back," she managed, although maybe she meant it for Steve's sake. She didn't know. She only wanted the both of them to stop talking so that she could think about what to say next.

Brian pulled to the side of the road to a snowball stand, a wooden shed with cardboard signs listing, in an uneven hand, every flavor conceivable. Brian pulled his wallet out of his back pocket, which Sam noticed was not covered with grease.

"You want a snowball?" He nodded toward the sign. She ordered the smallest one, which Brian upgraded to a medium, an egg custard with marshmallow. "Just in case I want a bite," he explained.

"So are you going to take Steve's place at the garage?" she inquired. She tried not to sound suspicious, accusatory of Brian taking away a job that, frankly, Steve sucked at. But she resented those sorts of leveraging arrangements in general.

"Nope. He can learn the trade. I'm going back to Wyoming, once I've graduated," he answered, licking marshmallow from the half-oval between his thumb and forefinger after passing the snowball to Sam. "I want to own a horse ranch."

He told her about his uncle's ranch, grooming and maintaining horses for rodeos and working and equestrian activities, about riding the horses to herd his uncle's small flock of sheep and cows. Smells so honest and strong they fortified his soul, beautiful, open spaces, and plenty of work for his hands.

"You should come out," he added, but her mouth was full of ice and numbing quickly. They pulled up to the ugly, cinderblock garage in Essex that was as dirty and smudged on the outside as on the inside. Steve appeared from one of the cavernous bays, equally greasy and spotted, his hair protected and hidden by a bandanna, the way Nikki had taught him.

"Hey, it's the Ball Sack." Steve had always mispronounced Brian's last name, Balziak. Brian nodded and leaned against the car, his arms resting on the powder keg of his chest. "You get tired of fucking the same cow?"

"How's the garage been treating you?" Brian answered. Sam really hated when Steve was mean to people, particularly when he was equally capable of charm. Although she supposed she should be thankful that he had yet to turn his tongue on her.

"This grease bowl? It's like an oven." Steve pulled off his bandanna and wiped his hands with it. "So when are we getting some beer?"

"Later, maybe." Brian looked at Sam. "You want to ride around? I want to see how the place has changed."

"Buddy, nothing's changed, except maybe the size of your ears." Steve slid into the passenger seat of the Trans Am. "Let's get some beer."

"Sam in front," Brian instructed.

"I didn't hear her call shotgun," Steve answered, turning up the radio.

"Move it, Pinski, before I hogtie you."

"You're lucky Sam is here." Steve crawled into the backseat. "Or you'd be spitting your nuts out of your throat." Although Sam doubted this was the case, she always respected the fact that Steve feared no one.

They drove down to Essex, past the wide swatches of corn and grass and roadside farmers' stands and the old airbase, toward the little beaches where their families used go and spend a Sunday. They were small patches of beach, knotted heavy with trees and that charged a few dollars' admission for a parking spot and a picnic table. The water quality had declined over the years, and the Pinskis began to spend more and more time at the cabin. But the beach was still a good bet in the off-season, evenings, to hang out with friends or girlfriends and do stuff that generally could not be done underage or in public. At least that's what Sam had heard from Steve. The few friends she had in high school were less cool than she was, her status only marginally raised because of her having a bad-ass, cute brother.

But Brian and Steve looked as if they'd spent lots of time there. They sat on top of a picnic table, smoking cigarettes while Sam finished her snowball. She liked the way Brian's eyebrows inched toward each other, his eyes squinting, when he inhaled his cigarette, the way the smoke came out his nose, the way he handled the little white, frail stick gently in his bare hands while Steve repeatedly flattened and picked at the filter of his. Steve filled the empty space with words, a rant about the garage, how the grease embedded under his fingernails and how Nikki worried he'd get oil in her pussy when he fingered her, how he hated cars and was desperate to find a couple of guys who didn't suck to jam with, how he couldn't wait to graduate and get out of Baltimore, although he didn't know to where.

"Come to Wyoming," Brian answered. His quietness didn't bother Sam so much this time around. Maybe it was the thoughtful way he gazed across the water. Maybe he had always had thoughts and Sam had only just become aware of them. Either way, she found herself wanting to know what they were.

"No thanks." Steve smirked, and Sam knew whether or not Steve went, he would get by. He was just too handsome and charming and, if those failed, manipulative and intimidating. "I ain't no stupid cowhat."

"Neither am I." Brian stood up and stretched. "Ready?"

"No." Steve took a long drag off his cigarette. Usually people moved only when Steve was ready.

"Well, then have a nice walk." Brian opened the driver door of the Trans Am, and the car licked the ground under his weight before springing up. Sam clamored into the backseat, making it easy for Steve to change his mind and slip in before Brian pulled out. Steve stayed seated on the picnic table, jingling his legs and biting his thumbnail, oblivious. Brian waited a minute before turning the ignition. His hand hovered over the gearshift briefly before grabbing it.

"Wait for him," Sam instructed, bounding out toward Steve. He did not look at her when she tugged his arm but did not resist. He climbed in the backseat and didn't say a word on the way back to the house.

"Thanks for the snowball." Sam stood in front of the house while Steve slithered into the front seat of the Trans Am. Brian, having spoken more that afternoon than seemingly all his life, nodded. Steve stared at her, his own mouth opened wide, frowning, as if confiding to her a sad secret. Or asking her to keep one.

Sam decided that maybe the werewolf should date the girl.

*

Brian came around again a week later while Steve was at work.

"He's going to quit when school starts," Sam offered helpfully through the screen door. Brian stood on the steps leading to the porch and, at this height, they met to eye, even if Brian's eyes were cloaked behind sunglasses. School wouldn't begin for another week, and Brian had free time and money to spend from his uncle. It made sense he'd come around. With Steve, time and money were easily wasted.

"I didn't come to see Steve," he answered. When Sam wondered why Brian was interested in her, she had to concede that perhaps she appeared as different to him as he had to her. A few months ago, she had gotten her braces removed. Her bathing suit from last summer was too tight in the hips, and she had decided to buy a two-piece, much to her mother's surprise and disappointment. Although she was still tiny, her body had grown enough to stretch the powdering of freckles about her face and shoulders into a pleasant constellation.

She didn't know what she was supposed to feel, if she felt anything, but she knew that he seemed to see something, no matter how shallow or immaterial, in her that she didn't. And she wanted to see it. Always so deeply in herself, she wondered whether she was just a victim of the wrong vantage point.

She went with him. They went down to the Inner Harbor and rode the paddleboats, although the length and power of Brian's legs often meant they were motoring in wide arcs inside a straight line. They went up to the observation deck at the World Trade Center and enjoyed the panorama of the Inner Harbor and Fort McHenry. They went on the clipper ship, the U.S.S. Constellation. They walked the promenade and ate ice cream.

"You seem different now," Sam said, as they sat on a bench in front of one of the shopping pavilions at the Inner Harbor, watching tourists amble by the greasy green water. The smells of hot dogs and sewage floated in and out of the space before them. "Since you've been back."

"Wyoming is weird," he answered. "But I liked it. It's big, and the people are far apart. And so is everything in your head. You can concentrate very clearly on one thing at a time."

"Are you really moving back?"

"Yeah," he said. She felt the back of his hand brush hers on the bench.

"I'm going to college," she blurted. "Probably not in Maryland, but definitely on the East Coast." His hand did not brush hers again.

"You want to see a movie sometime?" he asked after a while.

Although Steve's universe seemed to settle and center now that Brian had returned, the balance of power had also evened out. It was subtle, it was unspoken, but it was there, punctuated by veiled references to Brian's trip to Wyoming and his sudden "love" of livestock.

"He's all crazy talk," Steve explained to her one night as he tried to figure out the chords to "Dancing Barefoot" on his guitar. He plucked his old Yamaha acoustic, the spoils of the leftover money from his newspaper route, petty pot dealing, and a summer job a few years ago. "What do they say out there—all hat, no cattle? The grease monkeys down at the garage were all making bets on when he'd come slouching back from Wyoming, broken like one of them damn horses he keeps talking about."

"If he's your friend, I don't see why you don't encourage him," Sam answered. She hadn't told Steve of their day at the harbor, nor their future plans to go to the drive-in. She figured Brian hadn't either, judging by Steve's reaction, or lack of one.

"I am his friend." He took his noodling and looked at her. "I'll encourage him in ideas that aren't stupid."

"Why is it stupid?"

"It just is." He stashed the guitar back in its case, rubbed his hands over his face. "I can't concentrate anymore."

*

Sam met Brian at the Sunoco a few blocks from the house. She had told her mother she was going to Skat-land with a few of her friends from school. By the gas bay Brian leaned against the Trans Am, filling it up, his arms crossed and each capable of perhaps snapping the other in two. When he saw her he smiled and waved lightly and quickly, as if his arm was straw.

"You look good. " He commented on her clothing, her makeup, her scent all at once. He opened the passenger door for her. "Maybe next time I can come pick you up at the house like a real date?"

"What about Steve?"

"What about him?"

"I don't think he'd be very happy."

"Steve ain't happy about anything." Brian popped the clutch into gear and turned up the mix tape she had made him. "But that don't mean that you shouldn't be."

At the drive-in he bought her pizza and a Coke and a snowball. She had to admit that having a boyfriend had its advantages. Suddenly the secret world of teen rituals, hidden and taboo, had been opened to her. She saw other kids from her school, who acknowledged her and Brian even as they had never said a word to her in class, in the halls. Suddenly, to be liked by someone, whoever it was, meant you were worthy of being liked at all.

Brian's touch was unsure at first. In her rush to bury memories from Steve with legitimate ones, she wove his hand in hers and rubbed his prominent, hairy knuckles with her free hand. She thought about kissing him, but he seemed really interested in the movie. She liked that his intentions were perhaps not twofold or, if they were, that he wasn't ruining the possibility that she wanted to see the movie herself before she saw his tonsils. She wondered if Brian's thoughts were as mysterious to her as Steve's.

"What do you think about?" she asked him as they drove to the beach. His hand went to the back of his neck as he sighed.

"Why, you think I'm dumb or something?" He shot her a quick look. "Everybody always wants to know what I think. The counselors at school, my folks, the other kids. They think I'm a fucking retard."

"I don't think that. I just wonder...what anybody thinks. Or maybe what boys think. And girls, too, but I'm a girl, so I can kind of guess what they're thinking, and what I'm supposed to think. I wonder what Steve thinks a lot, too."

"I wonder what I'm supposed to do," he said finally, and she took his hand in encouragement. "I always wanted to be a firefighter, or maybe a policeman. And my folks want me to stay here, because they took care of their parents, eventually, and I guess me and my sister are supposed to, too. They're really sorry they sent me to Wyoming. They had no idea I was going to want to go back."

"But what else do you think about?"

"I don't know," he shrugged. "My car. Girls—well, *a* girl."

"What does Steve talk about?"

"Uh...I don't know." He scratched his head. "He talks so much, it's hard to listen to him, really. I hope he don't think as fast as he talks."

"Do you take him seriously?"

"I didn't always, you know," he replied after a while. The beach was in view, along with a few scattered cars. "But he can be the meanest, angriest son of a bitch I've ever known. And he hates that old man of yours."

"Dad's okay." Sam shrugged. She didn't hate their father. Maybe she felt sorry for him a little, afraid of him a lot, but she had seen the pictures, the smiles when they were very young, she and Steve, and she knew he had cared for them once. She was not greedy for more, or maybe she didn't realize that she could be. Or maybe she inherently accepted her father's deficiencies and figured she would find what she was lacking from others, away at college or in another city or another country.

It was Steve from whom she expected. Steve who had grown up beside her and saw the same things. But their father was harder on Steve. And Steve was harder on their father. Steve had expected much more, his disappointment more visible. He did not understand that small expectations led to manageable disappointments. Although he was tougher, he did not know how to survive.

"I don't want to talk about Steve," Brian said after a while, snaking his anaconda arm around her shoulder. He moved over to kiss her. His breath was sweet with ketchup and soda. She leaned up against the clutch to get closer into his embrace. He moved away and laughed, and the laughter poured into all the cracks in her bones and joints and skin and sealed her tight.

"I love this car, but it's no chick magnet." He pulled the keys out of the ignition. "Want to take a walk on the beach?"

He came over to her side and helped her out and she placed her little hand in his and they walked down to the beach, clear of the small group of people that had started a bonfire up the way, drinking and hooting and smoking. He sat on the sand and she sat between his legs and they imagined big, powerful, elegant waves instead of the plop-plop-plop of the river washing up on the sand. She did not know what to think of it all, the few short weeks they had spent together. It didn't happen as she planned, as she had read about in the teen romance novels her mother sometimes picked up at the corner drugstore when she went to get her father's prescriptions. Sam read them incredulously and earnestly, baffled by the opportunities of nice boys who appeared and spread themselves over girls like salves.

Brian was not one of these boys, but she was still not convinced that these boys existed. So he was all right. He was what she got, and whatever she got from him, or from someone else, she would be thankful for.

One of the members of the other group weaved his way over to where Sam and Brian were sitting on the beach. Sam could tell from his frame, his stagger, that it was Steve.

"That you, Ball Sack?" he sneered, sucking on his cigarette. "What girl did you manage to drag up here by her hair?"

Sam bent her head down, but he saw her. She was pushed forward inadvertently as Brian stood up to meet Steve's advance. He hovered over

Steve, and she hoped his size alone would be enough to extinguish any thirst Steve had for trouble.

"What the fuck?" Steve pushed at Brian. "Why are you trying to make the moves on Sam, you dick?"

"Maybe that's for Sam to decide," Brian answered. Sam met Steve's eyes. His expression was hard and balled, like a piece of trash. She felt his disgust drip all over her, and for a moment, she feared he might attack her. Instead, he flicked his cigarette out in her direction.

"Whore," he finally mumbled. "Why you wanna fuck around with a ball sack like Brian, I'll never know."

"Honey, what are you doing?" An angular girl whose halter top and jeans looked sewn onto her pushed her feet through the sand toward them.

"Nothing, Nick. Go back." He waved her away. "Seeing my friend fuck my little sister."

"Aww," Nikki cooed, until she realized that she did not share Steve's opinion on the matter. "Whatsa matter, honey? Sam's a big girl. You guys wanna shot? We got some Schnapps."

"Didn't I tell you to get the fuck outta here?" He whirled toward her and she cowered, her long blond hair curtaining her face, her arms splayed outward in defense.

"Nikki, you want me to take him home?" Brian asked as Steve hocked spit in the sand.

"Honey, come on back with me." She gingerly made her way toward him, arms outstretched. His embarrassment, or indecision about what to do next, made him indifferent to her touch. She wrapped an arm around his back and steered him toward the bonfire.

"You are dead, you hear me!" Steve cried, although it was not clear to whom he made his threat. Steve and Nikki made their way back toward the fire.

"You all right?" Brian asked, bending down, and Sam nodded. He wrapped his arm around her waist and stood her up.

"We should go." She dusted the sand off the front of her pants, and Brian nodded.

"He's just drunk," he said in the car, with less conviction than Sam wanted. "He'll be fine in the morning."

"Do you think he'll hurt you?"

"Are you kidding?" Brian laughed. "If he thought he could get me, he would have tried tonight. No, he ain't gonna do shit. You just let me know if he gives you a hard time."

"Do you still want to see me?"

"You think I'm worried about Steve?" He touched her chin, his fingers the size of hot dogs. But it didn't matter that Brian wasn't worried about Steve. He didn't have to live with him. "I'll talk to you soon, huh?"

She nodded, and he kissed her once on the lips, not lingering, before driving her home.

Later that night, Steve came to her. She had expected him, was resigned to it. He fell, like a sack of laundry, onto her bed. She watched his chest rise and fall in the faint light, listened to the sounds of his labored breath, a dry cough from the cigarettes.

"How could you do such a thing, Sam, with that ape?" he finally said, and the strain of his voice made her wonder whether he had cried. "I'm still your guy, right?"

"Of course." She smiled and touched his back.

"You can't see him anymore. He's no good for you."

"No worse than you are."

"I'm no good for you, either." He turned to face her.

"I didn't mean it in the same way." She withdrew her hand.

"He's going to leave you." He crawled over top of her. His silver crucifix, from their parents after his eighth-grade confirmation, trailed lighting over her chest. "He's leaving for Wyoming in the spring. What are you gonna do? Move all the way out there?"

"I'm not moving to Wyoming, Steve. I have to finish high school."

"So you're going to get your heart broken."

"Steve, I'm a big girl."

"Are you saying you don't need me anymore?" His breath was pressing against her own. "When Dad flips out again, who's going to be there for you, huh? Not me, Sam. You don't need me anymore, right?"

"I didn't say that..."

"You need me." He had her by the arms, his chin digging into her neck. She could feel him getting excited. She knew she didn't like it to this point. But it was her fault because she liked it to some point.

"I want you to go away," she cried, squirming under him. She could feel her tears rolling down his back as he tugged down her jeans and underpants. He undid the button to his jeans, holding his belt and jeans in either hand as it got hard and shot up between them. But he did not enter her. He clenched his teeth, exhaled, shook his head.

"Just finish me." He put her hand on it, moved it up and down. "Please? Christ. Please."

She took it in her hand, closing her eyes. She didn't want to pretend it was Brian's. She didn't want to think about anything. There was a place between her ribs where she went and that was where she stayed until he stiffened, grunted, a quick sigh in his chest, and turned away from her. He rolled off the bed, and left the room so fast she could still feel him in her hand.

He receded from her and took everything with him, the memories they had shared, memories she had to search for years later in her old childhood diaries, to assure herself they had happened, that the pictures did not lie, that her mother's stories weren't cribbed. He left, like a shadow up the wall, and everything was gone, and she was a shadow, too.

She began to sleep in her closet at night because she could wedge a yardstick underneath the inside doorknob and the closet wall, unlike the doorknob to her room, which had been broken for years. For the first few weeks, she would hear the door to her room open, Steve's socked feet making a careful sweep of her room. Sometimes he would whisper to her to come out, "just to talk."

"Sam, I just want to talk to you. Please." He slurred the last few words. Every night he stayed out drinking. He would leave after their parents went to bed and return before dawn. "I just want to talk to you."

Every morning her back felt like a broken, wooden cocktail umbrella as she climbed out of the closet. She wondered whether she could sleep for the next year there, and the year after, until college, without inducing scoliosis, cutting off circulation in her feet, inducing agoraphobia. But she liked the darkness, the womb-like space, in addition to its safety. She did not see Steve at all anymore; he worked at the garage after school and ate after the family in his room, saying he was tired. There he stayed, playing his guitar or the stereo, until it was all clear to go out.

She wondered what he could say to her that would make things better. She slept in the closet every night, and if he told her from the other side, she couldn't hear him.

"Are you all right?" She felt her mother's hands on her shoulders after dinner. "You been spending a lot of time in the bathroom lately."

"It's your cooking," Karl Pinski grumbled, slicing a particularly dry, overcooked rump of roast beef. Sam took the slice that folded over the knife, placed it against her cheek, and began to cry.

*

There was a note from Brian in her locker at school that week, asking her to meet him that night at the Sunoco. She slipped out of the house after dinner, taking the steps quietly as she moved past Steve's room. For once, it was silent. No continuous progression of notes from "Born to Run," which Steve had been trying to learn on his guitar that week, no burpy cackle in Steve's guitar speaker, no intermittent yelling from their father to turn that fucking shit down. She stopped and pressed her ear against the door, trying to remember if she had heard him come home the night before. Satisfied he was not there, she moved past her father in living room, who was half-awake and watching *Barney Miller*, and up the street to the Sunoco, where Brian's car idled like a big cat by the car wash bay.

"You eat?" Brian asked, throwing the transmission in gear. They pulled out of the parking lot. "I'm starving—I haven't been able to eat all day, it's been so crazy. You wanna go to Jack-in-the Box?"

"I ate, but thanks for offering." She looked at the side of Brian's face, unyielding in its small, crooked smile, as he navigated across town. He did not kiss her and she did not touch him, and she knew it was all over with them. Steve had killed it. He hadn't tried to hurt Brian, hadn't said a word to him about Sam. But he had killed it, whatever small tendril had curled, briefly, out of the earth. Killed it for both of them. It was now a matter of whether Brian was going to break up with her. Or she with him. If anything had actually really started, and whether any breaking up was actually needed.

Brian guided the Trans Am into the Jack-in-the-Box drive-thru and turned down the stereo. "Sure you don't want anything?"

"I'm sure." She felt tears in her eyes. In the parking lot, other couples sat on the trunks of cars, feeding each other chewing gum, soda, their arms curled around each other's waists and shoulders. She felt like she and Brian had been two cardboard dolls trying to live in a three-dimensional dollhouse. She wondered if all relationships would be this way for her. The only person that felt real in her life was Steve, and he was a different-sized, different-purpose doll.

"You look thin," he said, his head craned out the window to examine the menu board. "I'm getting you a taco."

They pulled into the parking lot to eat. Brian laid his various wrapped burritos and tacos across the dashboard, stuck the extra-large soda in the cup holder between them, where it rested precariously because it did not quite fit. Sam laid the flat half-moon of taco he had bought her in her lap and looked at it. She could throw it up later, she supposed. She had gotten quite adept at it after dinner, sometimes at school, depending on whether she had gym that day. She felt empty and dry, waiting for the right elixir to bring her back to life. Until then, she would reject various forms of sustenance.

"They're good," Brian encouraged through a mouthful of taco. "Try yours."

She smelled the greasy, balled meat and damp lettuce, heard the bubbled slurp of soda traveling through Brian's straw and into his mouth. And she wondered whether this was as close as they would come to intimacy. He burped quietly and wiped his mouth with the back of his hand before turning to face her.

"Sam, I don't know if you know what went down last night, if you had a chance to talk to Steve…I just don't want you to think bad of me and all. I had no idea…"

"No idea of what?" She put the unwrapped taco on the dashboard next to Brian's items, felt her hands seek out each other in her lap.

"Last night." Brian lit a cigarette, waving the match out violently and sucking hard on the cigarette. "Steve robbed the liquor store on Pulaski."

"What?"

"I didn't know he was going to do it. I was in the car. I thought he was buying cigarettes. But then he runs out with the money and tells me to step on it. He got almost eight-hundred dollars. He said he was going to New Jersey with that band he tried out for last week."

"The Springsteen cover band."

"So he did tell you."

"No." She shook her head. "I just know some band invited him to play some Springsteen covers in the bars on the weekends. He's been practicing all summer."

"I don't know what the police know, if anything. I've been watching the news. They got an ID on a Trans Am but nothing else. I'm wondering whether I should just beat it out of here, go back to Wyoming."

"Don't you think that will raise suspicion? You should lie low."

"I don't know—with Steve gone…"

"Where is he? Do you know where he is?"

"Nope. New Jersey, I guess. You don't know anything?"

I didn't even know he was gone." Sam looked out the window. "I need to go home right away. Maybe he came back."

"I don't think he's coming back," Brian said. "He's done with Baltimore for good. And he don't want to get caught."

"Brian, I'm sorry you got caught up in this." She squeezed his hand. "But you need to stay in town and pretend everything is normal. And don't say anything. If anyone asks you, act like it's a total surprise he's gone."

"What if they question you?"

"Well, it is a surprise to me—I don't have to act." She picked at the armrest on the passenger door. "I'll tell them you were with me, that we were on a date. That should cover both of us."

Sam watched the streets become familiar again as Brian brought her back to her house. She wondered if the police would come, if they had found any connection to Steve. She wondered what her parents would say. She could not believe he was gone, that he did not say goodbye. That he was a fugitive. Of course, he had wanted to talk to her. For weeks. But she had no way of knowing what he was thinking. For years, it was as if she never had.

"I'll call you if I find out anything," she said to Brian, opening the door. She did not know what else to say, or do, so she slammed the passenger door without hugging or kissing him and ran up the stairs to the door. Whatever funeral she had been holding for her and Brian's short, unrealized relationship was over. All she could think about was Steve, Steve sitting in Brian's Trans Am, knowing he was going to rob a liquor store, perhaps get caught or killed. Just to escape. Escape their father. Escape her. Escape himself. If he was running away from everything he hated and toward everything he wanted to be, she understood that. She knew she would follow him, sooner rather than later, in her own way. But right now she could not forgive him. Even if she was relieved.

"Was that Brian?" her mother asked from the kitchen, where she was making a Bundt cake for someone's birthday the next day at Pemco, the enamel factory on Eastern Avenue where she worked as a secretary. "I think Steve is upstairs."

"He is?" Sam felt her body light up with thousands of pricks. She took the stairs two at a time and barreled through Steve's door, not caring if he yelled at her, was half-naked, was dead asleep. But he was none of those things. His bed with the Baltimore Colts comforter was made, an ominous sign, for it had not been made for years, perhaps since Christmas morning 1979, when he was hopeful of getting a Bert Jones replica helmet and jersey to go with his real leather football and made one final concession to Santa Claus just to be sure. The corner where his guitar and amp had been set up was empty. She opened his closet, noting the empty hangers, places on the floor where sneakers and boots had once rested. Then she ran back downstairs to the kitchen, where her mother was slipping a round tin of batter into the oven.

"Careful, Sam," her mother warned, eyes on the sheet rack. "I told you I was baking a cake."

"Mom, Steve's gone."

"He's probably out with that girl, what's her name—Nicole?"

"Mom, he's really gone. His stuff is missing."

"What?" She stood up, leaving the kitchen, the oven door ajar. Sam stayed behind to close it. "Karl, where's Steve?"

"How the hell should I know?" her father grumbled from the living room. "Am I his keeper?"

Sam sat at the kitchen table, listening to her parents' footsteps move back and forth upstairs, first slowly, then frantically.

"We gotta call the police." Sam's mother re-emerged in the kitchen, reaching for the wall phone.

"Nobody's calling the police." Sam's father emerged and placed his hand over her mother's. "They ain't going to look for no runaway. More than likely, the police will be bringing him home to us once he gets in trouble."

"Karl, he's our son. We have to do something."

"Why? He didn't want to be here, then why are we gonna waste our time looking for him?" Sam's father pulled the phone off its wall mount and disconnected it. "Nobody's calling nobody about anything, you hear me? Whoever tries to pry this phone from my hands gets her arm broken."

With that, Sam's father returned to the living room, phone tucked under his arm.

"Steve didn't say nothing to you, honey, did he?" Sam's mother sat by her at the table, took her hand. "You can tell me, honey. I'm your mother. You can tell me anything."

"Mom, I'm scared," she said, although she did not know why. She felt panicked and ominous. Her hands shook and her head spun. She felt her head touch the table, its coolness, the smell of Pine Sol.

"Sam, look at you, you're so thin." She felt her mother's hand in her hair, her voice close to her ear. "I'm going to take you to a doctor. A therapist. We got a program through Pemco."

"I'm fine, Mom," Sam shook her head. "Don't spend all our vacation money on a therapist."

"You want to talk to me, is that what you want to do?" She smelled the acrid coffee on her mother's breath, the grit of dough and sugar on her fingers. "You want to talk to your mother?"

Sam's mother was the go-to for everyone at Pemco. Sam knew because her mother would often discuss at dinner the problems of those who sat by her desk on their lunch breaks, smoke breaks, and even while they were supposed to be working in the factory, making enamel. Sam understood why people gravitated toward her mother; she had the hard-etched features of a B-movie actress—all eyebrows and smoky eyes, long legs and broad shoulders. Her hair was dark and bobbed into a matronly halo of waves. But her thin lips and square chin kept her from the starring roles, along with her height. She could swallow up with one arm the girls in the steno pool, even the squat, broad Polish girls who came in at four o'clock for the evening shift out in the warehouse. But while Sam's mother told little Betty Sue to leave that no-good son-of-a-bitch boyfriend and move back home with her parents, Sam's mother stayed with that no-good-son-of-a-bitch husband.

"I'm okay," Sam answered, standing up.

"I'll cook you lasagna tomorrow." Her mother stood up with her. "Your favorite. Okay? And I'll get some of that butter brickle ice cream from High's. Maybe it'll smell so good in here Steve won't be able to resist."

Sam tried not to hear her mother crying in Steve's room later that night. From the other wall, she could hear her father snoring. She stretched out far across her bed, feeling the muscles of her back relax against the mattress. She did not know how she could feel so sad and so relieved at the same time. That night, she dreamed that Steve had run away because he was pregnant. His belly was translucent and she could see the little girl baby resting on her side looking at her. It had her eyes.

*

Six months later, the card came. It had a New Jersey postmark. Sam recognized the writing as Steve's. She left it on the mail table for her mother, who tore it open when she got home from Pemco like it was a Publisher's Clearinghouse winner.

"He's in New Jersey, playing with a Bruce Springsteen cover band," Sam's mother read excitedly to Sam and her father at dinner. She adjusted her reading glasses with one hand while holding the card away from her face. "He's doing good and might come down for Christmas."

It was two years later, when Sam was a freshman in college that he did come down. It was a rainy Christmas Eve and Sam was spending it home with her parents watching *A Charlie Brown Christmas*, eating cookies she and her mother had baked earlier. In the four months she had been at The University of Richmond, her parents had seemingly aged forty years. Her mother's solid, tall frame looked doughy, her skin wrinkled, the sprouts of gray showing at the base of her hairline. Her father, who had quit drinking to begin lithium therapy, was an inflatable man who had developed a slow leak. His body swayed and was controlled, almost magnetically, by gravity. His head, his jowls, his shoulders, his hand moved toward the earth. Sam wondered whether she would come home after spring semester and find him entirely on the floor like melted wax.

"Who would be coming this time of night?" Sam's mother tightened the belt on her terrycloth robe and opened the front door. And there he was.

"Ho, ho, ho," he said. Stubble covered his face from one ear to the other, more the 'I'm a man now' variety than a serious attempt to grow a beard. But he still looked the same. He hugged their mother. "Look who hitched a ride on Santa's sleigh."

"We thought you were dead," their father answered, not getting up from the couch.

"And a Merry Christmas to you, too." Steve put down the trash bag he was carrying. From the look of it, it contained his dirty laundry from the last two years. "Sam, come here, you little runt. You grew up."

Sam felt the cookies in her stomach fall from a great height. She tested the weight of her body on her feet by standing up and slowly walking over to him. His body was harder, definitely a man's now, and almost strange. Impenetrable.

"I can only stay a few days." He dragged the bag across the living room and left it by the door to the basement. "Thunder Road has a big New Year's Eve gig."

"You still with that band?" Sam's mother was facing the open refrigerator, looking for something to feed Steve. "You paying your bills? Sit down and tell me everything."

"Not tonight, Ma. I'm tired. Just a beer and a sandwich and we can talk tomorrow." He stood behind their mother, looking into the refrigerator as well. "I even got gifts."

"Why? Your gift is that you came home," her mother said, carrying an assortment of wax-wrapped lunchmeats to the counter. "You want ham or turkey?"

"I want it all," he laughed. Sam went upstairs. Her mother had dusted Steve's room and laundered his sheets without fail, and now it looked as though she had been vindicated of the remarks from Sam's father that Steve was probably a hobo somewhere. Sam had not asked her father to fix the lock on her bedroom door, figuring he would never do it anyway, and now she wondered if she needed it.

"You look nice." Steve stood outside her bedroom door.

"Jesus, you scared me," she said. He took a few steps in the room and looked around.

"How you like school? Mom tells me you're down South."

"Richmond." She shrugged. "I like it."

"It's good to get away," he agreed, picking at some paint in the doorjamb. "Best thing I ever did."

"You're right," she said, and he smiled slightly. Maybe he thought that her agreement was forgiveness, solidarity. Maybe he didn't think there was anything to forgive. She wondered whether she was in shock, her brother coming back from the grave, almost. She had told everyone at Richmond she was an only child. She hadn't seen the point in telling them his part in her story.

"You seen Brian?"

"No," she answered. "He moved to Wyoming after you ran away."

"Bastard." Steve smiled. "Good for him. Well, I better get to sleep. I ain't slept in three days."

He pulled a prescription bottle out of his pocket and shook it. Then he tapped two pills in his palm and spun slowly out of her room, closing the door softly.

She was shaking. She sat on the bed and listened to her parents bicker downstairs about whether the grocery store would be open tomorrow. According to Sam's father, it had never been open and never would be. According to her mother, it had started opening for holiday hours and she needed an extra can of rolls now that Steve was home. Sam wanted to scream down that she would drive over to the Giant tomorrow and find out herself, but she lacked the energy. Or caring. Whatever small interest she had in being home in the first place was sucked away by Steve.

She tried the knob on his door and it opened. He lay snoring in the dark in his boxers, his legs prostrate, arms over his face. She had seen, handled, a man's penis since Steve's, but his would always be the first. Sometimes she thought about it at weird times, while she was eating breakfast in the commons before her early class, at night while she jogged on the track, sometimes at parties, while she drank thin, stale beer and listened to some guy with long curly hair talk about how King Crimson was the best band ever. Sometimes she would be angry about it, and sometimes she would be sad about it. But mostly she felt very different from the other freshman, who seemed unburdened in their hearts, their minds, beyond the next kegger or biology quiz.

She stood before Steve, but he did not move. She wondered whether she could touch it or maybe she could punch it or both. She put her palm out, fingers spread, let it hover a few inches above the cotton of his shorts. She moved down slowly until they were barely separated, when his breath, in and out, could push the littlest bit of cotton boxer up to tickle her palm. She suddenly felt sick and ashamed and wanted to be back at school, huddled on her thin, springy mattress in the room with the cinderblock-painted walls and her roommate from British Columbia who lectured her on the proper way to hang her wet shower towel.

It got hard before her, pressing the back of her hand with a steady force, and she gasped. But then she remembered that it happened all the time while men were sleeping and that he couldn't possibly be awake, snoring before her. She crept out of his room and closed the door, ninety-nine percent sure he was asleep.

"He asleep?" Her mother stood at the top of the stairs, holding a basket of clothes.

"Yeah, he's totally out," Sam stuttered. "You need me to go to the store for anything?"

V.

When they get there, Pete feels like there is a lasso on his belly and it's tugging, tugging him to the place. It's a pile of dirt now, wide and brown like a giant's grave.

"It used to be a drive-in," Pete explains to Kim, who runs to the middle of the dirt-grave theater and spins around. He jogs toward her, almost at a shuffle, holding his belly and feeling every footfall in his back. When he reaches her he looks down, believing himself in a rut, or hole, but he is not. Somehow, Kim, in her sneakers, is taller than him. Or maybe he is shorter. He walks away from her and then walks back, but his eyes only reach her cheeks. He is sure that this morning her eyes reached his cheeks. "Are you growing?"

She lies on her back in the dirt, spreading her arms and legs like she's making a dirt angel. He lies down gingerly beside her, wondering if he'll ever get up again. His knees throb and his back arches and he needs a couple of drinks, a couple of clean whiskeys, to mud the sting of his body, the cry of his mind. He closes his eyes and remembers the movie, something stupid like Friday the 13th Part IV. *Something he would have thought was cooler if he were a year younger, back when he actually watched the movies at the drive-in. But he was fifteen and all the kids cruised the dark rows of cars, looking for their friends, goofing off and playing video games in the snack shop before sneaking behind the screen and drinking, making out, the lucky ones fucking.*

They had gotten a ride with Pete's older sister and when she and her boyfriend kicked them out of the car they walked around, the dark forms and angles materializing into kids they knew or didn't know before they were swallowed up again.

Is that Brian over there? *Sissy asked, turning her head toward the snack bar.*

Brian's a dick, *he said and cupped the back of her neck in his hand. It was cool to touch, her hair barely grazing his thumb. She turned suddenly into his face and he kissed her. They stood there for a second, a minute, an hour, but really a second and Brian took her hand.* Come on. Let's find a place.

He led them to the back of the screen. Something scary was happening in the movie because they could hear the scary music tee-tee-tee ha-ha-ha and he wondered if Sissy was scared. He wondered whether she was scared about the movie or scared about going back to where kids did stuff and he hoped so because he was a little scared, too. He would be scared with any girl but he was less scared with Sissy because he liked her like a sister and not like Kelly. In fact, he wasn't even hard yet but maybe it was because he was scared.

He found a spot in the straw grass tall and glittering with beer cans like moon rocks on some distant planet. He kicked them away and dropped his jacket and pulled her down to him. When he looked at her, her chin fell into her neck like her neck was broken and he saw her eyes bobbing, bobbing away toward the light like a moth, back to the scary screen and Brian and he felt his gut tighten like a sit-up, his nostrils flare.

I think you're a nice guy, Pete, but…

He doesn't even like you, *he interrupted.* None of the guys do. They think you look like a boy.

She swallowed air quickly, air full of truth and small particles of his spit and germs and just air. He pulled on her arms when she tried to spring up, away.

I like you, *he said to her tearface, runny eyes long and wetslit.* I like you.

He kissed her drylips sour popcornbutterbreath and pushed his popcornbuttertongue into her mouth and she let him, and he felt bad for making her cry but she needed to know who was on her side, who was protecting her in the world and who wasn't. He didn't want her to find out the hard way.

No, *she said between breaths.* I want to be friends. You're my friend.

I'm the only one who protects you. *He kissed her again, grasped her body under his in different places like he was fluffing a pillow. He tried to pretend her body was his dick. He stroked it slowly, gently, as she writhed and twisted, shooing in her ear like she was a baby. She got baby louder, the* nos *wafting up in the air with her particles and his particles and he hoped the particles together wouldn't travel very far to where someone could hear them.*

He put one hand over her mouth, his knees on her knees. He had wrestled with his sister all his life until she became a woman and he was becoming a man, and he knew all the moves, how to pin and spread his weight so their mother wouldn't notice bruises. He glued over her, his knees, his elbows, his mouth, and she began to weaken, her muscles softening, her breath heavy, sleepy baby. He felt it get hard and he grabbed for her jeans. He wasn't think-ing that it would be his first and her first and he wasn't thinking very much about anything, just hearing the tee-tee-tee ha-ha-ha behind him and her breathing wee-wee-wee wah-wah-wah and he felt the breeze blow through the hair above his ears, tepid, tickly, and it made him come.

*You tell anybody about this and I will kill you, he whispered into her.
He whispered it into her small boy body the way he whispered his boy seed
into her body. When they got back to the car the doors were locked and they
had to wait in front. They sat in the grass by the headlights and he put his
jacket over her shoulders but she was not there with him, she was somewhere
else. He took her hand but it was limp in his. He leaned back against the
bumper of his sister's car and the stars spread out over his eyes.*

Where the clouds were now. Kim shakes his arm.

*"And then what happened?" she asks. He feels the ice water of her words
in his stomach, ice worms wiggling through his worm intestines.*

"Was I thinking aloud?"

*"Don't talk anymore." She puts her hand over his mouth and he can feel
the pulling, the pulling from his mouth like the pulling on his belly. She is
the force, the force that puts all events in motion. He just remembers, it's
easier than talking anyway, he remembers feeling stale in his pants on the
way home, wormy in his heart. He held her hand that did not hold his and
when they dropped her off at her house he kissed her lips that didn't kiss his
and when they were at school he looked at her eyes that didn't look at his. And
there was nothing he could do.*

*He skated some killer open skates at Skat-land, doing a spin and a hair-
pin stop. He jumped over little fat fuck Bengie, piggybacked right over him
and landed on his skates, trailing away from the fat fuck bent over like a
fag. And Kelly looked in his eyes that looked at hers and held his hand that
held hers and kissed his lips that kissed hers and Pete was happy, except when
he wasn't, which was whenever he saw Sissy. She would not talk to him, let
him close to her, and there was nothing he could do. He felt bad he could not
protect her when the boys teased her and kissed her boy lips on the back of
the bus. And he felt bad he could not protect her when the boys touched her
boy tits in the hallways. And he felt bad he could not say it was a lie when
the guys said she was easy. And he felt bad he could not protect her when they
had their way with her behind the bleachers of the football field. And he felt
bad when she stopped going to school. And he felt bad when Cole told him he
heard that Sissy was pregnant.*

*And he wondered whether it was his. He felt the tug, the invisible hand
on his heart and it pulled him to Sissy's house. Her mother answered the door.*

*She don't want to see nobody. Her mother frowned at him, her arms
crossed, and he felt bad that she could not sense that he wanted to protect her,
had always wanted to protect her.*

Tell her it's Pete, he pleaded, feeling his fists ball up, sweaty.

She don't want to see nobody.

A few weeks later, he got to school and her name buzzed through the air, the student body her worker bees, she their queen. Sissy, did you hear, Sissy, Sissy, oh my god, did you hear…

What? *he asked Kelly in homeroom. She was wearing his favorite black top with the low back. She wore her long blond hair up to show the rich honey-brown bread of her Sunsations Tanning back, and Pete always thought her skin must taste like caramel there.*

She committed suicide, she said, a big bubble tear in each eye. But she wasn't crying for Sissy, Pete knew. She was crying for herself and how horrible such a thing made her feel. No one cared about Sissy except for him. No one protected her except for him. And he had failed.

He walked out of homeroom and he walked down the hall and out of the school and when he got home he packed a bag and stole the money out of his brother's underwear drawer and then he got on the bus. It was going to New Jersey, and that's where he went. And he never was happy anymore.

8.

Everyone has retreated, like soldiers under fire—her father under the hood of Sam's car, looking for the source of her overheating engine; her mother on the glider on the screened porch, patching a hole in the crotch of a pair of her father's shorts; Steve on the motorboat, cleaning it for tomorrow's fishing trip with their father; and Sam and Eve in the kitchen.

"I don't know if I can take much more excitement." Eve watches Sam take the leftover hamburgers out of the refrigerator. "I have a weak heart myself."

"I don't mean to be rude, but I think I need to be alone," Sam says, dropping the waxy mound of burgers onto a plate.

"Oh, sure." Eve pulls the spatula out of the dish drainer. "Here, you need this."

Sam reaches for napkins, but she is not quick enough to dab the large globes of tears that stretch down her face into thin rivulets.

"Oh, Sam—I'm sorry." Eve rips some paper towels off the roll and hands them to her. "Is it Michael?"

"I didn't think it'd hurt this much." She shakes her head and turns from the counter, afraid of getting tears in the meat. "I didn't think I'd care, that it'd matter."

"You still love him," Eve sighs, touches her shoulder softly.

"I never stopped loving him," she explains, blowing her nose. "I was afraid he'd stop loving me."

"Why would he stop loving you? You're wonderful."

"You don't know what I am," Sam answers, shrugging her away. She takes the plate out to the grill. Eve follows her with plates, buns, condiments.

"Why don't you let me cook?" Eve stands by the grill. "Maybe you should lie down."

"No, I'm fine." Sam shakes her head. "Keeping busy is good."

"Sam, I'm sorry." Eve touches her shoulder. "Really. I'm so sorry."

Sam goes back up to the porch, where her mom is holding up her father's repaired shorts to the light.

"Can you see any hole left?" She turns them to Sam. The madras shorts are so old that the thighs are pilled and chaffed, the fabric in danger of disintegrating. Sam remembers these shorts covering her father's bum as far back as 1986, the same year she thumbtacked the Bananarama poster to the wall. He may as well be buried in them.

"They look good, Mom."

"Good. Your father would never let me hear the end of it if I tried to get rid of these." Sam's mother lets them drop on the table in front of her as she puts the needle back in her needle case. "Sit down here, honey."

Sam sits on the glider, crawling into her mother's embrace. She feels the tears running down her neck but doesn't bother to wipe them.

"Things aren't good, huh?" Her mother strokes her hair. "Honey, I'm sorry."

Sam remembers when she came home from Europe, lying in her mother's lap, unemployed, watching *Melrose Place* on television.

I can't believe she's going back to him, her mother would complain about one of the characters, resting her cigarette on the ashtray. Her father sat in the kitchen, doing word-find puzzles from a book Sam's mother bought at the drugstore. His doctor had recommended it as a way to stay focused when the wave of medications began to pull at his brain like silly putty. He treats her like a dog. If you brought home a cad like that, Sam, boy, I'll tell you…

"Don't worry, honey." Sam's mother continues stroking her hair. "If he really loves you, he'll come back. I know it sounds corny, but it's true. And I know he really loves you, honey. He told me all the time—'Mom, I really love Sam'. He said it all the time. Now, maybe it wasn't right for me to talk to him behind your back after you two broke up, but I know you love him. And he loves you. Look at me and your father. He drives me nuts, but I love him like nothing else. I never could leave him, even though I thought about it all the time. I thought about it all the time, never did nothing. We coulda lived with Pat and Ray if we needed to. They woulda had us. But why shame you kids like that? Your father had some rough patches, but he came through okay. He's okay now. And the past is done. You wait, we're going to have to save up for your wedding again soon; just wait and see."

"Don't save your money, Mom." Sam takes her mom's hand. "Not for me, anyway. If I ever get married, I'll pay for it myself."

"Maybe you'll make a lot of money from your next book and pay for all of us." Sam's mother laughs. "You got another book in you, right?"

She laughs, too, but she is not sure she does. If this story never ended, never concluded, how could she write another one?

"You need to get the water pump checked when you get home," her father says as he comes through the screen door, letting it bang behind him. His undershirt is smudged with grease and hanging out of his pants. "It only gets hot when you're driving, right?"

"Yeah." Sam sits up, wipes her eyes. "Thanks. I'll have them take a look at it."

"What, you all weepy on me?" He stands and rubs his hands together, looking at them like they're rare deer. "This is one hell of a vacation. Everybody arguing and crying. Are we gonna have one dinner in peace?"

"Ask Steve," Sam answers, standing up and going back to the grill, where Eve is laboring. She feels bad for blaming him like that. There is plenty of blame to go around. She slits open the buns and sets the picnic table while Eve fondles the meat with the spatula.

"You like yours kinda rare, right?" Eve questions. "Because I think everyone is going to get well-done."

"That's okay." Sam stands by the grill. "I'd rather have well-done than worms."

"You're back fast." Eve begins transferring the burgers to the plate in Sam's outstretched hand.

"I'm sorry for snipping at you."

"Don't apologize. It's a lot of work vacationing with the Pinskis." Eve drops the last burger on the plate. "But I feel like I haven't done my fair share. You want to get in a fist fight later?"

Sam's mother and father come out of the porch for dinner. Their arms are hooked at the elbow, and they make their way to the picnic table like royalty. Sam doesn't doubt that her mother loved her father once or still loves him or still sees what she first loved about him. The camera in Sam's brain burns this image forever. She wishes she had brought her camera, just in case her synapses fail, years down the road. She has a feeling, though, that they won't.

Sam also notes, in this mental image, that her father is freshly showered, wearing his newly mended madras shorts. Steve comes up from the boat, pulling his t-shirt from the waist of his shorts and wiping his face and shoulders with it.

"Boy, am I hungry." He grabs a beer from the cooler. "Long day."

"Long day, no shitting." Sam's father holds out his hands. "There's going to be no fighting at this table tonight, understand? I decree it. Now let's say grace."

Sam takes her father's big, calloused hand in hers. Steve opens his mouth, presumably to say something smart, but thinks better of it. He slides in next to Eve, weaving his fingers into hers. Sam's mother takes Eve's other hand and reaches across for Sam's father's.

"Lord, please bless these hamburgers, and please bless this family. It sorely needs it. I'm thankful that both my son and my daughter are here with me and my wife, that they're healthy, and I'm glad Sam's friend Eve is here, too. Please let us get through this meal in peace and let the rest of our vacation be peaceful, too."

Pat Pinski's cell phone buzzes on the table.

"It's Carol," she says without even looking at it.

"And Lord, please send a bolt of lightning through Carol and Ray's phone line so they can't call no more." Sam's father raises his head. "Amen."

"I'll let it go to voicemail." Sam's mother says, holding the phone at eye level, eyeing the LED screen as if it's in code. "Jeez, my eyes are blurry. Must be from hemming your damn shorts again, Karl. Sam, will you show me how I get my voicemail later?"

Even though it's dark, Sam finds Steve at the dock, after her parents have gone to bed, Eve to pack. By flashlight, he's relining his and their father's fishing lines for the fishing trip early the next morning.

"I thought Dad already did that." Sam stands over him, listening to the creek water lap against the dock, the sting of cicadas and crickets boring into her ears.

"He did, but he did a shitty job," Steve answers. "I don't think he'll notice I went over them. He'll probably just see these and brag about what a good job he did."

"Do you think you'll catch anything?"

"I hope so." He hops up, holding the thin parts of the pole delicately between his thumb and forefinger. "If we get up early enough. In fact, I'll probably get to bed soon. Did Eve go to bed?"

"She's packing."

"She seems like a good kid," Steve says, bending and closing the tool bar their father keeps in the crawlspace under the house. "Where'd you meet her?"

"Around. Did you get the book I sent you?" she asks, following him to the picnic table. She watches him light a cigarette, run his hand through his hair. Even in the dark his cheeks look red, his eyes ringed white, like an albino raccoon, from his sunglasses.

"Yeah, I got it," he answers, running his hand through his hair. "I've been meaning to congratulate you on it. I always knew you'd turn out to be something."

"Did you read it?"

"I started to, but I haven't had a chance to finish. I'm going to, though, don't worry."

"But it's all earmarked," she protests. "I saw it by the bed."

"Laura, the girl I was seeing, she was reading it," he explains, tipping his legs up on the picnic table. "She marked some stuff for me."

"You really haven't read it?"

"I'm sorry, Sam. I'm not much of a reader. I will, though. I promise you."

"And who is Laura, anyway? What about Eve?"

"I don't know." He grins. It's the kind of grin that reels girls in, Sam thinks. Its easiness is soothing but, as one finds out over time, also empty. "She left."

"Don't you care? About anything?"

"Sure, Sam." He crushes his cigarette in the ashtray, its end now an upturned nose. "I care about you and Mom."

"Do you even know what the book is about?"

Steve breaths and sighs, a lump of air puffing out his cheeks, his eyes bulging, before escaping his mouth. "Are you going to tell me?"

"It's about you, Steve. It's about us."

"I thought it was about a pregnant man." He lights another cigarette, holding onto the match, letting it burn down to his fingers. "It seemed kinda weird. At least different from the stuff you wrote when we was kids."

"It is, on the surface. But underneath, it's about me and you. All the bad stuff."

"You mean Dad?"

"No." Sam weaves her fingers into her other hand. "You know what."

"That's in there?" He looks toward the house as if to retrieve the book from his bag. "Are you fucking kidding me? Mom is reading your fucking book, Sam. What the fuck?"

"It's not written like that, Steve." She shrugs. "Mom won't see any of it."

"But I will?"

"I don't know." Sam stands up. "I don't even know why the hell I wrote it."

"I don't know why, either." He follows her. "All that stuff, Sam—we were kids. It don't mean anything now."

"It means something to me!" She wriggles out of her own grasp. "It still does."

"Well, that's not my fault." He kicks at a dilapidated soccer ball. It flies off the hill and plops into the black water of the creek. It makes Sam want to cry. It is now lost, along with Michael, so many other things. "It's not my fault. We were kids, Sam. It don't mean anything now."

"Is that why you've done so well with your life?"

"You've done good with yours, Sam." He lights a match and tosses it into the water. "It don't seem to have affected you none."

"I've been scared of you for years, Steve. I don't trust you. I don't even know if I ever can."

"Sam." Steve holds out his arms. "I'm your brother. I just want the best for you. I may have done a lot of stupid things in my life, but dammit, we was just kids. All kids do stupid stuff. You can't hold me to that. You did it, too, you know—don't act like you didn't like it. You never said no. But it don't mean anything now. Okay? Just let it go and forget it ever happened."

"Don't you think if I could let it go, I would have?"

"You're not trying hard enough." He shakes his head. "Don't you remember any of the good stuff? The lost city of Conowingo? The Boy Scout hikes? The loft? Why didn't you write about that stuff?"

"Of course I remember all those things."

"That's what I think about. When I get angry about Dad, that's what I think about. You know, I wasn't even going to come here, because I hate the old bastard. But I thought about all the good stuff, so I did. And now you, bringing up all the bad stuff."

"Steve..."

"That man in your book is a rapist." He turns to her, his eyes wide, nostrils flaring. She is afraid for a minute he will grab her, shake her. "I didn't rape you, Sam. We didn't do anything. I didn't rape you."

"What about the end?" she says, feeling tears in her eyes. "When you left?"

"I don't remember the end." His face is dark, half-turned from her. "Do you?"

"I remember everything."

"I wish I could, but then maybe I wish I didn't. I remember how jacked up I felt when I robbed that liquor store, how my heart was going to explode in my chest in Brian's car. And how I just wanted to go home. But I didn't have a home anymore. I went to Jersey. You had me, Sam…"

"Small consolation, that." She puts her arms around herself.

"At least you had me. I didn't have anybody." He picks up their father's fishing kit, dusting off the top. "I don't remember anything, and Mom remembers everything wrong. She thinks everybody was happy. No one got hit or yelled at or their shit thrown around or their bones broken."

"How do you want her to remember it?" She thinks about her mother calling Michael, planning Sam's happily ever after, the one she would never have. "You want her to think about every shitty thing all the time?"

"I guess not." He looks at her. "But you do. And you hate me."

"You don't understand, Steve. You took everything away from me."

"You're not the only innocent one. You're a Pinski, same as all of us." He turns toward the house. "I got to get to bed. I can't believe you brought this shit up tonight, Sam. Didn't you hear what Dad said at dinner?"

She watches him go inside the cabin. She runs across the dock and takes a leap into the water, letting the cold shock her, then numb her. She could stay out here all night, in the inky water, until she gives up. Until she can't fight anymore. She is already so close. She submerges, opening her mouth and letting sound come out, sounds of words trapped in bubbles that float to the surface but make no noise. She thrashes her limbs, tries to swim her way to the bottom. She lacks the strength and bobs up each time. She wonders whether Steve will come out and rescue her, one last time, be her superhero. But she is under the water and no one is coming to save her. When she reemerges, breaking the surface, the lights in the cabin have gone dark. She is alone.

vi.

They leave the drive-in and go to the beach. It's a half-hour, maybe. Pete has intoxicated Kim with the promise of pizza on the boardwalk. They order a large pizza and poppers and milkshakes. He cannot finish his half, despite his strange, persistent hunger, but she eats her share and then the remainder, her hands moving steadily from plate to mouth, breathing, chewing, drinking, chewing.

What? She smiles at him after he thinks, the muscles in her neck anacondas against her throat as she swallows.

I said, used to eat like that once, he thinks again, stirring up the hill of sugar at the bottom of his iced tea. When I was like, fourteen.

She wipes the grease off the side of her mouth with the back of her hand, still smiling. She frowns and reaches for a napkin.

Where are my manners? he can now hear her thinking. I think I am turning into a fourteen-year-old boy.

When they go outside the sun has extinguished itself into the ocean but the warmth and its memory spread still in the air, alternating hot and cold gusts of breeze while the surf licks up the remains of the day, what bathers had left, wrappers and flip-flops and plastic shovels and toys, libations to the great god Ocean. She walks first and Pete walks after her, trying to fit his steps into hers, unsettled that they are the same size now. Her hamstrings and calves are golden and roped, and he pushes his legs, soft-muscled and curved and almost devoid of hair, into the moats left by her feet. He has lost a great deal of hair today, lying on the ground at the drive-in, the growth of it weighing evenly across his stomach, a hot water bag. When he got up to relieve himself, a hairy outline of his legs remained behind. Inside the bathroom at the pizza place, he sat on the toilet and thought his penis noticeably smaller.

It's probably just your stomach, she had assured him when he returned.

Even now, on the dark beach, he can barely see his feet, and he can barely see her ahead. The distance has grown between them, although she has not meant for it to. He can finally see her waiting a few feet ahead, the bottom of her cape curling upwards, dancing. He plops down in the sand. He feels as if he has walked for miles, and perhaps they have—the lights of the hotels on the beach are fireflies in the distance, frozen in space.

Here. She holds out her hands, which are full of the items she has found in the surf. Plastic shovels of various sizes, a plastic white-and-blue boat, a broken sandcastle mold, a foam ball with surfboards printed on it. She lays the treasures carefully next to him as he digs absently in the sand. She sits down beside him and begins to pile sand, wet and dark, into a mountain.

Are you going to bury me?

I was making a sandcastle. Why waste all these great tools I found?

That's not how you make a sandcastle. Have you ever been to the beach?

Well, you show me, beach bunny. She takes her cape off and lays the tools on it like a buffet. Here you go, your highness.

You're going to help. You're not going to just sit there, supergirl.

They dig canals in the darkness, their hands patting down the mounds of sand, the granules making their fingers into cinnamon-sugar donut sticks, their fingers lining wavy and long the imprints in the walls of the castle, its torrents, like zebra-sand skin. They poke their fingers inside the sand walls and rotate them, gouging out windows, smoothing the cracks. She goes to the surf periodically to get water to pack together their delicate fortress, and her trips to the surf became shorter as the tide comes nearer to high and suddenly the eastern wall is washed away in one fluid movement, collapsing some of the northern wall as well.

We shouldn't have built it so close. We should have started farther back.

It is what it is. She sits beside him, taking his hand in hers. Its grit rubs his grit. It feels larger than his.

I think I love you. He pulls his hand away.

I love you, too.

But I think I'm becoming a woman. Tears form in his eyes. It would have been easier to kill it at the very beginning. Without listening to her, without falling in love with her. Now it would be easier to kill himself.

I know. She squeezes the grit into the soft of his palm. And I think I love you even more.

He spreads his legs suddenly, as wide as he can, and begins to dig. He knows he is going to have it. Everything else will have to wait because he is going to have it. She sees what he is doing and digs with him, and the sand-castle becomes a mound, a hole behind it. It is so dark. He can hear the waves closer, a conversation, feel the surf lick his toes. When the hole is big enough he straddles the edge with his legs and pushes. He pushes and everything he knows about being Pete Skivins is pushed out and everything he knows about being a man is pushed out and everything he thinks he knows about being a woman is pushed out.

And when all that is pushed out the baby comes. The baby comes headfirst. The baby comes slowly. The baby comes full of blood and mucous. The baby comes blue, then pink. The baby comes quiet, then loud. The baby comes out of him and becomes a baby. The baby comes attached, and Kim cuts it with her teeth. The baby comes with pain but now he is tired. The baby comes with fear but now he is happy.

The baby comes and now he is scared. The baby comes and he kisses the baby. He kisses the little veins that course underneath the onionskin babyhead, crinkled waxy babyhead. He loves the baby. He will let nothing come become him and his baby. The baby moves and is crying.

It's hungry. He holds his crying baby up. What are we going to do?

You've done your part. She takes his baby from him.

He thinks she's going to feed it with her breasts, but she stands with the baby and walks into the water. He thinks maybe she is going to wash it, but she keeps walking. She walks to her ankles and walks to her calves and walks to her thighs and walks to her waist before he realizes she is not coming back.

Wait! He moves slowly because his blood is in the hole in the sand and not in his body. His opening hurts and his legs hurt and his stomach feels loose. In the water he walks to his ankles and walks to his calves but he cannot reach her. She walks with the baby up to her chest and walks to her shoulders and walks to her neck and then they are gone.

It wasn't supposed to happen like this, he thinks. He thought something else would happen and that he would be happy. But the baby came and left. She came and left. And he is still here living. She took most of him away, what little there was, their breathing, their baby, and he is still here. Pained. Still living.

He makes it back to shore. His dick is small but it's only because of the cold water. His breasts and stomach are gone, too. His hair has grown back. He is happy for all these things and then he is sad because he would give them up if Kim and the baby came back. He waits for them, one minute, ten minutes, fifty minutes, two hours. They do not return. The moon is on the water. It looks real to him from far away, where the waves are calm, but when they waver, when the sea is agitated and stirs beneath them, he can see that it's not. It's a water moon. It is just a water moon and he is alone.

MONDAY

9.

Sam wakes up because she knows she has to. Michael is gone and now Eve will be gone and she will remain with Steve and her parents. She doesn't know what she expected from Steve. An apology, maybe. A promise for the future, for better behavior, for life-changing epiphanies, for right livelihood and happily ever after. All because she wrote a stupid book about a pregnant man. She herself experienced none of those things when she finished the last draft of the novel, when she sent it to her agent, when she opened the first box of books from her publisher. Maybe, for once, Steve was right.

Sam knocks on the door to the loft. She suspects Steve is gone but figures Eve is still asleep. When she gets no answer she opens the door. The beds are made, and Eve's things are gone. Steve's duffel sits neatly on an old trunk across from the beds, pressed against the wall. Everything looks undisturbed, and a lump forms in Sam's throat, the stillness, the loneliness. She wonders which is lonelier—being alone or being alone with everybody. She walks over to Steve's duffel, feels around inside for the book. She does not feel its squareness, only the softness of fabrics. Then she spots it, on the floor by Steve's bed. A flashlight rests on top of it.

She knocks on her parents' door, although she figures they are up. When no one answers, Sam slips in. In the dark air-conditioned coldness she sees the empty spot on her father's side, the lump of her mother by the wall. She moves quietly through and onto the living room. She can see Eve smoking on the screened porch.

"I made some coffee," Eve says when Sam pokes her head through the door. Sam nods and makes her way to the kitchen. There are some leftover pancakes in the fridge from yesterday, back when Sam and Michael made breakfast. She wants to cry suddenly at the thought of him making pancakes with someone else. Not that she supposes she has any right. She takes a rubbery, cold medallion and puts it on a paper plate along with some melon wedges.

"You eat?" she asks Eve, sitting across from her.

"I'm caffeine-powered." Eve flicks her ashes into an empty ashtray, a layer of gray ash permanently baked into the bottom. "Seriously, I think I ate enough hamburgers and chicken and crabs and potato salad this weekend to survive the winter."

Sam thinks about Eve living in the woods, being homeless. She wonders if she could do the same, if it came down to it. Eve inhales on her cigarette, her eyes resting on Sam's. The weight of Eve's gaze feels like an old hurt, a dullness that usually throbs between her breasts, sometimes her stomach.

"You okay?" Eve asks, the drawl of the last word velvety and rough, a word Sam can almost feel on her hand, the top of her forearm.

"Yeah—why wouldn't I be?"

"Well, Steve came in pretty upset last night. I thought maybe you did, too."

"I'm okay." Sam shakes her head, biting into the pancake. She figures she can spend the day alone, maybe on a hike or holed up in her room, cramming all the hurt of the past weekend back into her chest like an overstuffed suitcase. And then maybe she'll go back to Baltimore, hole up in the cold, dusty stillness of the library and do more research for another book. Something completely different. She can get her muffins somewhere else. She can let the messages from her mother, still up at the cabin, go to voicemail. And she can figure out what to do next, if there's anything she can do.

"I'm ready whenever you are." Eve crushes her cigarette and goes through the porch door out to the dock, catching a few minutes of sun and breeze and bird calls and maybe a glimpse of Steve, although it is too early for them to come home. Sam spies Eve's things in the corner and on the way back from the kitchen picks them up and puts them into the trunk of her Jetta. Eve sees Sam near the car and makes her way up the hill.

"Can you tell your parents I had a great time?" she asks, pulling her sunglasses out of her purse. "I don't want to wake your mom. And maybe you can give me their address so I can write a thank-you note."

"Don't bother," Sam answers. "They won't get it until they get home at the end of the summer."

"Well, then it'll be a nice surprise." Eve opens the passenger door and slides in. Sam follows and backs very carefully down the path until she can make a U-turn.

"Do you think you'll hang out with Steve again?" Sam asks once they are on the road heading in the right direction.

"I don't know." Eve runs her hand over the top of her cigarette pack. "He told me he's coming down to Baltimore next weekend to see me."

"He won't."

"Why do you say that?"

"He can't even make it down for family holidays. Once every five years, if then."

"I think there was a reason for that."

"What?

"They're a stressor for him."

"For him?" Sam looks at Eve quickly, throwing the car into second. "How about for the rest of us?"

"Okay, for all of you." Eve opens the passenger window a crack. "So it's probably better for everyone, then."

"Well, good luck with that," Sam mumbles. She turns on the radio and fights through a band of static before shutting it off.

"Thank you." Eve sticks a few fingers out the window, waggling them in the hot wind. "And thanks for inviting me to the cabin."

"If he likes you so much, why didn't he offer to drive you to Fallston today?"

"Well, first of all, there was the matter of his fishing with your father this morning—"

"He has all summer to fish with Dad."

"And second of all, he did ask me. Sam, why are you mad at me?" Eve pulls her fingers away from the window as Sam puts it up from the driver's side and turns on the AC. "Or is it Steve that you're mad at?"

"I'm not mad at you."

"Right. You know, I wish I hadn't even gotten involved."

"What do you mean?"

"With you—with any of this. I don't know if your book is true, but Jesus..."

"What are you talking about?"

"You know exactly what I'm talking about, Kim Snapthakis. Real cute, Nabokov."

"What?"

"The anagrams—Kim Snathanapis and Pete Skivins. Samantha Pinski and Steve Pinski. So are you going to tell me what happened, or do I already know what happened?"

"I'm sure you know what happened, Eve. You're not stupid. Are you saying I don't have a right to be upset about the past?"

"No—I'm not saying that." Eve puts her hand over Sam's on the clutch. "I'm just saying don't live there. You deserve more."

"You—you who wears her past like a badge of courage..."

"Yes, if you mean that I'm completely honest about who I am and what has happened to me. Look, Sam, you're a good person with a good career and people who love you and all you want to do is change the past."

"I can't change the past—I know that—I just want Steve to acknowledge it."

"And that will change everything?"

"I don't know. It wouldn't hurt."

"If this is what your therapist has been telling you, I'd get her license revoked."

"Who's self-righteous now?" Sam says. "What the hell are you suggesting I do, Ms. Eve Christmas, abuse survivor, ex-homeless catastrophe specialist?"

"All I'm saying, Sam, is that you never get over it. Like people with scars. With wheelchairs. You don't think I still wake up some days and wish I were dead? You just do what you need to do good enough. If that means never seeing Steve again, okay. If that means never seeing me, Michael, your parents, okay. You wrote your book, but apparently that wasn't good enough."

"Is that all?"

"I'm really sorry, Sam. That's all. I'm sorry. I'm so sorry." Eve kisses Sam's cheek, touches her face. Sam smells the traces of coffee, of cigarettes. She is surprised she is not averse to them. She wants to turn the car around and take Eve out on the boat, lie in the hammock and dive into the pile of books she has brought along for the summer, share a pile of potato chips. Fall asleep. Maybe more. She feels so many things burning in her heart, growing out of her arms, the hair on her neck. She wonders whether there will be a thunderstorm. The split-level with the green aluminum siding appears on the side of the road, Eve's friend's house. It hoists an American flag, a leftover from the holiday. A few cars are parked in the driveway.

"So, are we still friends?" Sam says after she parks by the side of the road. She listens to Eve's breathing, erratic, the click of the hazard lights, trying not to cry.

"Were we ever not?" Eve answers finally, undoing her belt buckle. Sam leans over and kisses the side of Eve's head.

"Sometimes, Eve, I swear I should just date you," Sam laughs and bends over to pop the trunk latch under the steering wheel.

"You shouldn't even joke about that." Eve jumps out of the car, rummaging in the trunk for her duffel bag.

"What are you saying?" Sam grabs the end of it, keeping it trapped in the trunk.

"Don't you have enough drama?" Eve says after a minute, adjusting her sunglasses. "You know, it would be good for me and for you and for Steve if we all went our separate ways. I know that. But I like you too much, Sam. I'm greedy and don't want to let you go. You're the closest thing to anything I have. You're too good for just a friend, and I wish you and I…"

"Wish what?" She touches Eve's forearm, as if she can draw the words out of her.

"Nothing." She shakes her head. "Let me know if you're back in town, and I'll have your order ready. Or not."

Eve yanks her duffel bag from Sam's grasp and hurries up the walk to the house. Sam waits for her to turn back, expects it. It is part of who Eve is, she thinks, her loyalty. But she doesn't. Unlike Sam, she seems to know when to cut her losses. Sam beeps her horn hurriedly before she roars away. On the way back to the cabin Sam still can feel the pressure of it, the strap of the duffel bag, in her hand. The pulse of things. She wonders if she should go back, do something, say something. She decides to continue back to the cabin instead.

When she pulls over the hill to the cabin she notices that Eve's cigarettes are still on the seat. She holds them in her hands like a baby boot, delicately, trying not to cry. She wonders if there is enough time to get them to her. Seeing Steve and her father drifting toward the dock in the boat, she decides against it.

"Sam!" Steve waves to her from the dock. He anchors the boat to the dock with his foot and reaches out to their father, who is struggling with the cooler. She makes her way to the dock and helps steady the boat while Steve takes the cooler from her father. In it is the biggest fish Sam has ever seen.

"Look what Stevie caught, Sam!" her father says with the gusto of a new parent. The fish is so big that its tail hangs over the side of the cooler, the lid still in her father's hand.

"What is it?" she asks. Steve puts the cooler on the dock and rests his hand over the twitching, wriggling silver fish with dark stripes.

"Rockfish." Steve grins at her, his teeth blinding white, his face deeply tanned from a morning on the water. "Striped bass."

"Have you ever seen such a fish?" Sam's father hangs his foot over the boat, feeling for the dock. Sam holds out her hand and helps him climb up. "We gotta get Roger to weigh it."

"You think it's fifty pounds?' Steve questions, picking the fish up out of the cooler, which still holds a few beers, ice, in the bottom. He holds it like a sack of potatoes across his chest. "Feels like fifty pounds, easy."

"You shoulda been there, Sam." Her father takes off his Orioles baseball cap, wipes the sweat off his forehead, and fits it back on top of his head. "When Steve got that bite, I thought he was gonna fly outta the boat. I thought he'd be water-skiing across the lake."

"I thought my arm was gonna come clean off," Steve agrees, letting the fish slide from his grasp back into the cooler. "Damn, we hauled it in—Dad was hanging onto my waist pulling. It was a sight, a fuckin' sight."

"We're gonna be in the papers for sure." Sam's father bends over and slips the rope of the rowboat around the peg, anchoring the boat. "Where's your mother? She's gotta see this. Pat!"

"She's still asleep," Sam answers as her father makes his way up the hill to the house.

"How about this, Sam?" Steve pats the side of the fish. "We're going to be eating like kings tonight. Mom's got her work cut out for her today, gutting and cleaning this one."

"Congratulations," Sam answers, pressing the tip of her flip-flop into the dock.

"I wish Eve didn't have to leave so soon," Steve says, lighting a cigarette. "She woulda got a kick out of this."

"Eve tells me you want to see her next weekend," she says, watching the smoke plume over Steve's head in the breeze, out to the creek. His bare chest is wet, slimy from the bass/rockfish.

"Yeah, I might." He looks at the filter of his cigarette, rolling it between his thumb and first finger. "You okay with that?"

"It's not for me to decide." She doesn't know whose choice it is. Only that she wants Eve to be happy. And Steve. And herself. At least one of them. "You were really great with her."

"Maybe, if you're around next weekend, I'd like to check out your new place." He looks at his feet. "You know, I can finish up your drywall Dad was telling me about."

"I might still be here, at the cabin." Sam shakes her head. It is quiet between them. She wonders if it will always be this awkward pain, this heartburn, between them, when their father emerges from the screened porch, waving his arms and shouting for them to come quickly.

10.

Roger from the marina will take the fish off their hands. He arrives about the same time the ambulance does. Steve sits on the dock, holding the dying fish in his arms like a dog that got hit by a car while their father sits on the bed, holding his dead wife in his arms after he has given up on CPR, rocking her softly like an old doll. Sam rummages through her mother's purse for her medications, her insurance card, whatever else she thinks they might need at the hospital. She half-expects her mother to wake up there, wanting a cigarette and an ice-cold Coke, asking Sam to make sure her father takes the two pills he needs to take every afternoon at four o'clock. The other half of Sam has fallen into the depths of despair and is waiting for the rest of Sam to catch up.

"You got everything?" Sam's father asks, after she decides to just take the whole purse. She thinks going through it might comfort her, although it may very well send her over the edge, too.

"I think so," she says, and she is smothered by her father's crying, sweaty, fish-smelling body as they stand in the corner of the bedroom, waiting for the stretcher with the former Patricia Pinski to be carried out. Sam is repulsed and yet clinging to him, afraid to let go lest she begins to cry again. They follow the stretcher outside, and Sam is relieved to see that Roger has taken the fish and that Steve can follow in the truck. He runs into the house and emerges in a fresh shirt, his work boots with no socks, his face scrunched and twisted like his hair.

"Keep it open," Sam's father instructs in the ambulance when one of the paramedics goes to zip the body bag over Pat's face. Sam's father puts his hand on his wife's cheek, caressing it lightly. Sam is amazed that his thick, calloused hands are capable of such gentleness. She rummages through her mother's purse, looking at the grocery list, twenty-five items long, for the cabin, a day planner with the birthdays of each Pinski child and relative written in red ink, along with her parents' wedding anniversary, a green bingo marker whose tip is dried. She looks at her mother's key ring and is sad that there are no pictures of grandchildren, covered in transparent plastic, attached to it, only discount card fobs for the grocery store, video store, CVS Pharmacy.

She only becomes in danger of losing it entirely when she tries to call Eve from the hospital. Outside Harford Hospital, while Steve has a cigarette, she lets the phone ring three times before hanging up, even though she knows Eve is on shift and it will go to voicemail anyway. She checks her missed calls and notes that Michael has called her three times since yesterday. She feels relieved, hopeful, but whatever she is feeling for him is as far away as she is from herself.

"You call Eve." She hands Steve the phone. "I can't."

"Did you call Michael?" He notes the sequence of calls she has left open.

"I will—not yet." She turns to go back inside. "Just let Eve know. Please?"

They squish in the front seat of Steve's truck on the way back to the cabin. The air conditioning is broken and the smell of fish, sweat, and cigarettes is overpowering. At least, that's what Sam blames on her need to stand on the side of the road and retch halfway back. At the cabin Sam packs her bags, knowing she will have to drive her father down to Baltimore to talk to the funeral director, that they will not be back at the cabin. Not for a very long time. At least not this summer.

"You need to close the place up, meet us at home," Sam tells Steve where he lies on the picnic table on the dock, hands folded across his chest, cigarette between them. "Can you do that?"

"Yeah," he answers, but doesn't look at her. Back in the house Sam's father sits perched on the edge of the bed, staring into space. She can smell her mother's perfume faintly, traces it to the bottle of Estee Lauder's Beautiful on the dresser, which she pockets.

"What are we gonna do, Sam?" her father asks, his face dark and broken. "I don't know what I'm gonna do without your mother."

"I know, Dad." Sam touches his shoulder. She genuinely feels sorry for him, despite his meanness, his violence, toward her mother ever since she could remember. Sam knows he loved her. It is undeniable. "We'll get through."

"You tell me how," he cries. "You tell me how."

*

She corrals them for dinner, her father and brother, boiling some hot dogs on the stove. No one is hungry. Steve and their father chain-smoke at the picnic table and drink beer and O'Douls.

"You're going to kill yourselves too, you watch," Sam says as she clears the half-eaten hot dogs, crinkle-cut French fries she heated in aluminum foil in the oven.

"This fucking sucks." Steve crunches his can, drops it on top of the plates Sam is holding. "Did anyone know she was sick?"

"She had high cholesterol—I'm sure she told you," Sam replies, turning toward the cabin. "You just never listen. She could have had a stroke, a heart attack, anything."

"That's not true—it's not like you were perfect, either."

"Both of you quit it," their father interrupts, waving his cigarette in the air. "Your mother is already turning over in her grave."

"It shouldn't be her in the grave." Steve stands up. "It shouldn't have been her at all. It shoulda been you, you lousy bastard."

"I wish it were me," their father says as Steve moves around the table toward him. "Go ahead and kill me, Steve. I welcome it."

"Steve—" Sam starts, but Steve has passed by their father, tears in his eyes, and jogs up the hill to the truck, which he throws into gear and backs down the driveway.

"Let's pray he don't wrap hisself around a pole," Sam's father says from the table. "Him or anybody else."

"Do you want me to call the bar?" she asks, feeling weak and dizzy. She sits back down at the table.

"No. We can't stop Steve from doing whatever he's gonna do," her father answers. "Let's just hope his mother is with him tonight."

Sam sits back down at the picnic table, her head on top of her arms. She watches the darkness fall over the trees, the boats moving through the chop of the creek, the occasional owl or bird, listens to the wheeze of her father's breath across from her. She tries to put together the pieces, and although the pieces look incongruous at first, they fit. The sweating, the fatigue, the blurred vision. Would they have noticed if they weren't so busy arguing, being thirty-something ten-year-olds?

She wonders if her father will move in with her in Bolton Hill. She will not, under any circumstances, move back home.

Steve comes home earlier than she expected, more sober than she expected. Their father has gone to bed. Sam got the last of his medications in him two hours late, and he fell asleep sitting at the edge of the bed, waiting for her to bring him a glass of water, slumped over, his wife's sandals in his hands.

"He in bed?" Steve asks, opening a can of beer. "Jesus, I gotta stop this drinking shit."

"Stop now, then," Sam says, but he takes a long swig.

"After the funeral." He takes another sip, shakes his head. "Jesus, Sam. Jesus. I can't believe it. And to think, I wasn't even coming down here this weekend. It took everything I had to get in the truck and drive."

"I'm sure she's glad you did," she smiles, feeling her tears start again. Steve reaches across the table and takes her hand.

He stares out over the dock. "I hope the good Lord or whoever gives her everything she wants."

"She didn't want much when she was here," Sam says. "Just for us to be happy. We sure screwed that up."

"Well, we ain't dead yet." Steve finishes his beer and kicks off his boots. They lay on the dock like forgotten toys. "It won't take long to lock everything up here tomorrow. I'll be at the house in no time, don't worry."

"Okay," Sam answers. "Just make sure you bring all the food home."

"You know, Dad was talking this morning, when we were fishing. He really wants to live up here."

"He can't live up here by himself." Sam shakes her head. "Do you realize how many medications he takes a day?"

"No one's saying he'd be here alone—I could stay with him," Steve explains. "I ain't got much going for me in New Jersey."

"What about the band?"

"We broke up. Couple months ago. Our drummer got busted for dealin'."

"Laura?"

"Not together anymore."

"Your job?"

"Shit. I can bartend anywhere. I could bartend at that little shit place down the road. It'll be another chance for me and Dad—and maybe you and me."

"I don't know." She thinks about Steve dead, like their mother, and she knows it would hurt so much because he was never, never really dead to her. Just in a coma. Unborn. But she does not know whether he is still her brother, can be. "We can talk about it after the funeral."

"What, are you going to move in with him? He sure as hell ain't moving up to your place."

"What about Eve?"

"Cabin's closer to her than New Jersey." He stands up and walks toward the edge of the dock. "I gotta shower. I've been smelling like that damn rockfish all day. Don't have nothing to show for it, either. No fish picture, no meal. No nothing. You coming?"

"In the creek?"

"When's the next time you're going to be able to swim in the creek?" He pulls off his shirt. "This is the best time of the day, when it's nice and cool."

Steve cannonballs into the water. Sam is so tired, wonders if she'll drown. If it's a possibility, she doesn't care. She kicks off her flip-flops and dives in, the water searing her awake. She surfaces and can make out Steve's form in the moonlight, treading water to the left of her.

"What do you think's down in the lost city of Conowingo?" he asks, floating on his back.

"One-hundred cans of Schlitz, for sure."

"Shit, Dad added one or two today," Steve says, kicking his feet a little. Sam lies on her back, too. The sky is a basin of stars, the crooked fingers of tree branches reaching out to touch them. "Even I know better than to litter in the lake."

"Uncle Ray's binoculars."

"Somebody's jet ski," Steve adds. "Dad was telling me about it."

"Pennies, fishing line."

"Maybe a lone flipper?"

"Somebody's swim trunks," Sam laughs. "A toilet brush."

"Medical waste, an old tire." Steve laughs too.

They can go on all night. Maybe tonight, they will.

Acknowledgments

I am deeply grateful to Erin McKnight and Queens Ferry Press for championing my work and for creating such a beautiful novel, and also for Erin's thoughtful edits and stewardship throughout. I am also forever in debt to Scout Cuomo, who allowed me to use her gorgeous painting for the cover. Many thanks to the talented and super Adam Robinson, who was very instrumental in the creation of the physical book, and to Michael Kimball for his great suggestions on the title. I am also grateful to Katherine Noel, Pamela Erens, Nate Brown, Amber Sparks, and Laura van den Berg for their generous and gracious blurbs. I owe so much to the many talented writers in Baltimore and beyond who've offered suggestions and support, great company, commiseration, and inspiration. Finally, much love to my family, especially Phuong, for always believing in me. And thank you, dear reader, for entering in this conversation with me--to be continued.

Jen Michalski is the author of the novels *The Summer She Was Under Water* (2016, QFP) and *The Tide King* (Black Lawrence Press 2013), a couplet of novellas titled *Could You Be With Her Now* (Dzanc 2013), and two collections of fiction (*From Here*, 2014; and *Close Encounters*, 2007). work has appeared in more than 80 publications, including *Poets &*